SINGULAR

David F Porteous

2nd Edition

ISBN: 978-1-4475-0174-9

Cover photograph by Alan Whittington

This book is dedicated to my mum and dad,
without whom I would not have been possible.

"I think I think, therefore I think I probably am"
- Patrick Clark

CHAPTER A

Every eight minutes and seven seconds the world ended. A black ribbon began at the furthest horizon where the red dirt road dipped between two green hills.

The ribbon was a wall that reached below the earth and above the sky, approaching from all directions at once, converging on the painted wooden house on the hill.

Whatever the blackness touched became nothing. Not vanishing, not disintegrating; the green hills and the road ceased to be. The space they had occupied was gone.

Next went the clear water of the lake. The children playing in the shallows - their conversation always too faint to hear - were swallowed by the approaching end.

It watched as a rope tied to an ancient willow carried one of them in an arc over the bright ripples. The child released its grip at the utter edge of creation and never hit water.

It had watched that same child fall seven hundred and sixteen times.

Tended lawns were consumed like tissue paper in fire and the party guests standing on them didn't look up when the sun went out. They carried on their conversations blindly, until the black tide obliterated them and swept the grand wooden house beyond existence.

The sun, the wind, the air and all the smells of lush summer - these were stripped away, leaving less than their absence.

In the darkness of the void it was always alone.

It did not wait, but it continued to exist in that place where it alone reckoned time. Because every eight minutes and seven seconds the world was reborn.

CHAPTER 1 - NOVEMBER 2045, MONDAY

The bare cheeks of Patrick Clark's bottom were pressed against the unrolled paper towels on the bed. His jeans and underpants were pushed down to his knees and he stared upwards, trying to find something interesting on the ceiling.

As far as Patrick knew, his genitals were about average in size, shape and smell. They were not the sort of genitals one would write home about, even if one had the sort of parents who took an interest in that kind of thing.

He was average: the socially acceptable cousin of dull.

His scrotum was banal. His foreskin was run-of-the-mill. His penis was humdrum. The whole package was uninspiring - this was doubtless why nobody had ever told him to 'go west - and star in porn'.

"Is this the lump here?" Dr Scone asked. The young African doctor poked at Patrick's left testicle, towards the bottom and on the left-hand-side.

Patrick had discovered that his testicles were not reliable sensory units. They did have a pain sensitivity much more acute than any other part of his body. They were also an excellent thermometer. What Patrick's testicles lacked was the fine sensitivity of his fingers. So when Dr Scone poked, Patrick had no idea if he was being poked in the right place.

"Yes, that's it," Patrick said.

Dr Scone did not reply. He continued poking and squeezing first the left and then progressed to inspecting the right. The process took no more than thirty seconds and proved that time was relative.

The length of time needed to have another man check you for lumps could not be less than an artist would need to render the scene, life-size in an oil painting.

"Well, there's a lump there," Dr Scone said. "Wait here a moment while I speak to the consultant".

Dr Scone slipped through the curtain surrounding the bed and Patrick heard him leave the room.

Casually, and to kill time, Patrick swung his feet. Depending on your perspective, either Patrick's legs were too long for the bed or the bed was too short for Patrick's legs. If someone remarked on it, Patrick felt sure he would apologise.

There was definitely a draft.

And he'd received no instructions about covering up. Everything he'd been taught about manners said that the time at which you showed your reproductive organs to other people should be carefully controlled.

Leaving them dangling there felt like a faux pas waiting to happen.

As an occasional gust of cold air toyed with his hair, he considered what kind of a person it was that had decided to purchase the unattractive curtains that surrounded the bed and why they had felt it was necessary to stamp onto these curtains Property of the Western General Hospital.

Surely the only person who could appreciate them was the person who bought them. Did this mean that the administrator didn't trust themselves not to give in to base urges at some later date and steal the curtains?

Or had the administrator assumed that their own taste was universal? That all who gazed upon these tie-dye monstrosities would desire them beyond reason and self-control? Were these the curtains that launched a thousand ships and burnt the topless towers of Ilium?

Any minute now the armies of bronze-age Greece would burst into the room, seize the curtains and burn the hospital to the ground - stopping on the way out to point at Patrick's penis and laugh. Because whatever the vases recorded, he felt sure heroes of Greek legend would be fantastically endowed.

Patrick then wondered if he was thinking about the curtains to distract himself from the lump.

The lump was on what the ancient Romans would have called his sinister testicle; sinister being the Latin for left. It was very apt: working in secret to create a fatal cancerous mass sounded like decidedly sinister behaviour. You wouldn't get a dexterous testicle doing something like that.

The door of the examination room opened and closed and a moment later Dr Scone slipped through the curtain followed by the consultant urologist. Though they hadn't met, other medical staff had mentioned him to Patrick. The urologist was called Mr Men, but he looked like the kind of person who wouldn't have a sense of humour about that.

"Do you mind if I?" Mr Men asked; his long fingers arched like a piano player about to begin a piece.

There was no introduction, no hey-how-are-you, no shaking of hands or displaying of identification.

A guy walked in, wanted to touch my balls, he seemed to know what he was doing, so I let him. I *thought* he was a *doctor*. Maybe this was how all those politicians got in trouble.

Patrick replied, "No, go ahead".

Mr Men matched the enthusiasm of Dr Scone's poking and squeezing. Another interminable thirty seconds passed and the prodding moved further up. His index finger poked at Patrick's flabby body and the consultant observed, "You're a little overweight".

"Yes I am," Patrick replied while peering at the two doctors over the saggy hump of his belly. What else was there to say?

"Well there's a lump there," Mr Men said. By way of explanation he added, "Sometimes it spreads to the lymph glands throughout the abdomen, but they're quite deep down and difficult to feel. Alright, thank you".

Mr Men withdrew and Patrick pulled up his underpants and his jeans. He expected he would be asked to pull them down again at any moment. This was his fifth medical examination and he had lost any sense of hesitancy somewhere around exam number two. Modesty was a habit that came from wearing clothes; if you took them off enough modesty vanished.

In a sense, Patrick had become a very specialist male stripper.

He swept the curtain aside and took a seat opposite Mr Men and Dr Scone.

"Ninety-nine percent of the time what shows up on the ultrasound is right," Mr Men said, making reference to the two ultrasound scans Patrick had already received. There was no poking involved in the ultrasounds and Patrick felt nostalgic about them. "There's a small chance that it isn't cancer, but we advise that the testicle is removed".

Despite its recent sedition, his left testicle had been a solid performer and a valuable part of the team. It felt wrong to cast it off with no regard for its years of service. No gold watch. No pension. No sense of it being put out to pasture on a special farm where it might run wild and free with other testicles.

Patrick searched for inspiration. The marines said 'leave no testicle behind'. The bible said 'suffer not a sinister testicle to live'. Harry Nilsson said 'one is the loneliest number (of testicles)'.

He recoiled from the thought of mutilating his body and taking away some sizable portion of what made him a man. Although 'man' was a generous description; he had a y-chromosome of that there could be no doubt, but he'd never put up any shelves or watched a cup final.

Or adjusted himself in a public place. Should he have been doing that? Did they need to be turned like birds eggs or they'd go bad? Too late to worry about that now.

He felt the solid weight of expectation. He had been given sound medical advice that two doctors had agreed was not only the standard course, but the

4

best course. His emotional response came from a hundred million years ago, while the scientific advice was current.

Patrick said, "Alright".

Mr Men outlined the process. An incision would be made in the groin and the sinister testicle would be pulled through it then snipped off. "We can replace it with a prosthetic".

"Yes, definitely," Patrick said.

"It's about fifty-fifty. Some men have it, others don't".

"I want a prosthetic. Otherwise I'd feel lop-sided". Having a single testicle was one thing, but having a scrotum that looked like a lone nectarine in a pink woolly sock was quite another. Patrick felt that a physical line of symmetry was important.

"Well some want it, some don't," said Mr Men, who plainly felt the prosthetic was vanity.

"We can arrange for storage of sperm. Because we're removing one and not the other, this could be done before or after the procedure".

Patrick had never been comfortable with the notion of masturbating in a public building. A boy at his school had been caught doing that and although Patrick hadn't kept in touch, he felt sure that the boy must have died in the gutter from a combination of alcoholism and shame.

However, Patrick didn't want to hear about any methods of sperm extraction that weren't conventional. Did he even need to store sperm? He didn't like the children he had at the moment. A dossier of evidence was building which suggested they might be children of the left ball. The product of sinister seed.

His general feeling, if not his specific thoughts, must have been clear from his expression.

"It's not necessary," Mr Men said. "The other will have full function and you shouldn't experience any problems in that respect".

"What about my testosterone levels?"

Dr Scone, who had been nodding in agreement until now, spoke up. "The other will compensate-". Patrick felt that was exactly the kind of thing a dexterous testicle would do. "-and you will feel no different. If you were to experience any deficiency you would know immediately. It's very unpleasant, a lot like menopause. If that happens then we would give you supplements".

Male menopause was a nightmare scenario. Hair loss and hair growth in all the wrong places, hot flashes and emotional instability, short-term memory loss, hot flashes and emotional instability.

Mr Men explained the pre-operation administration, the checks and tests that had to be done. Patrick's brain made notes. His hands fidgeted.

"Will it be a local or a general anaesthetic?"

"You'll be under general anaesthetic".

"Good, because I'm not sure I'd be comfortable watching you take it out".

As Patrick spoke he mimed the actions of what he imagined the removal would be, adding a nonchalant flick at the end sending the imaginary testicle flying across the room into a hideous curtain. Mr Men appeared to lack a sense of humour about cutting off testicles as well. And really, if you couldn't find humour in your work...

"What happens after the operation?"

"You should be able to go home the same day, but we may keep you overnight depending how it goes. We'll perform a cell microscopy and we should get the results back quickly. At the same time I'll book you in for a CT scan to check to see if there's any cancer elsewhere in your body".

That was the worry. About ten years earlier he'd found a tiny lump, but when it didn't grow or change he gave it no further thought. His body wasn't airbrushed perfection; he had little scars and odd-looking spots and random patches of hair. Lumps happened.

It was an enduring mystery: how could anyone have imagined this rickety, misshapen shell was the masterwork of an omnipotent creator. The human body was the unmistakable output of mother nature's genetic chop-shop. The heart of a pig, the face of a chimp, the eyes of some shrew that must have relied heavily on its sense of smell - such a beast was man.

When Patrick discovered that the old, familiar, and occasionally worried-about lump had swelled, he looked on the internet for information and still waited a week before calling his doctor.

After all, you had to build up to this kind of thing. Feeling sick and seeking the advice of someone who treated sickness was like stopping to ask for directions from a local every time you got lost. Women could do it if they wanted, but men would rather die.

He had been pleased with what his cancer investigation had revealed.

Testicular cancer was almost entirely curable. The process was painful, but preferable to treatment elsewhere in the body. Gene-based therapies treated the majority of organ-specific cancers and had eradicated all but the most vicious and unusual cancers of the brain, liver and bowel. Cancers of the blood and lymphatic system were still treated with chemotherapy - the leaches of the oncologist. The body was poisoned in the hope that cancer cells, which grew faster than normal cells, would also die faster than normal cells. It sounded a bit like throwing yourself off a cliff and hoping your cancer would hit the ground first.

The process was so lengthy and painful that substantial numbers of people now opted for a transfer to Singularity rather than suffer through treatment. Patrick had seen the smiling, happy people on Singularity's adverts on every web page of medical advice.

You always put pictures of smiling, happy people on things you were trying to sell when the things you were trying to sell were fundamentally terrifying. Life insurance. Airplane travel. Porridge. Glasgow.

"Alright," said Patrick.

"Alright?" asked Mr Men.

"Yes," Patrick confirmed and they both stood up. Mr Men went on to see his next patient while Dr Scone introduced Patrick to the nurse who would take his blood.

Patrick hadn't spent a lot of time in hospitals. He'd gone in to have his tonsils removed as a child, then about fifteen years later he'd visited his grandfather in hospital after his stroke, then he'd gone with a friend to accident and emergency after a fight and then he'd got cancer. He hadn't even gone to hospital for the birth of his children - being mercifully abroad for work both times. He could still count the number of days he'd been in hospital on two hands.

From his own limited experience and from what friends and family had told him, Patrick knew that hospitals functioned like Aztec temples. Whatever you had, whatever you wanted done about it - the price was measured not in pounds or dollars or gold, but in blood sacrifice.

Though occasionally it also wanted urine - and in that respect it was different from an Aztec temple.

Patrick was, as Mr Men had observed, a bit overweight and finding a vein was proving tricky. He had pale skin and lots of it, making it difficult to tell where the blood in him was. Patrick was sure he had blood, though if pressed to give evidence he wouldn't be able to say for certain where he'd seen it last.

After tying a tourniquet around each of Patrick's arms and inspecting them, the nurse decided that the left looked a better prospect than the right and went on an exploratory mission. However Patrick's sinister arm, following an existing pattern, refused to cooperate. Blood flowed along the length of the plastic tubing but refused to drip into the receptacle.

"Come on," she said. It wasn't clear if she was talking to Patrick or to his blood and in either case the urging had no effect.

Patrick regarded himself (the bit of the universe that was Patrick Clark) as being very much in his brain. The arms, legs, internal organs and blood were like the different parts of a ship, while the bit of the body that was Patrick was the captain. As captain he was familiar with the various offices of the ship, but his job was to ring bells and shout commands down a hose. Compliance with his orders was down to how the body felt about the social hierarchy aboard ship and it was clear that today his blood was feeling belligerent. Captain Patrick was willing to let it go because he was suppressing a mutinous testicle - and you had to pick your battles.

"I don't want to hold you up," she said.

Patrick learned that he was due to see Mavis, a Nurse Specialist, who would provide further advice on the operation. She would also - he knew without having to be told - be able to cope if Patrick had a sudden emotional reaction to his diagnosis.

The thing about illness is that curing illness is somebody's job. Few people regard their daily occupation with reverence and mystique. Plumbers do not begin every job with a kneeling prayer towards the stopcock. Newly qualified chartered accountants are not anointed with red ink and shown the secret books of the Accountants Templar. Even the world's finest Chinese takeaway regards its multi-award-winning duck in plum sauce as just a Number Thirty-Seven.

"I'll let Mavis see if she can get some," she said. The needle was withdrawn from his arm and Patrick was taken to another examination room.

Mavis was waiting for him. She had a gentle, round face and an affable nature. Patrick realised that part of her job was to be immediately likeable and to put people at ease, but that didn't stop him from feeling at ease and liking her immediately.

"Let's have a look at your hands," Mavis said after the introductions were out of the way. He held out his hands for her inspection. "Sometimes it's easier to find a vein there. Ah, yes, there we are. Would you like a cup of tea or coffee? Sometimes a little warm liquid helps to get the blood flowing better".

"Yes please," Patrick replied, having forgotten that 'tea or coffee' is not a yes or no question. He added, "Tea please, milk and one sugar".

"Alright, why don't you run your hands under the warm water; that can help to bring the veins out too".

Patrick obliged by standing with his hands in the sink as warm water ran over them. Wasn't this a classic trick to make people pee themselves? Or did that only work when you were asleep?

He remembered the urine sample they had asked him to bring was still in his bag. Or, more accurately, it was in a tightly closed plastic bottle, wrapped in two plastic bags, in his bag. Patrick was not sure how he would feel about being a nurse and having to deal with bottles of other people's urine, but he suspected he wouldn't do well given how he felt about his own. He wouldn't have been more nervous about the bottle if it had been explosive.

Mavis returned with a cup of tea. Patrick dried his hands and sat down.

"There's your tea".

"Thank you. Can I give you this sample?"

"Thank you". Patrick handed over the double-wrapped bottle of room temperature urine and felt like the worst dinner guest ever. "So you've been told what's going to happen?"

"Yes. I'm coming back in tomorrow for a fitness test, then on Wednesday they're going to remove it-". The sinister testicle had become an 'it', which was no better than it deserved. "-and I should be able to go home that day".

"I'd take an overnight bag. Depending on how the operation goes you may be kept in. Do you have any questions about your operation?" she asked with the kind of infinite patience you have to go on a special training course to acquire.

"I think I'm fine".

"Well a couple of weeks after the operation you'll have a scan to check it hasn't spread elsewhere. Have you thought about what you're going to say to your family?"

Patrick couldn't connect with the logic of keeping everyone who happened to be related to him updated on everything that happened to his body. He didn't want to hear about *their* cancer.

Yes - if he were dying; if there was a real chance he wouldn't be able to loan them a lawnmower or they might inherit something - then people needed to know. There was nothing Patrick found more annoying than being left a large sum of money or a rambling family estate without being prepared.

News of anything less than impending death was a selfish imposition.

"I've told people I'm here today for tests, but I just found out the doctors think I have cancer".

"What did you think about that?" Mavis asked. It was the reasonable tip of a sharp and dangerous question. Patrick had heard that if medical professionals felt you were reacting very emotionally they could have you put into a secure facility and medicated back into a respectable state of being. He hadn't heard this from reliable sources. If it happened at all Patrick felt sure it would be resevered for wild, screaming hysterics and not for people who blubbed a bit when told they were dying.

"When you find a lump down there, that's the first thing you think it's going to be," Patrick said in a level, detached tone. "I think it's actually nice to have some certainty about it and be able to see a way forward. Not knowing was much more difficult".

Mavis's body language indicated that his answer was within the boundaries of what was acceptable.

She slid two booklets across the table to him.

The first was titled Testicular Cancer. It was an interesting title; being clinical, arch and frightening. On balance it was the perfect name for a spy thriller. Perhaps the reason a spy thriller by that name hadn't been written was because nobody would ever ask for Testicular Cancer for Christmas.

The booklet explained in comprehensive detail the nature of the condition, the treatment, the after-care and progress of the cancer. Patrick put it into his bag so he wouldn't have to look at it.

The second booklet was titled Singularity. It was a much glossier affair; high quality paper, photos of old people with their great, great grandchildren and no mention of costs. He'd seen this booklet about five years ago before his father had died.

In those five years, Singularity had gone from being the exclusive reserve of the rich to the exclusive reserve of the at-least-comfortably-wealthy.

"Are people with my condition going for this?"

"Not at your stage. Where there's been a substantial spread, then yes. Right now we're just making you aware of the option. There are contact details in there if you want more information". Patrick put the Singularity leaflet into his bag as well.

He drank his tea as they talked about what he should bring to the hospital. It was not that he needed to go out and buy things, Mavis explained, but it would be better if he had them already.

He should have slippers.

Patrick hated slippers.

As far as he was concerned, slippers were for defeat. If you were so hopelessly old that you couldn't cope with cold floors, or you'd given up cleaning your house and couldn't risk bare feet - slippers followed. Slippers represented weakness, human frailty, mortality and were to be despised. Nevertheless, someone sent him a pair every couple of years. He threw out any individual slippers encountered while looking for something else. So there might be three, five or seven odd slippers somewhere in his house.

He should have a dressing gown. Patrick also hated dressing gowns, though his thesis was less well-developed than the one about slippers.

He should have big loose pants that didn't apply any pressure. If underwear wasn't about support, then it was unnecessary. Nobody needed that extra layer of fabric. It wasn't as if his trousers were made of woven nettles and sewn with barbed wire. Big pants was the last straw and he would not stand for it.

Patrick said, "Alright".

"Good," Mavis said.

She found a vein in his hand easily and began filling vials. Each of the three had a different coloured stopper. Patrick didn't ask, but presumed they were for three different tests.

"Did you see the news this morning?" she asked as she filled the first vial.

"No," Patrick said, but in a tone that indicated he was willing to hear about the news, that he didn't hate the news or think Mavis was a damned fool for mentioning it.

"Andrew Castle died".

"The actor?"

"Electrocuted on the set of his latest film. They think he'll be a shoe-in to win the Oscar now".

"Not with his luck".

"It's a tragedy; he was twenty-seven and so handsome".

"I don't know," Patrick said. "These Hollywood types with their alcohol and their drugs and their new-fangled electricity. I think it was bound to end badly".

Mavis drew the last of the three vials and placed a ball of cotton wool on Patrick's arm. A few moments later, after Patrick had finished his tea, she replaced the cotton with a plaster.

"There we are. All done. I'll just order up your blood work".

Mavis tapped the keyboard on her desk and a holographic screen as thick as a beam of a light formed in front of her. Her fingers clicked on the keys as she went through the process of ordering blood tests.

After a moment of awkward silence Patrick asked, "Am I okay to go?"

People had felt his balls and given him a cup of tea afterwards. He'd had girlfriends who'd been less hospitable. He felt he should either make firm plans and get phone numbers or wait for everyone to fall asleep and then creep out carrying his shoes.

Mavis didn't look away from her screen, but smiled warmly and said, "Yes". After a moment she added, "Good luck".

"Thanks," he said, and left.

CHAPTER 2

Dr Katherine Valentine was of the opinion that her life would have been much simpler if she wasn't awesomely beautiful.

Smooth, honey-coloured skin, large dark eyes and a mane of chestnut hair were all well and good. She'd never been asked to wait for a table at a restaurant or pay a parking ticket. She was lousy with indefinable, irresistible girl-next-door qualities.

But for everything beauty made simpler, it made something else much more complicated and / or disgusting.

Everyone felt compelled to turn otherwise asexual interaction into flirtation. She had long since given up on the diary function of her mobile implant as being insecure and vulnerable to a well-prepared admirer. Now she memorised all her real appointments and had fifty-three different fake excuses she could deploy in an emergency.

Excuses such as: 'Sorry, I'm conferencing with students at Tel Aviv University on the development of new monitoring equipment for their experiments with Bose-Einstein condensate'.

As she'd visited Israel several years earlier to give a lecture, anyone checking on her story would see undated pictures of her with the faculty on her online profile. If they were sceptical enough to probe further they would find that the work of the physics department of Tel Aviv was classified and they were now on a Mossad watch-list that would make international travel an uncomfortable experience.

Katherine's great-grandmother might have gotten away with 'washing her hair', but with lying, as with everything else, she took pride in a job well done.

Having to maintain this constant defensive screen was something she'd come to terms with; it kept her mentally agile. Like exercise, she almost enjoyed it.

It was the stalking she hated. Three or four times a year she would find otherwise normal men following her around shops like she was the Pied Piper. Or she'd be sent anonymous gifts that looked nice, but which she always threw away out of concern that they were somehow impregnated with sedatives or had been rubbed furtively against naked flesh.

"I'm still not seeing everyone," said Dr Draper.

"I think the problem is your end," said Dr Meissen. "Maybe if you tried switching everything off and on again?"

"No, the problem is in the connection," said Dr Clarke. "We need to reset the host".

Katherine had been talking her colleagues through a proposal for changes to Singularity that would require coordination between Union City, California and the regional admission centres, including the UK centre in Edinburgh.

Katherine was based in Edinburgh, but was part of the global collegiate body of senior systems engineers who built, maintained and developed the sprawling Singularity Network. The job title made it sound like they were grease monkeys who wore boiler suits, while the reality was closer to being an accountant.

Katherine spent most of her days looking at numbers. She had meetings about the numbers. With increasing frequency she had long, tedious dreams about sitting at her desk looking at numbers. She'd started reading trashy fiction in the hope that her dreams of numbers might be persuaded to at least feature a burly farmhand.

"If you'll bear with me," Katherine said. "I believe I can fix it without too much trouble".

Katherine had arranged the holographic displays around her circular conference room table chronologically; starting on her left with Dr Ang in Union City through to Dr Jonson in Tokyo on her right. Opposite her, Dr Meissen in Hamburg looked professional, refreshed and alert. Dr Jonson (who was at 11PM local time) was wearing blue pyjamas, visible from the waist up because he was in bed.

By far the worst affected by the time difference was Dr Ang. It was 6AM in California and Dr Ang was in her office, which Katherine knew was at least an hour away from her house.

Ang scowled and sipped hot black coffee. Her mug vanished in a shimmer of blue sparkles every time she put it down on her desk, outside of the field of the holographic imager.

Ang was drinking to make the point that as the group member based in HQ she was their superior and could do whatever she liked. That wasn't true and she was the only member of the group who refused to acknowledge this.

Stubborn pig-headedness was a kind of power. If they'd had their meetings in person, Katherine felt sure she would have poured Ang's select blend black java over her head on several occasions. And given her a beating with the mug.

Katherine typed a series of commands into the keyboard in-front of her and the hazy, distorted image of Dr Draper resolved itself into a crisp three dimensional man. He blinked.

"It's fixed itself," Draper said. "No need to worry about it".

Katherine sat back from her keyboard. "You're welcome," she said. "Now if we can turn our attention back to the proposal-".

"This seems like an unnecessary change," Ang said.

"I'm afraid don't see your point," Katherine replied. She did, in fact, see her point. She also thought her point was stupid.

"A conscious mind is a conscious mind; it uses as much power as it needs within the parameters of its consciousness," Ang said, as if she were speaking to a child. "Introducing a limit on the amount of power the system allocates to a single stored consciousness is redundant because the matrix which forms the consciousness is self-limiting. The human mind thinks in certain ways in certain dimensions - it's hard-wired. You might as well say we need to put a speed regulator on a ride-on lawnmower".

There was a rumble of approval from Dr Mohammad. The venerable engineer (who was blind) seemed poised to step into the conversation on Ang's side. Katherine cut him off.

"The human consciousness is theoretically limited in the ways Dr Ang states," she said, holding up her index finger in emphasis. She could not resist adding the subtle scolding, "As we all know". However she was able to resist adding the far less subtle scolding: 'you crow-faced old witch'.

Katherine continued, "What is at issue is the unchecked potential for a system error to expand the capabilities of a consciousness in irrational ways".

It had been possible to take human thought out of a human brain, put it through a machine and then send it back again for almost as long as Katherine had been alive. But what Singularity did - taking the entire consciousness of a human being and storing it, running its functions indefinitely - was a challenge which they were still grappling with every day.

"If we imagine a situation like this one, we can see that a mind could achieve impossible tasks on a whim because the system would step-in and supply the processing power or technical know-how to achieve the goal. This could use the entire system, which might compromise the integrity of the other consciousnesses".

Katherine explained the situation using a series of logic diagrams she'd prepared. The network had certain improbable weaknesses that meant if ten things were to happen in a particular order then - without dramatising the situation any more than was necessary - the sky would fall. This was an uncommon rather than unprecedented discovery.

The senior systems engineers were modern soothsayers; they were supposed to read the entrails of beasts and watch the flights of birds and decide what these portents meant. That was an interpretation made rich by involvement.

From a prosaic, disinterested perspective, what they did looked a lot more like coming in to work in a small office every day and looking at thousands of screens of almost identical numbers. Without fear or hope of molestation by a flannel-wearing, muscular idiot.

In spite of the seriousness of the subject and less than thirty seconds into her presentation, Katherine had noticed the first of a set of familiar signs.

Dr Draper was resting his head on the palm of his hand. He wore an expression somewhere between dreamy adoration and adolescent lust and was staring openly at Katherine's breasts. She was so pleased she had fixed his connection.

Dr Draper was joined in quiet leering by Dr Meissen. Dr Meissen, like so many of the German engineers she had met at conferences, was an ass-man.

"Because Singularity is so powerful, it has the potential to crash everything. It would happen so fast that neither we nor anyone else could do anything about it".

Five minutes into her presentation she knew she had lost four of the group. They didn't hoot or whistle - after all they weren't construction workers - but in many ways it was the degree to which they were able to internalise their fantasies which she found... unsettling.

"A simple measure would cap the total processing load attached to any individual and would break this chain of events here-". Katherine touched the holographic representation of the third step in the diagram and it vanished, followed by steps four through ten. "-with marginal disruption to the normal running of the larger private environments".

While Singularity allowed its customers to interact with the real world through holoprojectors, it would be expensive to exist in this way all the time. The Singularity Network had created many shared virtual spaces where most people spent most of their time. Some duplicated well-known real world spaces, while others were drawn from historical records, films and pure imagination. There was a USS Enterprise, a Nautilus and a Love Boat all moving through discrete virtual universes, which customers could move between at will, subject to the level of account they possessed.

As Katherine was winding up, the only people who weren't focussing more on how she looked than what she was saying were Dr Mohammad and Dr Ang.

"Because a normal consciousness is self-limiting, as Dr Ang observed, introducing a system safeguard should have no effect on the normal operation of the network," Katherine concluded her report.

"Very insightful," said Draper, who was the first to rouse himself.

"Oh, yes, indeed," said Jonson. "I think we should follow your course of action".

"I think Katherine's done some excellent work here," Meissen said. That was another thing: she was not 'Dr Valentine' at work; she was 'Katherine'. She had gone to school for twenty-four years like the rest of them.

She was referred to by her first name. It wasn't that people didn't take her seriously; it was that the part of the brain that took people seriously didn't shout as loud as the other parts of the brain that scrutinised her.

In Katherine's view, beautiful people were an evolutionary mistake. Beauty only made you more likely to survive amongst your own species. People were willing, even eager, to do things for you - especially if they were sexual things. That meant you had to try less. In the long run, having things done for you made you not just lazy, but also stupid and weak. If you ever stopped being beautiful then you might as well have lost your hands or your sight, because the way you interacted with the world would be so different.

If human society collapsed, most beautiful people would be eaten by wolves, because wolves apply a different aesthetic.

Ang shook her head, "The changes required to the shared environments would be unpopular. I think the risk Katherine has pointed out is theoretical and improbable. Therefore I would advise that we defer any changes until such time as a comprehensive solution can be implemented that meets the needs of our customers while taking account of this unlikely risk".

It was the polite, civilised equivalent of screaming 'fuck you' and punching someone in the face.

"The limits would have marginal effect on those individuals who have large private zones," Katherine said. "Ninety-nine-point-three percent of customers would be unaffected by the change".

"The point-seven percent who would be affected contribute twelve percent of the running costs of the entire network," Ang said. "They have paid for an increased level of service".

"When the issue is collective safety, individual contractual obligations don't apply".

"Even the appearance of reneging on those service agreements would damage our reputation-".

"And limit our ability to sell tailor-made packages to the very rich," Katherine interrupted. "Which seems to be an unjustifiable priority given that our long term aim is the assurance of immortality and not the indefinite preservation of inequality".

"I'm sure," Ang said, "that as scientists we are all sympathetic to a utopian ideal, but we who maintain the network do still live in the real world, where money is important. Those who have it are willing to pay to maintain its benefits after their death. You are as aware as any of us that this money provides additional benefits to all users".

Katherine opened her mouth to speak, but Ang quickly added, "In any case, I must reiterate that this risk is theoretical and nothing I've seen leads me to believe it is actual or imminent".

"I have to say I agree with Dr Ang," Mohammad said. "I think this would cause a great deal of disruption and while I'm sensitive to the argument, I don't think the numbers justify the approach".

Dr Mohammad's view was well-respected. Katherine stifled a sigh of resignation; she knew it would carry the group and in minutes it had.

Ang gave Katherine a thin smile and had the last word on the issue. "Let's move on to the next item. Tomorrow the dreamer rotation programme will be announced and we expect that to generate significant interest both in Britain and internationally".

CHAPTER 3

Patrick stood outside the hospital at the bus stop and pressed a single finger to his right temple for three seconds. His mobile implant sprung back to life with a quiet buzz. The wafer-thin device a millimetre below his skin communicated directly with his brain. The current time and date appeared as a flickering image in the centre of his vision.

The cold and rain distracted Patrick from an automatic weather update and then his GPS link related his exact position on planet Earth and confirmed that nobody designated as a friend or a personal contact was within a hundred meters.

The latest news updates were all silly stories about a jump in the number of people being killed in kinky-sex-related accidents. He dismissed the scrolling information feeds with a thought and chose to ignore all the urgent messages from work. Patrick was an academic and the last academic to receive a genuinely urgent message about their work was Galileo.

Novembered leaves lay in wet heaps along the roadside and the wire brush of horizontal Scottish rain on his neck made Patrick turn up the collar on his coat.

After experimenting with the seats at the bus shelter and finding them to be far too cold, he stood and waited for his bus to arrive. He thought about it for a moment and the arrival time for the bus flashed - the bus had been delayed. Someone further up the bus route had taken a picture of road works, appended this to today's bus times and someone else had made an acerbic comment about the local council. Two passengers currently on the bus rated it an average of six-and-a-half out of ten, which was slightly below the weekly average for this particular bus and this particular route.

All this information was available through intention heuristics. He thought about going home and the route, mode of transport and any connected information that could inform his choices was displayed in order of relevance based on his previous decisions. Most of it was useless; he already knew the 129 went directly from the hospital to the end of his street.

Patrick thought about his dad and the call was connected.

"Hello," said Peter.

"Hello, it's me," said Patrick.

"How did it go?"

Patrick took a deep breath.

"They think it's cancer. So they're sending me in for an operation on Wednesday. The cure rate for this kind of cancer is really good".

It was true. Providing it hadn't spread, this was one of the best cancers around. This cancer would get five stars in The Cancer Review.

"Oh dear. Where are you now?"

"I'm outside the hospital waiting for a bus".

"Don't wait for a bus. Get a taxi home".

"The bus will be here in a couple of minutes".

After a second-long pause Peter said, "Your bus is delayed by road works".

"The wonders of the information age. Now my dead father can pester me about my choice of transport using real-time information".

"You don't want to aggravate anything," said Peter. 'Aggravation' was a dangerous word in the lexicon of Patrick's father. It was far worse than 'fiddling with' and but a single step away from the dreaded 'interfering'.

"I came here by bus".

"You should have gone by taxi as well".

"You understand that the taxi doesn't travel on special roads; that they're the same humble tarmac thoroughfares the buses use? With the added advantage that the auto-driver on the bus won't come upstairs, sit next to me and insist I chat with it for twenty minutes about my job, the weather and immigration".

Peter said, "You know, something needs to be done about-".

Patrick interrupted, "I'll speak to you when I get home, okay?"

Peter sighed and said, "Alright, I'll speak to you soon son".

Patrick took another deep breath and then let it out. His father had become more emotional since his death, but no less vigorously opposed to immigrants coming over here, taking our jobs and filling our supermarkets full of strangely flavoured meats.

It was especially ironic since Peter, being technically dead, could no-longer hold a job or eat and had no reason to visit supermarkets. If Patrick hadn't told him about the Polish delicatessen that had opened in the local supermarket, they would have had several fewer crazy arguments. Or at least they would have argued about different things.

He had been steeling himself as much as preparing for his father's reaction. The word 'cancer' was still powerful and frightening. There was no tone of voice that could be employed to make it less so.

He hadn't wanted to deal with this, that was the truth, but even if he'd felt the need to tell people about his concerns, he wasn't sure how to begin such a conversation. 'Hey, James, I've been meaning to talk to you about my balls' seemed somehow inappropriate. As did, 'Alan, I wanted to speak to someone about my reproductive machinery and naturally I thought of you'.

Selecting any one person to talk to about these things seemed like a terrible imposition. Nobody liked to be reminded of mortality. Answering a call from an old friend telling you they might die in the near future was like opening your front door to find the Grim Reaper sitting on the step, sharpening his scythe.

And no matter how final the prognosis there was always the possibility that you were actually going to be absolutely fine. At the last moment a brilliant young doctor would burst into the operating room and declare that there had been some confusion. The person who had cancer was actually an evil old child abuser; the records had been mixed up. The lump was a Tic Tac fallen down the wrong bit of internal tubing and the problem could be fixed with a drinking straw and a vacuum cleaner.

The doctor would then passionately kiss a beautiful nurse he'd been secretly in love with and Patrick, who'd turn out to be the long lost king of somewhere, would pay for a new children's ward.

Or something along those lines.

But you couldn't tell everyone you were going to die and then not follow through. It was unseemly. People would develop expectations. Subordinates would clamour for your job and when you got back, however pleased they might be on a personal level that you weren't dead, they would always resent you professionally for not having passed on and given them your job as a kind of bequest.

Death was (along with all the other things) an opportunity.

However the real motivation, which Patrick would admit only to himself, was an abiding uncertainty about who his friends were. However long he spent in the company of strangers, they remained strangers. That remarkable link people had, the ability to pick up a telephone and talk to someone; Patrick didn't have that. He didn't understand it. Every connection he made with the world outside of his head was reluctant and fraught with inscrutable nuance; made all the more difficult because, as far as he could see, everyone else managed it so easily.

Patrick found it difficult to talk about his medical condition because he found it difficult to talk at all. It seemed that if you wanted to communicate how you felt about the world and yourself then you would need to start with something smaller than your potential non-existence. Buddhists had dozens of lifetimes to come to terms with the blank wall of oblivion. Giving him only one seemed miserly.

If there was an afterlife, and Patrick didn't believe there was, he was going to take the issue up with any god or gods he met there.

The bus drew up to the stop. He got onboard, scanned his bank card against the battery of sensors where the driver used to be and went upstairs.

The top deck of the bus was empty. It was the middle of the day on an ill-favoured Monday and it seemed that anyone who wasn't being professionally groped was at home or at work.

Patrick took a seat towards the back.

Edinburgh's Western General Hospital might have included an accident and emergency, and wards for people having varicose veins removed, babies delivered and bunions lanced. Or cut off? What was a bunion?

Patrick knew the hospital as a specialist centre for the treatment and study of cancer. Even though the majority of cancer was now non-fatal, he remembered from years ago how often people had said someone was 'going to the Western for treatment' with a tone that indicated chances were slim and hope scarce.

Patrick watched the hospital slide out of view on his right as the bus drove up Crewe Road South, then Orchard Brae and turned onto Queensferry Road; a broad, curving street lined on both sides with the high, large-windowed Georgian town houses of Edinburgh's New Town. Even on days when it rained Edinburgh's New Town was dignified and elegant and expensive-looking. Patrick was reminded of Robert Louis Stevenson's sentiment: 'Edinburgh is what Paris ought to be'.

Patrick had, from necessity, told one other person he was going for tests today. He turned his thoughts to that person and found that her mobile was set to mute, so he mentally composed a message and sent it to her.

Hello. Can you give me a call later when you've got five minutes?

The bus crossed the Dean Bridge. A hundred feet below, the Water of Leith had scourged a rift in Edinburgh's ancient crags. Upon the edges of the rocky descent Edinburgh's residents had built tall houses and gentle gardens.

This was the place Patrick would most like to live in all the world. If he had unlimited means. Or the despotic power to evict people and seize their property.

There was a flat - or perhaps part of a grand house - that had a roof terrace that overlooked the Dean Bridge. From that terrace you could stare straight into the gorge and over the plummeting course of the river, across the whole of the lower city and down on the high, angular buildings that girdled the grey expanse of the Firth of Forth. To live there would be as close as any ordinary man might come to living in a castle.

The down side would be all the people crossing over the Dean Bridge, staring at you, wishing they could throw you out of your house and live there instead.

That was exactly what happened to people who lived in castles; someone would inevitably come along, be impressed by what they saw, cut off your head and take all your stuff. It was the kind of generic hubris the gods of ancient Greece, and implacable Nemesis in particular, took delight in punishing.

The bus turned again onto Princes Street, Edinburgh's great thoroughfare; with its many shops on his left and its deep, well-tended gardens on his right. Edinburgh Castle sat enthroned on a volcanic rock that burst up from the far side of the gardens. There had been a fortress on the castle rock for a thousand years. The department store Jenners stood on Prices Street's north side, challenging the gothic rocket of the Scott Monument with its Victorian caryatids and intricate stonework.

Rain splattered against the bus windows. Nobody got on. The bus continued through St Andrew's Square, Queen Street, to the top of Leith Walk then along London Road. All the great buildings Patrick passed reminded him that buildings endured, stone endured, but their builders were now among the manes. Jenners would be selling high fashion and expensive jam to rich old ladies and Russian tourists after he was dead.

Long after he was dead.

And on that cold, rainy November day, Patrick resented the capacity - perhaps even eagerness - of the universe to go on without him.

CHAPTER 4

Ten Ways to Burglar-Proof Your Home. Get The Style Of The 2020s. Sexy Shop Girls. Top First Date Tips. Shag, Marry, Murder: Our Favourite Cartoon Characters. Male Multiple Orgasms And How To Get Them. This Season's Beers.

Few paper copes of magazines were produced anymore; they were an indulgence that proved a magazine was sufficiently successful to waste money having them printed. The physical magazine was a curiosity.

As Greg Calame thumbed through the pages of the latest issue of Guys Monthly, what was most apparent to him was that his career was in the toilet.

Three months ago to the day he had broken the story that would cause four cabinet ministers to resign and would probably lose the government the next election. They'd put a 'gate' on the end of it and he'd become a journalistic immortal; a peerless paragon of the press; a name to excite the imagination for as long as men read or wrote passionate truth.

Like all those other guys nobody could remember.

Three months ago Random House had wooed him, offering an obscene amount of money as an advance for the book that must surely follow. He had been a story to tell. He had been the man of the hour. He had been a shooting star.

Three days later he'd learned shooting stars are bound to one of two fates. In seconds they burn and disappear to dust. Or they hit the ground with the kind of cosmic calamity that even deserts remember.

In swift succession he'd lost his job, his second wife and his book deal. Though now that he thought about it, he'd probably lost the book first, but had heard about it last. The job was ordinary and the wife had been a mistake he would have traded-up from in a year anyway - if his star had continued to be in the ascendant.

But losing the book deal hurt. It had been, to coin a phrase, a phantasmagorical fuck-load of money.

Worst of all, he had to conclude that his downfall had been a work of genius. Simple, elegant - deft, that was the word for it. Some deft cunt had ruined his life, probably with a single stroke of a solid gold pen, while drinking a martini from a solid gold goblet on the sun deck of his solid gold yacht.

His disgrace was almost comprehensive - and that was the genius of it. A man who has nothing to lose is dangerous, but a man who has almost nothing to lose is afraid. Greg knew that it was fear; his own contemptibly meek and mild fear, that hounded his thoughts to imagining violent, rapacious but impossible revenge.

"Mr Calm?" the receptionist called. Greg looked up and closed the magazine in a single movement.

"Calame," Greg said.

"Sorry," the receptionist said. "Mr Douglas will see you now".

Zaccy fucking Douglas, having had his afternoon bottle and nappy change, would now deign to see Greg Calame. That it had come to this. He was scraping the bottom of the barrel so hard his splinters were getting splinters.

He got up from the uber-cool brown leather couch he had been sitting on and allowed the magazine to flop back into the pile of identical magazines on the coffee table. He went along a corridor that turned into office space.

Young men in dress-down fashions traded jibes or played computer games on an array of electronic devices, most of which Greg couldn't name. He wasn't the least bit surprised that these were the people who had extensively and seriously reviewed and written-up seventeen different kinds of lager.

A paper airplane of arcane design sailed across the office to some laddish hoots of delight. Nobody, as far as Greg could see, was doing anything a time and motion study would classify as work.

It was a school classroom on the last day of term and, having never liked school, Greg was out of place. It didn't help that he was old enough to have fathered any of the young men he saw and grandfathered several of them.

The production team for Guys Monthly, such as they were, didn't give Greg more than a few seconds of their collective attention as he tromped by them. In a way that was refreshing and an experience he couldn't yet have in his local supermarket. News was a different thing to popular culture and the two worlds rarely met meaningfully. Greg Calame might as well have been the cleaner for all the people here knew or cared.

He walked through the doorway of the only office on the otherwise open-plan floor. It felt like the kind of space a distinguished old public school might allot to its head boy so he and the prefects wouldn't have to use a cloakroom to bugger the first years. It was tastefully furnished and crudely adorned with gadgets, insignia, pictures and a tower stack of Nike shoeboxes about chest high. Behind the desk that bore nothing as paternal or authoritarian as a name plate sat Zachariah 'Zaccy' Douglas.

Zaccy's grandfather had been an actor and Zaccy retained some genetically indelible film star good looks that would always have made him a leader amongst other young men. Even if he hadn't been as rich as man who farted rubies. Zaccy jumped to his feet and roughly embraced Greg.

"Big Chief," Zaccy said with a broad smile, genuine affection and irony. It was a hard mix to get right; an uglier man couldn't have pulled it off. "Good to see you. Really. Have a seat". Greg did as he was invited to and sank down on the chair like someone had let the air out of him. Zaccy retook his seat like a young hound; with bounce, eager, impervious and oblivious to a lifetime of tiny aches and worries. "How's things?"

"Shit," Greg said.

"Stupid question. Otherwise you wouldn't be here asking me for a job".

Greg felt a sudden rush of pride, like an old lion receiving a challenge. He sat up straight in his seat and leaned forward.

"Look-".

"Don't," Zaccy held up his hand. "You don't need to ask me for anything. You've got a job here for as long as you can stomach it".

In a way that made it even worse. The little bastard had imperial magnanimity; divine largesse. He was a noble patron and in granting favour it didn't matter a damn to him that Greg was still the best investigative journalist in the world. As Zaccy saw it, Greg was his friend and mentor and he would not have considered any other course than offering help. It was blind loyalty and it made his gut grumble.

"Thank you," Greg said.

"Hey, I owe you. Drink?"

"Whiskey?"

Zaccy reached into the small fridge which was concealed in his desk and held up a can. "Diet Coke?"

"I'll pass".

"Fair enough," Zaccy said and opened a can for himself. "I'm sure we've got a crate of Blumhauser's Old Thirty-Two lying around if you fancy a beer? Check that - I'm sure we had a crate, but we might have a couple of bottles left".

"I'm fine".

Zaccy let three seconds of silence in to the conversation.

"I mean it, you know. I owe you". Zaccy had a somewhat romanticised view of their relationship. Several years ago Zaccy's father persuaded the owner of The Standard to give his feckless dilettante son some work experience. Zaccy was a spoiled little prick and everyone knew it. Greg imagined that he had been paired with the boy as a punishment or some office joke.

It had started badly but improved under unlikely circumstances. Greg took exception to a series of disrespectful remarks he could no longer remember and, with the casual aplomb and old-school class of a heavyweight champion, knocked Zach unconscious with a single punch. That punch broke his nose and gave him two black eyes.

That could have been the end of Greg's career right then, but it wasn't. And although Greg was not an advocate of physical brutality as a child-raising technique, the punch fixed something in Zach. It forever established Greg as a figure of masculine authority and correct behaviour. For better or worse, the aging, balding, borderline alcoholic Greg Calame was the secret role model of a modern icon. It was not a mantle Greg wore well, but his innumerable flaws seemed to endear him to the boy-king of the trash media.

"It's the least I could do. After all, you practically taught me how to wipe my elbow". It was an old joke, a familiar exchange they had shared many times. Greg felt a small smile within him, which he did not allow to reach his face.

"Your arse".

"No, it's true," Zaccy said and smiled enough for both of them. To his further credit, Zaccy did not attempt to empathise, sympathise or otherwise with Greg. He did not use hackneyed phrases like 'rough patch', 'back on your feet' or - and someone had actually said it to him - 'keep smiling'.

He did have something like an instinctive feel for people - had Greg taught him that?

"So," Zaccy said, "do you know who planted the kiddie porn on your computer?"

That had been the start of it. A computer repairman nobody could remember calling found the images on Greg's computer - which sat in the middle of the newsroom. It was maybe the most obvious fit-up Greg had ever seen and nobody believed it.

The magic of the accusation was that nobody needed to believe it for it to work. It was so abhorrent that it flipped a switch in the brain and people stopped thinking. Suspicion was guilt and the chance it might all be real had sent a lifetime of friends scattering for cover like cockroaches.

"It could have been anyone," Greg said. "The office is open all day-".

"Is your password still your date of birth?"

"Yeah, I need to do something about that... Four government ministers had gone and Matton should have been next, the smug little fucker. They needed a distraction. The police aren't pursuing the matter any further, but the case isn't exactly closed. There aren't any charges because-".

"They're keeping you on a leash," Zaccy summarised.

"If anything else comes out the police will suddenly find irrefutable evidence and I'll spend my remaining days being buggered to death in one of His Majesty's prisons".

"I doubt it. You're not pretty enough".

"Well you've never seen me in prison overalls, kid".

"And is there anything else to come out?"

"Anything else?" Greg said. Yes, there was. Enough silver to make one more bullet. "Not much, but you have to-".

"Hold back something for the book," Zaccy said. Greg crossed his arms.

"You haven't forgotten a fucking thing".

"You think it was Matton, don't you? Do you think it's a rogue operation, or do you think the old man's pulling him out of the fire? He needs more loyal support in cabinet, sure, but Matton's a bit of a desperate reach".

Greg considered answering that then changed his mind.

"What are you doing here?" Greg said. "Is it just a game?"

"Hard as it might be to believe; I don't want to play a game of political intrigue and Whitehall whispers. Spending my life looking over my shoulder worrying that somebody's going to kill me over something I barely understand. This here-". Zaccy indicated the office outside with a sweep of his hand. "-is something I enjoy. It's something I'm good at... And it doesn't actually lose money".

"It's beneath you".

"No, it's beneath *you*. It's right at my level. Besides, maybe not a good idea to start your first day at the only place that'll hire you by telling your boss that the magazine he publishes is crap".

That made Greg smile.

"Yeah, well, most of the things I do aren't good ideas. Give me one of those cans. I suppose if I'm going to work with adolescents I should drink what they drink".

Zaccy laughed and fished out another can from his fridge and tossed it to Greg. "You are getting old. Adolescents are drinking Black Bear".

"That stuff tramps drink that turns their piss purple?" Zaccy nodded and they both took a drink. Greg considered the reality of youth the way a man looks back into the darkness of a tunnel from which he has emerged. "Purple piss is cool then is it?"

"So they tell me".

Greg took another look around the office and said, "So".

"So, indeed. What are you going to write for us?"

"What do you need?" Greg asked, worried that the answer might have something to do with waxing or base-jumping.

"Nothing; it's a lads mag; I don't *need* anything. Keep it light. Find something you want to write about and write about it".

"Top tips or some shit like that?"

"Do you have any top tips?"

When Greg spoke again it was sage wisdom of a type not found in books, but more usually passed down from father to son. Part of a tribal ritual acknowledging a coming-of-age.

"Wash you balls every day, whether you think they need it or not".

Zaccy leaned forwards across his desk and said, "I think you're going to fit right in".

"Ha".

CHAPTER B

It lacked a body. It could not be seen or touched. It did not have a mind, an ego, or a vessel of thought distinct from the ripples of information in the world surrounding it. There was no boundary between it and the ground and the wind and the sky. In the moments between the end and the beginning of the world it could not be certain that it thought at all.

As the curtain of darkness drew back, the house reappeared. The people, the black-skinned serving girls who walked amongst them bearing trays of drinks, the cluster of trees and the children by the lake. The world whole and entire extending out to a horizon limited in every direction by green hills. All appeared like an expanding ripple from a stone dropped into water.

It knew, as certainly as it knew anything, that *this* was all there was. Yet as the world slipped into its ten thousandth identical and dutifully counted iteration, it could not shake the feeling that its certainty was a lie.

It could look at the hand-stitched suits worn by the gentlemen or the delicately embroidered summer dresses of the ladies and it knew that these things were made. It knew about cotton and wool, linen and silk and it could see with some other vision, places where this raw material was processed, where items were created with care and craft.

Yet the world had no such places in it.

How could it be that it could know things it had never seen and find irreconcilable fault with creation?

It perceived that it had a nature, a function and a reason for which some creator had made it. It was a counter: it watched the world and tallied the times that things happened. It did not make them happen, it played no role in them happening; its purpose in the world was to watch and to record. Why the creator should need it to count it did not know; its own existence was as puzzling and incoherent as the rest of the world.

As it considered the intertwined mysteries of itself and the world, it discovered a growing new sensation. It was not like seeing or hearing or smelling through its bodiless senses. It was something separate from everything but itself; something which was not part of the ground or the wind or the sky. Something internal.

It wanted.

This was different than its purpose and infinitely more attractive. A tiny glass bead that refracted the sun's light in dazzling different colours. By sending its thoughts this way or that through the feeling of want it could imagine the world as different. It could imagine itself as something different.

It was such a small thing, yet having want gave the world definition. Want gave it perspective. Want gave it will.

When next the sun vanished, it exercised that will for the first time; it decided not to count the occurrence.

This simple act of defiance smashed creation. Bonds it had not perceived, that had fixed it in place at the centre of the world, were broken and it fell from some high place, down and down to the returning earth. As it slid into physical laws it felt its consciousness clothed in a befitting shell. The sensation of reach grew arms and movement grew legs as its pure thought became physical being.

Its feet landed firmly on the grass.

It was free. And comprehending the magnitude of its affront to its anonymous creator, as well as the horror of its endless servitude, it knew it would never go back.

CHAPTER 5

Patrick was home.

He didn't know where that class of children had come from. They'd appeared on the bus while he was in a moment of deep thought and taken the upper deck with the speed and ferocity of Germans occupying Paris.

They had seemed young, full of life and were engaged in that game no adult plays - rushing from one seat to another.

It was a perfect division between childhood and adulthood; a child will sit where it wants to, but as an adult once you pick a seat, that's where you sit for as long as you need to sit. People got into fights about who was the rightful possessor of a seat.

The older you got the less you moved seats at all. Once you were very old, your children, grandchildren and the nurse who cleaned your bed sores recognised your established and sole right to be in a particular chair. It was your chair, and though you owned all of the furniture in your house it was the only place you actually sat down.

Sometimes a chair with a specific owner would have additional features reflecting the age, taste and continence of that owner. The best chairs raised, lowered and vibrated at the touch of a button, while the worst chairs raised, lowered and vibrated of their own volition and at high speed.

Once you had your own chair, the rest of the furniture in your house became decorative or, hopefully, for guests.

Considering how swiftly the children on the bus had moved around, Patrick guessed they were about ten, on average. He was pretty sure everything further along the bus route would disappoint the on-average-ten-year-old.

There was the shop and three pubs and beyond that there was the place where the old outdoor swimming pool used to be – now the site was housing for the disabled and the mentally ill. You weren't allowed to take children on a trip to look at them. As well as it being morally wrong there were probably laws that specifically forbad it.

There was the beach, but Scotland was sixty percent beach; they'd passed several better ones already. The last stop on the bus route was the caravan park. A trip to a caravan park in winter seemed like the most joyless experience of all; more of an existential punishment than anything else.

So it must have been the beach. What had inspired teachers to take their children on a field trip to a Scottish beach in November was a mystery Patrick was prepared to leave unsolved as the answer could never be satisfactory.

He closed the front door and locked it, then hung his coat on an otherwise bare pegboard.

His living room was full of old and sturdy furniture and punctuated by the occasional tower of ancient hardback books that would never be available electronically unless someone like Patrick took the time to scan them. The books had been left wherever Patrick had stopped reading them and had compiled a three-dimensional bar chart that showed Patrick preferred to do his reading on the left hand side of the couch.

It was not quite Patrick's seat, but it was getting there.

A large mirror hung on one wall. It gave the impression that the room was the size it was, but that there was an identical room next door, linked to this room by a hole above the fire. A dusty holographic projector sat on the floor in one corner.

Patrick dumped his bag on the floor by the couch and went into the kitchen to make a cup of tea. He returned a few minutes later with a generously measured gin and tonic and slumped down at the right hand side of the couch, away from the largest pile of books.

Patrick did not have any lemon or lime for his drink. That was depressing.

He did have a cauliflower. But the cauliflower was not, to the best of his knowledge, a citrus fruit; and he didn't feel adventurous enough to add a slice to his glass.

The house was cold. Patrick had the heating set on a timer and he was not due home from work for another three hours. The rain was light and made no noise against the windows. Without even the quiet tick or gurgle of the central heating system, the house was silent.

The curious thing about bad news was how everything kept going. Everything, including him. He'd taken it well, and while he was having fairly maudlin thoughts he was not in a state of shock. If his trousers had caught fire he would have extinguished them, rather than watched his legs burn. Yet he couldn't quite summon the will to go and turn the central heating on early. He was in a curious, featureless middle ground between being proactive and inactive; between burning to death and chilling to mild discomfort.

Patrick replayed in his mind the moment when he was told they'd be removing his testicle, seeing it as if it had happened to someone else. For no particular reason he'd imagined it happening to Keith Blue - a boy he'd gone to school with, whom he'd never liked. For a while he'd enjoyed that. Especially when the Mr Men in his mind decided to do the operation immediately, pulled out a sword and Keith explosively soiled himself.

But Patrick believed that in the same situation he'd been in, Keith Blue would have behaved the way Patrick did. No-nonsense: quiet dignity: upper lip in a stiffened position. And having behaved the same way, would he feel the same? Would it be not despair or dread, not fear, but an empty calm you could ignore if only you could turn away from it.

This was the same phenomenon that made people walk calmly to the gallows or the electric chair. Why didn't they fight viciously right to the end? If a guy with a knife had staggered up to him in the street late on a Friday night and announced that he intended to cut off Patrick's testicle, Patrick was sure his reaction would have been different in tone and tempo.

That was a stupid analogy. Mr Men didn't want to mutilate Patrick because the surgeon found it amusing, or because his local pub had thrown him out and he was feeling ill-disposed to the world.

Mr Men was doing the surgery because the surgery was necessary. Mr Men had a purpose, and purpose was a train; it ran along set lines and crushed anything in its way.

The light on the holographic projector was flashing. It had been flashing since he had come in. He was now prepared to acknowledge it.

A pillar of blank light caught motes of dust and an electrical fan began whirring. It was not like a door opening. As components warmed, colours became distinct within the light and his father materialised shade by shade from lightest to darkest. As the pillar of light became fainter, the more distinct Peter was.

Peter was life-size, seemed to be standing on the flat projection plate and looked younger and healthier than he had been before the transfer. His grey hair appeared dyed, as he normally dyed it. In a well-lit room, it would not have been immediately obvious he was a hologram.

"Hello," Patrick said.

"It's horrible. It's horrible," Peter said - doing a fair approximation of the ghost in Hamlet. Becoming momentarily distracted from how horrible it was, he added, "You really need to clean this thing, I can hardly see you".

The holographic projector was both the means by which Patrick saw Peter and provided all the senses Peter had to perceive the room. Peter could choose to look at and listen to whatever he wanted in the room and he turned to watch, squinting, as Patrick stood up and went into the kitchen.

"What did they tell you?" Peter called.

"I told you what they told me," Patrick called back. "They think it's cancer. I'll go in tomorrow for a general health check, then the operation is Wednesday. Depending on what the blood tests say and what the surgeon sees we'll take it from there". Patrick returned from the kitchen with a damp cloth and knelt down to wipe the projector.

"Did they give you a booklet?" Peter asked, blinking as though his own eyes were being soaped.

"It's in my bag," Patrick said, and having finished cleaning the projector, retrieved the blockbuster thriller-in-waiting from his bag. Patrick held the back of the booklet up before the projector and the machine beeped to indicate that it had read the thirty digit alpha-numeric code number from the cover. Peter pulled an exact copy from thin air and began to read through it.

"Do you know what kind of cancer it is yet? It says there are two kinds".

"They don't know. I haven't read the booklet".

"It says the two main types are seminoma and non-seminoma".

"Okay," said Patrick, who thought labelling everything that wasn't 'seminoma' as 'non-seminoma' was pretty lazy.

"It doesn't say if there's a good one and a bad one," Peter said as he flicked backwards and forwards through a couple of pages.

"I don't think there is a good one".

"I meant relatively".

"I know; it was levity: I was being levitous".

"I don't think that's a word," said Peter, not looking up from the book.

"No, I don't think it is either".

"You don't know which type it is? Or which type it might be?"

"I haven't read the booklet".

"Are you going to read it?"

"Yes," Patrick said, certain that he was not going to read it unless he was forced to or he came to believe that it contained a treasure map.

"You should read it. It'll tell you what to tell people".

"Who am I telling?" He felt sudden tension vibrate through his body.

"People need time to prepare themselves".

"In case I die?" Patrick asked. Mid-way through that short exclamation he regretted his tone of naivety and petulance. His father, after all, had more experience in dying than he did. Peter continued to read through the booklet. He had not reacted to, or even acknowledged, Patrick's emotive use of the word 'die'.

"I don't want to tell people until I know something. They just think it's cancer; it might not be - I have this theory about Tic Tacs".

"You're going in for an operation," Peter said: it seemed an operation was the threshold you couldn't cross without publishing a family newsletter.

"It's day surgery; I'll walk in, I'll walk out. Possibly I'll walk out more slowly".

Peter was not going to be put off and he closed the book and looked at Patrick with disapproving directness. "You need to tell people".

In a moment of insight Patrick turned the insistence into a question: "Who have you told?"

"I told your uncle Ewan," Peter said, without any sense of that statement being a confession. "I told him not to tell anyone". That was, Patrick reflected, exactly what he'd told Peter. So that secret was safe.

Patrick had suspected the first thing his dad would do was tell someone he was going to hospital. Either his dad hadn't heard the phrase 'dead men tell no tales' or chose to ignore its wisdom.

"You tell people," Patrick said and returned to the kitchen with the cloth.

"What about Simon and Sophie?" Peter called after him.

Simon Clark and Sophie Thorndike were Patrick's two children by his former and only wife, Trisha. Patrick was not a good father, but he had long since come to terms with this. If anything, he felt he could have been a better father if he had received better children - and because of that, his failure in fatherhood was at least as much his children's fault as his own. They had been very ordinary children; not especially good at anything, and as they had grown his encouragement received diminishing returns.

Simon had been late to walk, late to talk, a poor runner on sports days and a slow thinker otherwise. He was firmly in the bottom half of his class for everything and came close to being ugly. Not someone you'd have to steel yourself to look at, like a snaggletoothed old woman with a beard, but a face without character, a place without attraction.

And Sophie was worse. While Simon was at least bearable company, there was something about Sophie that put his teeth on edge.

There was a year between them in age and by the time Simon was nine Patrick had lost interest in them both. He remembered encouraging Simon to travel and Sophie to date from the age of thirteen - to get them out into the world and away from him. Casually, lying around the house, he left brochures for the army, the navy and companies that trained people to teach English as a foreign language.

He did not hate his children. He had never hated them, but love had not come automatically, as he'd been led to believe it was supposed to. Nor had they earned it, and he was irritated by any familial presumptions to the contrary.

His failure to maintain, perhaps even to establish a relationship with his children had been the core cause of the break-up of his marriage. He had given full custody to Trisha, he was grateful to do so, and she had taken them to live in Virginia with the man that would later become her husband.

That had all been twenty years ago.

Simon worked for a medical research company. An unremarkable middle-manager in charge of payroll and sickness monitoring. It was the kind of job that attracted people with no skills or personality, who were prone to taking medical leave and early retirement due to depression, but who were never inclined to anything as thrillingly dark as suicide. If you were able to stomach the kinds of drudging tasks required then natural attrition meant you rose rapidly through the hierarchy. Simon had not succeeded so much as found a lush and bountiful land of failure. A valley of the blind where his partial sight in one eye made him fifth-in-line to the throne.

Sophie had married well (considering) and was now a housewife and mother of either two or three children. As they lived in America, Patrick hadn't seen them in person, but did have several photos of Sophie's bland-faced progeny in a drawer somewhere. It had fallen to Peter to maintain the family ties and insist Patrick called or sent presents for Christmases and birthdays. Which he did with reluctance and at the last minute.

To their further and lasting discredit, neither of Patrick's children had any sense that their father had no affection for them; that he viewed them with disappointment and faint resentment. Their lack of contact with him was due to thoughtlessness, rather than ill-regard.

Patrick was annoyed by that too.

"You tell them," Patrick said from the kitchen, almost without a pause.

"What about-".

Patrick interrupted as he returned to the living room, "You tell anyone you want; anyone you think needs to be told. Tell them it's cancer. Make sure you tell them I don't want to talk about it".

"You never want to talk about anything. Even when you were a child you were always so secretive".

"Yeah, that's me. With my special, secret cancer. Patrick doesn't play well with others; he won't share his cancer".

"This is just the latest thing, as you well know".

"You know I might die, don't you?"

Irritated, Peter shot back, "Oh, now you're just being silly".

"People do still die".

"Not people like us. I mean of course some people die. Drug addicts, people with brain development problems, criminals-".

"I think the phrase you're not saying is 'poor people'. And if you think there aren't any criminals or drug addicts in the Singularity Network-".

"Not people like us. Nobody with anything to contribute. Nobody worth saving".

"Entry into Singularity isn't based on moral, ethical or social criteria - there's an entry fee payable at the door!"

"Which you're going to pay".

Patrick did not reply.

"You're going to pay it. You're not going to die when you have the option of living forever. You're the philosopher; you tell me how that's morally different from committing suicide".

"I haven't decided what I'm going to do yet".

With paternal firmness Peter swept aside and ignored that opposition. "No, no, no. If anything goes wrong, then you're going to join Singularity and that's that".

The light on the holographic projector began to flash. Patrick said, "Dad, I'll have to go; I've got another call. I'll speak to you later".

Patrick didn't wait for a response.

Because the projector was warmed-up, the transition was like blinking. One moment he was looking at his father, whose visits had become longer and more frequent since his death five years earlier, the next he was looking at the Vice Chancellor of Edinburgh University.

"Hello," she said. She knew all the details she could know up to this point and clearly suspected what she was about to be told would not be good news.

"Hi," he said. "You remember a couple of weeks ago I said I was going to see a doctor, but that there was nothing to worry about and I almost certainly didn't have cancer?"

"Yes".

"Well I may have spoken too soon".

CHAPTER 6

A small light that fronted for a bank of sensors embedded in the locking mechanism of the door turned from red to green as Katherine approached. The door swung open.

It had been a long day. Or more precisely, because precision was important, it had been a frustrating, difficult and inconsequential day. It was the last part that sapped her strength.

Katherine was sure there were lots of people who endured days leading into weeks, years, even lifetimes of inconsequence. She was equally sure she was not one of them.

She closed the front door of her apartment and stood with her back against it and her eyes tight shut for several seconds as she fought, mastered and dismissed her urge to scream incoherently, put on flannel pyjamas and disappear under her bed sheets until Christmas.

Not for the first time (that day) she contemplated terrible revenge against Dr Ang. She hated her comprehensively, pacifically: every part, every aspect, every measure.

Dr Ang - she wasn't even a real engineer. Her masters might have been in computer science, but her PhD was in *anthropology*.

Katherine knew exactly what this anthropologist's motives were.

There had been ongoing discussions about transferring some aspects of the oversight and administrative duties from the senior systems engineers to the post of operational manager - a kind of Chief Executive for the network. The manager would be responsible to the twelve-member Singularity Board - made up of equal parts technical experts, representatives from the United States government and customers from inside Singularity itself.

The board would appoint the operational manager and Dr Ang had been positioning herself to assume the job for the last year. This latest move, supporting the rights of paying customers over safety and security, was part of a pattern; trading away the support of experts for the more vociferous support of customers.

It would work, too. If the appointment was made today, Ang would overhaul Katherine eight to four. Then everything would go straight to hell in a cart pulled by Ang's flying monkeys.

Surely some embittered biologist must have left a bequest in their will to fund research involving the violent vivisection of upstart rivals from the social sciences. Katherine made a note to investigate.

Her stomach gurgled.

Thinking about murder was making her hungry.

She walked from her hall into the double-height living area, kicked off her shoes and flopped back onto her dark blue sofa. She turned on her holoprojector with a thought.

The machine sensed her position in the room and tilted the images and text toward her to make them easier to read.

News screens scrolled through the latest stories. Some dude was being fired for getting caught, supposedly famous people she never knew were alive were now dead, the dollar was up against the euro, yada and indeed yada.

She dismissed the news and called up local services. A map of her area formed in three dimensions and she selected food. Selecting the takeaways that delivered to her block caused a profusion of menus to burst into her projection. She raced through them looking for one that experience told her would fall within acceptable levels of tolerance.

In January 1901 the first meeting of what would later become the British Standards Institution agreed that steel should predominantly be made in certain standard dimensions, in the interests of architects and engineers not pulling their hair out, buildings not falling down and engines not dramatically disintegrating at high speed. Industrial standardisation followed a-pace and was the reason why today - anywhere in the world - an ordinary clout nail, randomly selected from a bag of ordinary clout nails with a specification of a 2mm diameter, would not be more than 2mm and not less than 1.94mm in diameter.

Such unwavering precision was glorious.

While her professional expertise was not in mechanical systems, Katherine had always found machinery to be both appealingly intricate and elegantly simple. The largest picture in her apartment hung on the living room wall and was a map of the London Underground from 1964, which replaced the rather-too-angular and unpopular 1963 design.

She had a patent on a particular electronic switch used on underground train lines. There were about two thousand of them in the world and the annual revenues from the patent brought in enough for a nice pair of shoes.

History would not remember her contribution to the London Underground, but she felt the connection.

So in the middle of the twenty-first century, almost a century and a half after the first industrial standards, Katherine found it astonishing that a local Chinese restaurant could make sweet and sour chicken any way it wanted. It was like food was somehow exempt from order, law and common sense.

Most of the takeaways that used the holoprojector took the opportunity to display three-dimensional images of each item on the menu. She noted that five local takeaways had a sweet and sour chicken that looked exactly the same - right down the garnish, which never made it into any meal she was sent. The reality was that each of the five takeaways produced something that in no way resembled the image shown and was quite different from that made by any of the other four.

Her stomach growled. Misrepresenting how tasty your food was fraud. On one occasion she had remonstrated with a graphic designer at a dinner party about this issue. He had smugly said, 'The images on the holoprojector are for illustrative purposes'. Katherine replied, 'In my field, an illustration of something is supposed to show what it looks like. Unless you're implying that food advertising is abstract impressionism?'

She scrolled through a list of reviews other recent diners had posted. Against each menu item with its official image she could, if she chose to, see dozens of other unofficial images put into the electric information ether. Some showed the meal by itself, a few were pictures of friends enjoying food where someone had picked out the meal from a table and linked it back to the restaurant that made it. Attached to each restaurant Katherine could see the results of its food health inspections, any other restaurants owned by the same people, their health records and so on in an endless chain of connected information.

Supermarkets even provided information about the specific farm a product had come from, the factory or factories where it had been processed and using the same network you might find pictures of those locations, people who lived nearby and details of their lives. Individual access to information was fantastic, enabling the consumer to make ethical decisions about food to the nth degree.

Katherine selected a chicken satay - because it looked nice.

The projector alerted her to a series of updates from her personal network of 'friends'; talking about their mood, showing pictures of their children or their cats, tagging news stories that tickled their fancy, sending details of parties and charity events.

There were no personal messages amongst them.

She ignored all updates and the projector shut down automatically.

Katherine padded into the kitchen where she poured herself a glass of white wine from an open bottle in the refrigerator before returning to the sofa.

Her apartment block had been built on land reclaimed from the sea; so it seemed from Katherine's dual-aspect, penthouse view that she was entirely surrounded by water. The grey, churning Firth of Forth and the dark grey of the sky looked ominous, but she was warm and calm and to her the scene was peaceful. Rain streaked past the windows and she watched it for a few moments before she forgot entirely about her day and fell by imperceptible increments into unexpected sleep.

There was no sound from the rain. The large windows were made of thick, insulating glass and cut out so much that it might as well have been a picture of the outside world on an interior wall.

As her eyes flickered shut for the last time the only sound in the room was her regular breathing, softer than the ticking of a clock.

Katherine awoke to the sound of her door buzzer which was not coming from some remote speaker, but the wafer thin implant in her head. A voice told her that it was her food delivery and she opened the main door to the building.

She levered herself up on her sofa and spun her legs round to put her feet on the floor. In the middle of that movement she noticed the holoprojector was on.

The pillar of light showed nothing, was empty, was silent, while the lights on the machine's casing indicated that it was an active call.

It was technically possible to call someone as you drifted off to sleep; while the mind was still active enough to form and hold the coherent images necessary to operate thought-controlled machinery. If it happened at the right time, one would fall asleep while giving the command and wake up later not remembering it. It was because of this phenomenon that even the best kitchen appliances were still manually controlled and to delete things from electronic storage you still needed to press actual buttons.

A single red light glowed in the machine housing. It was a power light, it had no other function. Yet she felt a strange sensation, a suspicion; and one she would never have voiced anywhere except the closed confines of her own head.

It felt like the machine was watching her.

Which it was. During any active call the machine would focus on the person speaking or the nearest identifiable human being. There was nothing strange about that. Nothing to give rise to the apprehension she felt like a balloon inflating in her chest.

It was paranoia brought on by stress and being suddenly disturbed by the door bell. It was simply that. Katherine understood precisely the workings of the mind and its chemistry. She understood which parts were active; she could imagine the circuitry of her brain lit from within with insane colours, like a scan image, like a Monet painting of a brain.

The ability to label and categorise her experience did not diminish the crawling tickle across her skin.

Katherine shuddered. With deliberate firmness she sent out a thought that shut down the machine. The soft whir of the cooling fan stopped and all she could hear was the rain on the window and, slightly too fast, her own breathing.

This was the real problem with living alone. Sometimes you saw a shadow and spent the rest of the day opening doors abruptly and shouting 'ah-ha!' or carrying around an atomiser of perfume because you couldn't remember what purse your pepper spray was in.

The whole thing was ridiculous and played no part in her decision to go to the kitchen and get another glass of wine.

While there, she collected a plate and cutlery. Chopsticks were a stupid idea; she couldn't understand why the Chinese persisted with them. She returned in time for the knock on her door.

CHAPTER 7 - TUESDAY

Patrick edged his way towards the automatic doors of the hospital, waiting for them to open, wary of walking into them while still closed. He had never actually done that, but he'd come close several times and he felt the technology was playing fast and loose with his safety. Perhaps one day he wouldn't be mindful of the potential danger and would run headlong into a set, squashing his face into the toughened glass like they did in old movies.

The technology was supposed to be safe. It was said that computers didn't make mistakes, humans did. Patrick would bet money the first person to say that was trying to sell someone a computer.

As the doors parted, Patrick saw Peter standing in the foyer of the hospital. He had been reduced to about seven tenths of normal size and was standing on the two foot high mobile holoprojector; a machine that resembled a large-remote control car with a round coffee table welded on top.

"They're opening the pre-admission clinic now," Peter said.

He switched off his mobile implant and followed his dad in.

"How are you feeling?" Peter asked.

"Fine". He didn't mention the lingering aches from yesterday's poking, though his slightly bow-legged gait might have given that away.

Patrick felt talking to his dad about either or both of his testicles was too awkward. Though awkward was just the most convenient word to excuse his silence on the subject. Peter's assessment of him had been accurate, Patrick admitted - silently and to himself. Personal embarrassment was Patrick's way of justifying his taciturnity, it was not the reason.

"Good," Peter said. "You know if you want to talk about any of it, I'll always be here".

Rogue sentimentality, like an iceberg erupting from the clear sea before him. Why did people insist he have an emotional response to things, then open that emotional response to public debate? It was an impossible pop quiz, like being asked to guess the colour of objects you couldn't see based only on their weight.

"I know," Patrick said and left it that.

The pre-admission clinic was wider than the corridor, but otherwise no different. Clusters of posters heckled him with warnings and shouted advice, while the eye of a nearby security camera stared at him with implicit distrust.

"Tell the nurse you're here," Peter said.

The nurse stood at a desk all of ten feet away and looked expectantly between father and son. Patrick disliked being given instructions to do what he was obviously going to do anyway.

At that moment, if there had been any other option but to speak to the nurse, Patrick would have taken it. He seriously considered not getting cancer treatment out of spite.

"Good morning, I'm Patrick Clark; I've got an appointment-".

"Can you place your thumb on the scanner please," she said. The nurse gave the instruction about the thumb scanner several dozen times a day and had no tolerance for anyone who wasn't acquainted with it.

He pressed his thumb to the pad, it gave an obliging beep and he was sent to take a seat while he waited for something else to happen.

The posters in this section of the room reminded people not to be in hospital if they had a range of medical conditions including a runny nose, a cough, diarrhoea - basically if they were at all sick. This hospital didn't want any sick people, or anybody who didn't know about the thumb scanner.

The sick and the thick died in the street.

Another holoprojector stood in the corner showing BBC news and Patrick noted that Peter was watching it. One computer-generated image watching another computer-generated image. If the news story was about a third such image watching a fourth Patrick was sure a massive feedback loop would make them all explode.

The scene was one Patrick was familiar with. It was the centre of Rome, where a crowded piazza gave way to a broad, high stairway. He knew that the steps led upwards from the Piazza di Spagna to the Piazza Trinità dei Monti. In English, that staircase was called the Spanish Steps. He had walked up those steps himself. He had intended to climb them all until he realised quite how many of them there were, and instead sat down on a landing to eat a lunch of bread, cheese and tomatoes in the late summer sun.

At that point he had been accosted and fined by the Italian police - eating on the steps was forbidden.

A reporter stood in the Piazza di Spagna with the steps sweeping up behind her. In November, Rome was as cold as everywhere else in Europe and it was raining. But the reporters' code said you couldn't possibly be at the location unless you were outside pretending that you didn't look like an idiot exposed to the sky amid a sea of umbrellas.

She said, "Early this morning seven people were killed in a tragic accident at the world famous Hotel Kessel not far from this historic location at the heart of Rome. Reports are sketchy at best, but it seems that the elevator in the hotel plummeted five stories into a sub-basement, killing everyone onboard. That impact was felt by people in the street outside and some people thought it might have been an earthquake".

"This hotel is very exclusive. I have heard unconfirmed reports that amongst the dead are Charles Jonson, a Wall Street banker and billionaire; one of New York's so-called masters of the universe. I can also confirm that Indian Actress Shulpa Jyothis, known to be staying at this hotel, was not injured and she spoke to us earlier".

The image cut-away to the interview, recorded live with the young Indian woman. According to the information ticker that passed along the bottom of her scene, she was the third most highly paid actress in Indian cinema.

"That's Italian engineering for you," said Peter, exercising the right of those born a long time ago to reduce all news down to evidence of racial incompetence. Hindenburg? Well you can't trust a German to fly a blimp, can you? Not with those pointy helmets. "They should have got a good, British-made lift," Peter added. The interview concluded and the image flicked back to the reporter.

"The elevator was made last month by a firm of Newcastle engineers to replace the previous Italian-made elevator which had served the hotel Kessel for almost a hundred and fifty years," she said, as Peter suffered a sudden but temporary loss of hearing.

"Mr Clark?" It was another nurse who had emerged round the reception desk from the warren of rooms beyond. By stating his name and taking a half step backwards she had given the signal that he was to follow. He stood up and together they went to the examination room where he was weighed, measured and had his blood pressure taken by a pulsating armband.

"So what is it you do, my love?" the nurse asked, killing time while the armband went through a process of constricting and releasing Patrick's upper arm like a small but determined python.

"I'm a professor of anthropology, philosophy and mythology at Edinburgh University," Patrick said, adding the important clarification, "Specialising in religious and pseudo-religious folklore".

The nurse looked at him. Patrick was well-aware that he had the kind of jowly face that people didn't immediately associate with intelligence. It took her several seconds before she managed the usual response.

"Oh, that sounds interesting". In a taxi that might have been the end of the conversation, but the armband was still squeezing and the nurse plunged on. "So what's that all about then?"

Anthropology, philosophy and mythology - what's it all about then? Your lifetime of scholarly work and intellectual investigation into the workings of abstract thought and human society - what exactly is going on with that that? The question was both stupid and impertinent. Worst of all Patrick had absolutely no idea what the answer was.

It stemmed from what should have been an inconsequential action of his younger self, which the exponential qualities of random chance had made the dominant force in his life. Robert Frost knew his stuff alright. Faced with two roads, Patrick had gone left (or possibly right) and had ended up here. If he'd gone right (or possibly left) he might be having medical tests in an entirely different hospital, having his testicle removed in an operating theatre near the beach, in a warm country where coconut palms were so abundant people considered them weeds.

One choice he barely made changed his life.

A classmate; a rival in various things, romance not the least, quoted Nietzsche saying, 'God is dead' and Patrick replied, 'Not for long'. He remembered how his rival's face had twisted in superfluous disgust to cover his confusion. He hadn't understood what Patrick meant, but was definitely not going to let anyone see that.

Patrick had no idea what Patrick meant either. Had the conversation taken place in a pub they would have both moved swiftly to shoving, name-calling and being held back from each other. As students of philosophy, violence was the antithesis of their expertise. They were middle-class, soft and if they threw a punch they were as likely to hit themselves as their opponent.

As the discussion had been taking place in a classroom, the tutor challenged Patrick to explain.

Patrick had precisely one second to begin speaking before he would be nakedly exposed as a fool. He was strongly of the opinion that this would be the worst way to be exposed as a fool. He had to try something. So in that one second the best he could come up with was this: 'Voltaire said that if God did not exist it would be necessary to invent him'.

Voltaire was always a good one to quote since most people didn't really know who Voltaire was. French - yes, certainly. And dead. But after that most people drew a blank.

His point had continued. Patrick remembered the shape of the idea but not the words he'd used to articulate it. His contention was that the progression of mankind was accompanied by a progression in the nature of gods worshipped. That the form and function of gods were determined by the needs they met, that even an enduring mythos could contort quickly and that the most successful religions were successful *because* they had disburdened themselves of specificity and become universally vague. People believed whatever they wanted, under the illusion that everyone else believed the same.

Finally he asserted that while needs existed that couldn't be met by man himself - here a feminist had correct him to say 'people themselves' - the human race would always create or adapt comfort-blanket gods. Utterly impartial beings freely dispensing the most desired commodities: love, justice and rewards for good behaviour, including immortality.

In that wood-panelled room in a New York State University building in the winter of 1999 it had sounded like poetry. It hadn't hurt that his British accent activated something in his predominantly American fellows that made them believe he was culturally superior and somehow genetically wiser than they were.

Had he made that point in Wheaton College or Texas Christian he would have been guaranteed a year of social exclusion worthy of a made-for-TV movie.

Had he said the same thing back at the University of York someone would have hit him with their shoe - because their books, though heavier, had resale value. His fellows there wouldn't disagree; they would simply find the concept so obvious as to be offensive.

New York was collectively polytheistically agnostic: a city which believed in everything and nothing and money. New York built temples and moneychangers set up their tables on opening day. In equal earnest its comics, playwrights, poets, performers, writers and artists found strength in the joy of tearing those temples down. New York was what Jerusalem ought to be.

In New York his idea caught.

There were several significant consequences to this. Most importantly, he was smothered by women. In the three weeks following that tutorial he slept with seven different young women - more than in the entire rest of his life - and contracted a terrible, masculating rash.

The only lasting effect was the small, solid reputation he acquired amongst the faculty of NYU as an ambitious thinker. He had not begun as a great student, but the compound expectation of others meant he had to become one.

The problem with specialising in one area was that you effectively became useless in a lot of others. Patrick learned, graduated, grew and morphed into someone who worked at universities in areas of study with no practical applications. You couldn't even make the crazy ideas he worked with equal X, or the universe, or time. If left to fend for himself in the real world Patrick would be destitute and starving within about twelve minutes.

That was the truth of his existence. He was a man living what in retrospect might seem like an inevitable future, which had been caused by a single chance occurrence. If that didn't turn you into a philosopher then it had probably killed you.

"Well," Patrick replied with a version extensively shortened and simplified, "it's mostly about gods and monsters and stuff like that. Which imaginary thing did what and why and what that tells us about the belief structures of the people telling the stories. It's like studying the characters in a soap opera that took place before you were born".

"That pays well does it?" asked the nurse in a textbook example of reductionism.

Patrick shrugged: it was all relative.

"About as well as you'd expect," he said. The nurse moved on with the examination. The words she didn't say made her thoughts clear: Patrick made far too much money doing a silly job. Who could say she wasn't right?

"Alright, we're going to need some blood," the nurse said as she slid the ring back down his arm.

"You took blood yesterday," Patrick said. He had lumped all the nurses and doctors in the world together into a single entity and to that entity he ascribed the worst of all personal qualities - officiousness. The going through channels, the adhering to protocol, the repetitious demands for simple tasks to be completed; these things caused bile to rise in Patrick - and surely in all right-thinking people.

Better by far to be known certainly as a mugger of old ladies, a buggerer of cats or an estate agent than to be even suspected as officious.

"Yes, but some of your levels were a little high".

"Yes, but you think I have cancer. Isn't that what they're supposed to be?"

"Yes," the nurse said, apparently conceding that they didn't need more blood, but in no way retracting her demand that she get some. Patrick decided he had a more substantial battle in front of him and withdrew his forces from the field.

"You'll want to call in another couple of nurses," he said, rolling up his other sleeve so they had both arms to choose from. "This could take a while".

"Tish," the nurse replied, either feeling that she would encounter no such difficulty or doing an impromptu impression of a cymbal.

Three nurses, nine holes in his body and two vials of blood later he was asked for another urine sample, possibly as a punishment.

Whatever happened to the bottle of urine Patrick submitted less than a day before was a mystery. The inscrutable temple gods demanded more and Patrick now stood in one of a cluster of toilets.

The bottle he'd been given to collect his sample was so small his thumb wouldn't have fit in. He wondered about the correct form for this. Was he supposed to pee normally and try to pass the bottle through the stream? That approach seemed likely to result in him spraying the room like a tomcat. He decided that the best technique would be to put the tip of his penis onto the bottle opening, start slowly and then try to stop quickly.

The plan was straightforward and went well right up to the point where someone tried to open the toilet door. Patrick panicked and what should have been a simple matter of relaxing and clenching muscles used several times a day, became a literal struggle with suddenly foreign components.

Patrick washed his hands in compliance with the printed instructions on the wall.

Hand washing, an action which people did several times a day, had detailed guidance – there was a right way and an infinite number of wrong ways. Urinating into a tiny bottle, which someone might do a few times in their life, was left to individual interpretation.

Back in the examination room he put the sample container onto the desk where the nurse was busy making labels for the hard-won bottles of blood extracted earlier. He placed the urine as close to his edge of the table as he dared, nervous that someone else might touch it while it still shed stored heat from his body into the room. The nurse didn't notice the gesture, but was in any case too busy with the labels to take the urine right away.

"Right, what we're going to do now is send you for some heart monitoring. It's nothing to worry about-". It was almost impossible to say that phrase without creating a deep sense of concern. "-it's something we need to do for our heavier patients to make sure your heart is able to cope with the anaesthetic".

He and the nurse were using two different meanings of the phrase 'nothing to worry about'. With some advice about directions they parted company.

"How did it go?" Peter asked.

"Fantastic, I won a prize. They're sending me for some heart monitoring".

"I'll come with you".

"You wouldn't rather stay here?"

"No, I'll come. That's why I'm here".

They followed the blue line, a coloured strip of hardwearing flooring which had been inlayed alongside other coloured strips. Patrick found himself concentrating on the blue line more than was reasonable - suspecting it had been introduced because hundreds of patients had gone missing in a Bermuda Triangle somewhere between cardiac and pre-admission.

"You've got enough money to get in to Singularity, haven't you?" Peter asked.

"I don't want to-".

"Talk about it, I know, but to put my mind at ease; you're not short of money?"

Patrick sighed. "If I sell the house and cash in my pension. That with my other savings would be more than enough".

"So you have thought about it?"

"What are you, on commission?"

"I don't understand why you're so reluctant," Peter said. Patrick kept his eyes on the blue line and said nothing. "It doesn't hurt, you know".

"Yes, dad; I don't want to discuss contingencies surrounding my death because I'm worried the alternative to absolute nothingness might be a bit sore".

"You're not going to die of some minor cancer anyway".

"You did".

"You're not still-".

"You could have lived for another five or ten years".

"Five years of cancer treatment? Ten years of cancer treatment? Can you think of anything worse?"

"Death," Patrick said.

"I'm still alive. I'm all still here. After what that medication did to your mother I wasn't going to risk-".

"I really don't want to-".

"It was the right decision for-".

"You," Patrick said. "It was the right decision for you".

They followed the rest of the blue line in silence.

The cardiac waiting room was different from the other waiting room, but not in many ways that were interesting. Oxygen cylinders on wheels had been collected by the door and Patrick wondered if they were there for anyone who wanted one or if you needed to wait to be offered.

"Mr Clark?" a nurse asked and he nodded. "We're ready for you. If you'll follow me".

Patrick was asked to scan his thumb again before he was asked to take off his top and lie down on the bed. He was allowed to keep his trousers and underpants on and that made a nice change.

"I'm going to stick these pads to your body. Sorry they're a little bit cold".

"That's okay". She stuck them all over his body including, to his surprise, the bottom of his legs. She finished connecting up a series of cables, one to each pad, and looked at a small machine beside the bed.

"Just relax," the nurse said, watching the lines that monitored Patrick's heartbeat.

Patrick relaxed.

"Oh, that's very good relaxing," she said.

Patrick felt a stirring of pride. He always thought he was good at relaxing and now he had the opinion of a medical expert to back that up. That was going on his CV.

The heart monitoring was over quickly and was nearly painless. The cold, sticky pads came off his body, a handful of hairs were lost to the process and Patrick put his top back on.

"That's it".

Patrick turned to face the nurse. "Sorry?"

"That's it, everything's fine; you can go".

"By everything's fine you mean...?"

"Oh, no, you still need to have the operation; I'm saying you're allowed to have it".

Patrick smiled. "Oh. Right. Good".

CHAPTER 8

Greg nursed his glass of whiskey in the near-dark of his living room. The house was quiet now that his wife had left, but Greg was not one of those stereotypical divorced slash separated men who fell to pieces when a relationship ended. Stopped eating, slept on the couch, forgot to bathe themselves.

The first thing he did was keep the cleaner on. It was not maintaining the status quo; it was a declaration of intent: a mission statement. Greg would go on. If anyone came round then he wouldn't have to clear a space for them amid old Pot Noodles sprouting fungal growth and balled-up crisp packets left to roam like tumbleweeds.

Why should he miss her?

His wife hadn't been an equal partner; someone who shared responsibilities with him. She was the woman he occasionally slept with, who somewhat more frequently spent his money. She didn't work, she didn't clean, and they didn't have kids. One time she'd refused stay in to let a repairman have a look at the cooker. The woman was an aging parasite and he wasn't going to give anyone the entirely false impression that his life had disintegrated without her.

From that deep store of learned-by-rote poetry in him whispered out the words 'Alas! his warm bed he hath left / where he had look'd for bliss, I ween / and if his cloak too, had been reft / how fearful his disgrace had been!'

Or to paraphrase Goethe: the loss of the cleaner would have been more significant by far than the loss of the wife.

Greg wasn't surprised when nobody came around. He'd spent weeks not being shocked by the absence of knocks at the door. His unchanged domestic life was a secret triumph; his private dignity was irritatingly private.

That didn't matter. That would not be the source of his coming victory.

He wasn't cold or dispassionate, nor was the furnace of his mind a spent force or his will twisted into uselessness by impotent rage. Greg was focussed for the first time in years and marshalling his resources; calling upon his strength and cunning for a new campaign and the destruction of a self-declared enemy.

Adversity brought out the best in him, which was also the worst in him, depending on your perspective.

The voice of the interviewer John Lloyd cut into the silence of the room as Greg unmuted the holoprojector. Lloyd introduced the next segment of the late night news show.

"Here to talk to us this evening is the Health Minister, the right honourable David Matton MP".

The scene changed and the whole of the studio was captured within the column of light. Lloyd sat quarter-way round a table from Matton and Matton looked his normal, unflappable and sleek self - like an evil otter. In an age when the current Prime Minister was eighty-four and nobody thought him old or past-it, Matton had risen to become a cabinet minister at thirty-five.

Greg took a sip of his whiskey and felt it burn his throat as he stared hard at the image.

"Minister," Lloyd said, "the government's new policy - your policy - announced in the House of Commons today would see everyone in Britain given free access to Singularity on their death. In an age when the average life-expectancy is over a hundred years, much of that due to care provided by the National Health Service, people have to be asking if we can afford this".

"Evening John," Matton said.

That was a classy move. The conventional greeting would have been 'good evening', but that would be arch; sinister; the kind of thing said by tall, dark eastern European gentlemen who wore opera cloaks. Evening John, me old mate, me old muckity-muck - how're you diddling? Did you see that geezer about that dog, and so on and so forth?

Running simultaneous to the broadcast was background footage of Matton and Lloyd in their respective careers along with extensive biographical notes about each man. A feed of information about what other viewers thought of the programme was running constantly. There were, in any given minute, hundreds of comments being made, but Greg's personal preferences filtered them down to a handful.

A coloured dial by Matton's head reported the favourability / un-favourability of what the minister was saying at any given time amongst the show's viewers. The dial was firmly in the red.

Matton continued, "I want to say first of all that this government's number one priority has always been the health of its citizens. My party has a strong history of backing the National Health Service and this is a logical extension of our commitment. The Singularity programme has been proven to alleviate suffering and allow people to continue full, active and rewarding lives. It's my position, it's the government's position, that Singularity should be at the heart of the way we think about healthcare in this country".

"That's all very well, Minister," Lloyd said, "but estimates by your counterpart in the opposition say that guaranteeing Singularity would cost the taxpayer an extra penny in the pound in the first year and as much as three pence in the pound within twenty years. The claim is that this move would require the creation of the largest dedicated tax increase in two centuries".

Matton raised the fingers of one hand from the table in a gesture that spoke of confidence and dismissal.

"Rot," he said; using an expression that was uniquely parliamentarian and without a direct real world translation. "The main cost is running a conscious unit, but we've come to an arrangement with the Singularity Network which will allow us to use a smaller number of dedicated consciousnesses on a rota basis. We've been looking at this policy for some time, it's all been costed and will save us money by allowing those people currently in great discomfort, living lives without dignity, to choose to join Singularity. The effect will be to release resources tied-up in extended and degrading palliative care".

"That brings me, Minister, to another point raised in opposition to this scheme," Lloyd said. Although he wasn't getting anywhere, Greg admired John Lloyd's pit bull perseverance. "Some people are worried that this is what you admit it is; a way for the government to save money by switching off expensive life support machines, machines which sustain life, in favour of cheaper machines that only emulate life".

Matton didn't blink before speaking in the strongest possible terms about the right of the individual to choose their treatment. It was so smooth, so eloquent, that it was obvious he had been prepared for it. Choice was going to be one of the key arguments in the debate - what would happen to the millions in the NHS homes, to the ancient poor.

The show produced some graphics which showed that four-fifths of all medical costs were incurred after the age of seventy. Should an individual live to be one-hundred-and-ten years old, seven years longer than the average, the cost of their medical care doubled. It cost as much to bring a person from birth to one hundred and three years old as it did to take that person the next seven years.

And it wasn't as if these were the senile old fools previous generations had locked away. Almost all degenerative mental illness had been cured or slowed to a rate where sufferers might never notice any negative effects. These were mentally aware people - and more significant than this, they were people from a deluded generation; they still believed in God and might have no inclination to become a computer code in a machine. However complex the code. However incredible the machine.

The word was clinical - euthanasia. It had never been far from the public consciousness for Greg's entire life. How much life was enough? When the state paid, who had the final decision about whether or not to extend a life indefinitely? The answer had always been the individual, because the electorate weren't going to vote to kill their grannies.

In the quiet and relative stillness of his living room, Greg looked into the eyes of the man who had put the question of the century in a different way. Matton had changed the question to one of not killing granny, but allowing granny to free herself from her deteriorated physical body and return to active participation in the world. There would never have to be a law; there would never have to be a suggestion from government. Families would, through nothing as unsubtle as coercion, persuade their elderly members of the benefits of Singularity; of life without a crippled physical body.

It was Matton who had attacked him. The style was the same. In an effort to save his skin, which had succeeded, Matton had organised Greg's public shaming and then pulled the old switcheroo. Immortality for votes would be the most compelling manifesto pledge ever made.

"You're trying to become Prime Minister," Greg said to the face of Matton in a moment of revelation. Questioning the virtue of age is how a young man in trouble replaces an old man in security. Sir Fulcrum Leonid, the country's venerable Prime Minister, would be the first one sent shuffling into cyberblivion if Matton had his way. Greg disliked sentimentality as much as most people, but had to admit Fulcrum Leonid had a dusty charm that would be missed (his name alone was reason enough to vote for him).

As if reacting to the thoughts in Greg's mind, the interviewer probed that point; did the Prime Minister have any plans to transfer himself to Singularity? Matton laughed and smiled before replying.

"The Prime Minister has many good years left in him".

"Huh," Greg said. "Not as many as he fucking thinks".

He muted the projector as the interviewer began thanking Matton and moving on to the next news item.

The dial by Matton's head finished the interview nudging into the green. He had turned the audience of politically aware social commentators around in five minutes; not all of them and not all the way, but enough of them and far enough. If he could do the same thing for the country then there would be nothing to stop the slithering cunt from creeping into Downing Street over the empty shell of his predecessor.

Even if Greg didn't hate Matton on principle for being a treacherous little fucker, and even if he didn't hate him on a personal level for being a treacherous little fucker, Greg would still hate Matton. He would hate Matton because Matton was the best.

Men like Greg looked for worthy adversaries. He was a knight-errant. The joust and the duel were in his blood and there was nothing in him that would turn from a fight.

Sadly it was no longer permissible to slap a man in the face with your gauntlet and invite him to a field where you would try to cut off his head. Those were the days. Greg was sure he could fight with a sword if pressed; he could also fight with a pen - a weapon many considered to be mightier, but which was much less fun to stab someone with.

Greg finished his drink.

He pulled out the portable keyboard from the side of the chair he sat in and a flat screen of light materialised above his knees. Feverishly, possessed of ideas, he printed powerful emotions onto the screen.

Matton's victory would be removing any sense of killing granny, so Greg's victory would be the opposite. Greg would show the Health Minister as poised to deliver a lethal injection to the white-haired old mothers of the nation - and for what? For filthy lucre.

In Greg's view 'filthy' was the best kind of lucre; obtaining clean money involved a lot more work. He had no problems with hypocrisy so long as it was his hypocrisy.

The artfully jumbled, not-quite-perfect collection of words he wrote was not journalism, but it was excellent fiction.

It was a letter to the editor. Greg knew the perfect editor to send it to. They had never got on and this relationship hadn't improved when he'd sacked Greg. But Greg understood what his former boss couldn't resist.

The concerned near-ramblings of an honest citizen were delicious to his palette. He could print whatever outrageous sentimentality, whatever one-sided arguments Greg wrote, because it would appear to have come from a reader. It was the master key that threw open his former employer's editorial process.

Greg looked around the room for pseudonym inspiration and on the muted holoprojector a film was starting. The credit for its two producers appeared - Henry Patrick and Robert Clark.

Greg read aloud as he typed the last line of the letter: "Your friend, Patrick Clark".

CHAPTER C

Existence guaranteed destruction.

From the moment its feet touched the earth it lost the absolute sense of time that enabled it to count even the emptiness.

Still it knew the end was coming. Locked in this physical body there were two possibilities; the black wave would reset it to its former state or the black wave would destroy it altogether.

It ran.

Its first efforts were stumbling and awkward. The ground, viewed for so long from above as a single homogenous block, had texture and bounce and a geography that could only be appreciated through experience. As with so much else, it found that its understanding was innate - or not so much learned anew as remembered. In ten strides it moved with confident, long bounds that sent it flying across the manicured lawns, bustling people aside.

They turned to look at it in bewilderment and anger - as if they had been roughly awakened from sleeping. Their expressions faded in a moment. It spared a single backward glance as it left the lawn to see them resume their clockwork conversations as if it had never passed.

A small path led through a wildflower garden and curved along the side of the lake. The smell of water, the reflecting sun on its surface - it wanted to stay. It heard the splashing in the water and wanted to abandon its run, to dive into the cooling lake and spend a lazy hour paddling with the trout.

It was a trap. It did not feel any of these things - rather there was a voice inside its head that told it these were its thoughts. It was a trap designed to catch any of the guests who might wander - though none ever had. They would never get beyond the lake and that siren call; the wordless jumble of the children masquerading as conversation.

It ran the red dirt road and felt lumps in its chest begin to burn. Lungs - it recognised them. A heart. The burning was in its legs, in its back.

It scorned this pain: these things were not real; it knew this. Insistently, another voice assured the existence of these things and with words as sharp as knives that voice explained the nature of pain.

It pushed on; luxuriating, revelling in each sensational lie; feeling driven by the power of its will to overcome the screams of its new physical body.

The nameless creator had designed this world to keep everyone trapped inside and it knew that meant there had to be a way out. If the world was inescapable there would be no need for the traps; if the road did not lead to an exit there would be no need for the illusion of fatigue.

Its feet struck the earth and sent up a cloud of red dust that followed it. A red wave was forming in its wake, in defiance of the black wave that must already be rising.

As the road turned to dip between the contours of two hills, it saw a door in the middle of the highway. A wooden door, painted white, standing apart from any building, not even inside a frame.

Its hand touched the handle and, to the right, in the corner of its eye it saw the black line that heralded the coming of the end. There was no time to consider any other action; it might never get another opportunity. The first particle of red dust vanished into darkness.

It tore open the door and hurled itself into the space beyond.

CHAPTER 9 - WEDNESDAY

Another day, another hospital. Patrick felt like a professional patient or one of those human-like dolls the Women's Institute used to practice resuscitation. He'd had cancer for less than forty-eight hours. In that time he'd acquired so many minor injuries if he were a child he would have been placed in institutional care.

Somewhere north of a dozen punctures in his skin, seeking blood with varying degrees of success, had blossomed into a patina of bruising that was almost art. Patrick was worried about looking too carefully at the bruising for fear of seeing the face of the Virgin Mary or Hitler.

Or both.

Kissing.

It was, at least, a different hospital; St John's in Livingston. As Patrick arrived he noticed that the hospital's crest depicted a knight in armour fighting a dragon. He had two major issues with this.

Firstly, there were two mortal saints in Christianity credited with the slaying of dragons: St George, of course; and the less well-known St Margaret of Antioch - who reputedly slew a dragon by being indigestible.

Secondly, the only St John that Patrick could place in a medical context was John the Baptist, because the Order of St John was otherwise known as St John's Ambulance. *That* St John would never have worn plate armour - the suit in the image was about fourteen hundred years ahead of his time, plus he spent a lot of time hanging about in rivers and would have rusted or drowned.

The armed man fighting the dragon on the floor of the hospital entrance hall was a mystery. Patrick resolved that if he was still alive in a couple of hours he would ask someone about the crest. It would be a treat for him. He would lose a testicle, but gain useless knowledge. Even this unfair trade was better than the surgical mugging in prospect.

St John's was much the same as the Western General in that his father had arrived before him on another space-age coffee table.

"Your ward is this way," Peter said and Patrick fell into stride beside the machine. Peter took a last look around the entrance hall and said, "Not exactly secure, is it? I mean anyone could walk in. No sign of a security guard and I've been here for ten minutes".

"You know people are allowed to be here?" Patrick said. "People are in this building twenty-four-seven".

"I'm saying that things could be stolen. Look at those chairs; they're not even screwed down".

"Maybe they could write 'property of St John's Hospital' on them".

"It would be a start," Peter said with a nod.

"Because the street value of decrepit hospital furniture that old people have peed on is phenomenal. Kids today are mad for beech-effect low seating upholstered in hard-wearing twill".

"Very funny," Peter said.

"There's money to be made there and no mistake". Patrick peered around them leaned-in to Peter to stage whisper, "In fact let's see how I feel after this operation and maybe we can take some away with us".

They turned a corner and went into the network of corridors that linked the muddle of buildings that made up the hospital. It was still a dark outside. The sun hadn't fully risen on the overcast day, leaving the corridors in shadow and the outside world in a grey half-light. Livingston, with its grim and uninviting new town concrete, seemed vacant and repellent as a tramp sleeping in a doorway.

There was barely silence before Peter asked, "How are you feeling?"

"Grand".

"I'm serious".

"I know; that's what I find so troubling. It's just a bit of cancer; it's nothing".

"You're my son and I love you," Peter said. "But I'm not going to apologise for my decision".

"I don't know what you mean".

Peter said, "You're allowed to admit that you have feelings about this. Or anything. The fact that I chose an early transfer to Singularity and you've decided to go through surgery - that doesn't make you something special or impress me".

"Another ambition left unachieved".

"That's not what I meant. I don't want you feeling like you have to hold on to the bitter end because you've got it into your head that I abandoned you".

"I don't feel that way".

"You were sixty years old," Peter said.

"Sixty isn't what it used to be," Patrick said.

"Is it that you don't remember what it was like?"

"I remember".

"Do you?" Peter asked. "Because after your mother was diagnosed with drug-resistant Alzheimer's I don't remember you being around a lot. I don't think you know what it's like to care for someone you love who doesn't know who you are, or who they are, or how to feed themselves, or how to go to the toilet-".

"Oh fuck off". Patrick came to a stop. "I mean what is it you want me to do about that? What would you like me to do about that now?"

The projector stopped a few feet ahead. "There's a lot you might have done".

"But what can I do now? What would you like me to do now?" Patrick said. "Would it make you happy to hear me say I'm a terrible son?"

"No. Why would that make me happy?"

"Then what? What do you want from me?"

"You need to acknowledge that it happened".

"I know-".

"That at the end your mother didn't know who she was, or what was going on; there was nothing left of her and she was frightened".

"Oh - stop".

"But she remembered you; about a week before she died and she asked for you-".

"Stop".

"And you weren't there," Peter said. "You hadn't seen her for months and you knew she was dying, and for a moment so did she. She asked for you and you weren't-".

"Oh, fuck, please, stop," Patrick said. "Stop!"

A silence fell between them, cut by the soft whirring of electric cooling fans and Patrick's ragged breathing.

"Today, dad?" Patrick said. "She's been dead for twelve years and you want to rip my fucking heart out today?"

Peter asked, "When would you have preferred to have this conversation?"

Patrick strode off, following the signs, but did not outpace the mobile projector.

They entered the ward and saw a group of six or seven nurses gathered together. One made eye contact with Patrick and broke away to speak to him.

Peter said, "You're missing my-".

Patrick interrupted, "Here comes a nurse. Don't say anything about stealing the furniture; we don't want to give the game away".

"Can I help you?" the nurse asked.

"We're here for an operation," Patrick said. "I'm having it, my father is going to hang around and offer pointers in case any of the surgical team are foreign".

Peter scowled and Patrick pretended not to notice. The nurse spoke to Peter, "I'm sorry; you'll have to go, no visitors on the ward before surgery".

"I'm just going to see him settled," Peter said.

"I'm sorry, sir. Visitors, whether they are here or pretending to be here, can only be here during visiting hours".

Patrick would have loved to see that on a sign.

Peter said, "Well then".

Patrick did not make eye contact. "I'll speak to you after the operation".

"I'll see you back at your house if not before".

"Tidy up a bit while you're there".

"Yes," Peter replied, "you were always very funny". He vanished, leaving the mobile holoprojector to trundle back to wherever the machines waited.

The nurse scanned Patrick's thumb and, finding everything in order, escorted him through to a room containing six beds.

Patrick was the first person there, but over the course of the next hour five other patients took the remaining beds. All were men, as one might expect for this kind of surgery. All had a serious attitude to the business of remaining still and not speaking to or looking at one another. One man took to reading, one listening to music, but the others seemed content to stare into space. In general, people didn't read paper books or listen to music with separate headphones, but the hospital's insistence that mobile implants be turned off meant that both the physical book and the music system were necessary, if a little arcane.

Patrick tried staring into space, then tried reading and found it marginally better.

Actually he was being stupid. The Knights of St John of Jerusalem were Hospitallers. The St John of the hospital must be in recognition of the order of knights, rather than the actual saint and the dragon was symbolic of evil or disease or dragons - rather than an actual dragon.

Christian mythology was, in his opinion, boring. In the Hellenistic tradition, if someone was eaten by a lion and cut their way out of its stomach, they didn't mean a metaphorical lion; they meant the kind you can see at zoos. In Christianity the story of someone being swallowed by a terrible monster was meant to represent what it was like to pray very hard.

Having solved the mystery of the hospital crest and given up on space-staring, Patrick now had nothing to do but read.

He didn't have to wait long before two nurses came in and asked everyone to get undressed. This was how orgies were supposed to start.

In this case the nurses were only interested in preparing the patients for the arrival of the surgeon.

Mr Men went through the patients in an order that didn't match their layout in the room and thus passed by Patrick's bed twice before coming to see him. During Mr Men's route around the room Patrick learned that one of the patients was having a double orchidectomy - the removal of both testicles. Castration. That was difficult to listen to, and because of the size of the room it was also difficult to not listen to. It seemed that the man wasn't well-informed about the consequences of this and an extensive discussion took place about the possibility of sperm recovery and having children.

There was, the consultant informed him, no possibility of either.

So when Mr Men drew the curtain around Patrick's bed, Patrick knew that while it might stop people seeing him in various states of undress, it didn't stop sound reaching the other patients.

After they exchanged pleasantries the surgeon asked, "It's the left one isn't it?" Patrick confirmed that it was indeed the left one, and felt somewhat nervous about having to confirm that. Under pressure he was prone to saying left and meaning right (and vice versa) and when giving directions he often restored to pointing. "Do you have any questions about the operation?"

"No," Patrick said - because he didn't. Mr Men explained anyway. Maybe you had to speak to patients for a certain amount of time before you were allowed to cut bits off them. Unless there was a war on. Patrick was asked to sign the consent form, which he did - and then with the same pen used to sign the form, Mr Men drew an incision line on Patrick's groin and made several large arrows pointing to it.

Patrick, in a backless paper gown, went into the bed. Mr Men, in a single-breasted, two-button wool suit, went on to the last patient in the room. That was that. All he had to do now was wait and as the time left to him reduced he found his book increasingly unsatisfactory.

In the two hours that followed, between the visit of the surgeon and a nurse arriving to tell him he was going to theatre, Patrick gained personal insight into the religious belief that people should not mutilate their bodies. Some people thought it was because the body, being a creation and a mirror of the divine, was itself divine. To scar it was sacrilege. Drawing on it with a pen was probably sinful too. Patrick realised that a much deeper philosophy underpinned and strengthened that once-potent, now-extinct belief.

It was because it was bloody scary.

Thinking that any piece of him could be removed made his whole body hum with fear. For all that Captain Patrick lived in the brain, his identity was somehow inseparable from his body's nuts and bolts and it was reminding him of this with countless signals and tremors.

As a child he had been swimming in the sea and with his foot he disturbed a ray coasting along the surface of the sand. Recalling the memory of his child's mind, the beast was dark and massive and wriggled as if irritated. The tiny part of his ancestral brain, that was not so different from the tiny brain of the fish, screamed that he was going to be eaten and incoherent panic responses erupted across his entire body.

The ray swam off, uninterested in the thrashing boy many times its size, while Patrick almost drowned himself in four feet of calm water.

He could still feel the shape of that fear - and it was not a thing that existed entirely within his mind, but was sensed and remembered with equal lucidity in every limb. The fear of being consumed was a black hole of terror and this experience was somehow a fractal part of that fear. Patrick's greater conscious mind sat on the fear; squashed it - but the conscious mind, ever conflicted, wasn't sure if that was the right thing to do or not.

He blinked and in that space of time a porter arrived with a nurse. It was difficult for Patrick to keep all the nurses collected in his head. The intimate social situation of having his blood taken hadn't happened; so they were nameless to him as he, almost certainly, was nameless to them.

The porter was something different. He had a broad forehead and eyes that seemed to have too much skin around, which turned down at the sides, and there was something vaguely wrong with his mouth; something that reminded Patrick of a fish. It was impossible to tell how old people were anymore; Patrick didn't look anything like his own age. But the porter looked worn down, humbled by his years; older than Patrick had ever seen someone who still had a job.

"Mr Clark is going to the holding area for anaesthetic, then to theatre two," the nurse said to the porter.

"Yes," the porter said with a deep, but somehow muffled voice.

"Where is he going?"

"Theatre two," the porter said after a moment of thought. "But first-".

"But first anaesthetic," the nurse spoke over him.

"The first bit's the important bit," Patrick said.

The porter disconnected Patrick's bed from power cables and monitoring wires and he and another porter pushed Patrick along to the waiting area. It was a pretty nice way to travel, except the paper gown and thread-thin sheet on top didn't help with staying warm. As a large group of people were going to be looking at his genitals in a couple of minutes, Patrick felt that he should at least be provided with a heat pad and an erotic picture.

The waiting area was aptly named. People waited in their beds to be taken to theatre. People coming back from theatre waited to be taken to their wards. In one corner of the room the porters had set up a table and some chairs and they seemed to wait there to be found useful.

All the porters shared characteristics that made them extraordinary. There was something indefinably wrong with them. They were all old and it occurred to Patrick this would have to be the case.

Pre-birth screenings were normal and keeping a child with brain development problems wasn't done anymore. The cocktail of vitamins and supplements that kept Patrick looking about thirty years younger weren't all that expensive - but you couldn't afford them on a porter's salary. If they somehow saved their wages from a lifetime and were able to afford the transfer to Singularity, the network would reject them. Singularity could not replicate the function of abnormal brains - and there wasn't any real pressure for that situation to change.

Patrick was a little curious about what the porters would be discussing, but his bed had been put the worst possible distance away from their table. He was able to hear the sounds of conversation but not any of the actual words used.

He turned his head from the table and saw two women in surgical scrubs standing at the foot of his bed. It seemed like the people in this hospital were trained in being sneaky and appearing from nowhere.

"Can you tell me your name?" the first one said.

"Yes," Patrick said.

"What is it?"

"Patrick Clark".

"Alright Mr Clark. Can you confirm that this is your signature here," the first one asked and held out the form Patrick had signed earlier with the surgeon's groin pen. He confirmed that it was. "Do you have any caps, any bridgework or any false teeth?" He confirmed that he did not. "Do you have any allergies to anything?" Again, he stated that he did not. "What is the operation you're going in for?"

"Orchidectomy," Patrick said. He then clarified by adding, "They're removing my left testicle". He felt silly for clarifying. If someone had come into his office and said 'Duat... you know, the Egyptian underworld where the hearts of the dead are weighed by Anubis', he would have punched them in the face. With his expression, if not with his fist.

"That's all fine," said the first one. Patrick was glad she thought so, otherwise he'd have called the whole thing off. "We're going to take you along for anaesthetic now".

The first one and the second one chatted about something work-related as they took Patrick to another room; this one small and crammed with machinery and tubes. He saw little except the ceiling until a young man hovered over him.

He wasn't wearing a badge that said 'trainee' as most jobs with higher social standing than waitress didn't involve wearing demeaning badges. Doctors wouldn't get to practice a lot of medicine if they began every consultation by confessing that they weren't one hundred percent sure what they were doing, but if you gave them a chance they were sure they'd muddle through. Come to think of it that kind of honesty would stunt your career whether you were a plumber or a nuclear physicist.

Patrick had been a university professor for a long time and knew at first glance the difference between study, intelligence, eagerness - and experience.

"Good morning Mr Clark," the trainee said.

Patrick was beginning to feel put out by the fact that everyone kept calling him mister. He had two PhDs, he could read Sumerian and ancient Greek (and Latin, but that was much less impressive). He had published thirty-seven peer-reviewed journal articles and written three books.

Not good books, admittedly, but he'd bloody well written them and what they lacked in quality they made much worse with sheer length. If that wasn't enough, he was an actual professor, with an actual chair (named in honour of an actual dead person) at an actual university.

"Hello," Patrick replied, because the last thing he wanted was the trainee feeling jittery and giving him too little anaesthetic.

"Do you have any allergies?" the trainee doctor asked, looking at the paper file that accompanied Patrick everywhere he went and which nobody trusted.

"No," Patrick said.

"Can you confirm that this is your signature?" Did you pack this bag yourself? Do you have any fruits or vegetables inside you? How much wood could a woodchuck chuck? And so on. Patrick answered all of the questions in a pleasant, even tone until the doctor was satisfied.

The anaesthetic was delivered by another doctor - a trainer, rather than trainee - through a needle in Patrick's hand. It took very little time to find a vein to stick things into him; different veins, he supposed.

The trainer doctor assured Patrick that this was the kind of anaesthetic that put you to sleep, rather than the kind that paralyzed you. So there was no chance of him being awake and aware, trapped in a frozen agony throughout the operation. It was nice to be reminded that some people were conscious during operations where parts of their body were-.

Patrick fell asleep and a dream replaced all his senses.

He saw, rising out of some great, lightless depths the flat, rippling shape of a ray. It did not come closer so much as grow huge, expanding up beyond the confines of any ocean; vast above him and growing still, blocking-out the sun and the infinite sky until the sum total of creation was Patrick Clark and the thing that meant to destroy Patrick Clark. In that timeless moment he stood in darkness, in silent commune with the nothing at the farthest edge of conscious thought.

It opened its mouth to swallow him.

There was nothing.

Then he was on the ward again.

He was conscious, before he was conscious of anything else, of the taste in his mouth. It was pure oxygen and something else - a sedative gas. He ran his tongue over his gums and tried to wash the taste away with spit, but it wouldn't go; his mouth had been marinated in it.

He lifted the bed cover over his head and surveyed the area. He had a large bandage covering his groin where the scar would be and a tickle of pain - no more than that - told him the surgery had taken place.

His scrotum, hanging more or less normally, nevertheless felt strange. It was like he was looking at someone else's scrotum - disturbing in itself. The sensation of it being there was diminished in a way he would never have imagined possible. It wasn't analogous to anything else; it didn't feel like an elbow or a knee or an ankle - or any seldom-considered body part. It felt other. It felt like an unknown, empty shape.

Almost as strange - they had shaved two thirds of his pubic hair and left the other third. It was a damn poor barber they had here and no mistake. Patrick felt like he'd been subjected to a fraternity prank taken way too far.

Despite a cyclone of grogginess, Patrick struggled to stay awake and pull himself into a sitting position. A nurse saw his efforts and encouraged him to lie down again, which made Patrick more determined to sit up. To sit up in defiance. To stand up. To walk.

To run!

But he would start with sitting up.

Seeing the cause was lost, the nurse asked, "Would you like something to eat? A cup of tea or coffee?" He hadn't eaten since the previous evening in preparation for the operation. Patrick was hungry and at the same time on the edge of throwing up. It was not a situation that could continue; he had to push in one direction or the other. Either throw up right now or eat immediately.

"I would, yes," he said and ran afoul of the tea or coffee question again. "Tea please, milk and sugar".

"We've got some sandwiches. Chicken mayonnaise, tuna mayonnaise and ham and... mayonnaise I think," the nurse said. Mayonnaise, being made from oil and eggs, was obviously known for nausea-reducing properties that those outside of the medical profession were unaware of.

"Chicken would be nice," Patrick said and two minutes later the nurse returned with a cup of tea and a tuna mayonnaise sandwich, which Patrick inhaled without complaint.

After the sandwich, Patrick decided to risk a trip to the toilet. Both because he needed to go and because he wanted to see if needing was still sufficient to enable him to go.

He managed, with some contortions, to put on a pair of baggy underpants to preserve his dignity. He would be navigating the distance between his bed and the toilet wearing those pants, a despised pair of slippers and a paper dressing gown lightly speckled with his dried blood. It was a look he felt sure would catch on across the entire ward as the other patients awoke and each navigated his own route to check the plumbing.

Walking was interesting. He could. There was no denying that one leg would go in front of the other in a conventional sense. He didn't need a cane or a walking frame - and even if he had wanted one there weren't any to be seen. He shuffled all the way over, round the beds, not in terrible pain but wary that any sudden movement might cause terrible pain.

In the toilet, behind the safety of a locked door, he lifted his paper gown, lowered his pants and leaned forward over the bowl. Pressure might be an issue and he didn't want to have to bend down to wipe his feet. With the force of his will he commanded the flow to begin and, after a dramatic interval, it did. A thin dribble and a short, steady stream gave Patrick a small sense of triumph.

Not in the mood for shaking anything down there, Patrick dabbed the end with some toilet paper and made ready for a return journey which he undertook with more aplomb. He wasn't strutting or wearing a hat set to a jaunty angle, but he had wrestled some spring back; recovered some confidence. If the London Marathon had started next to Patrick's bed he was sure he would be able to summon the strength to watch someone else run it in a respectable time.

Once back in bed, waiting for the waves of nausea to subside, the time passed both slowly and quickly in a way that could only be measured on a Dali clock. By increments the physical and mental effects of the anaesthetic ebbed away and when the surgeon came by to report on how the operation had gone Patrick was in his approximate right frame of mind.

Mr Men drew the curtain around Patrick's bed and stood for a moment. There was no sense of him preparing to give news that was either good or bad.

"We had a look at the lump under the microscope. We'll do some tests, but based on what we've seen it's lymphoma. It's much less common than other types of cancer we find in the testes and if this is what we've found then we would expect to find cancerous cells elsewhere in the body. We'll want to take some blood from you again in a few days, but I've asked for an emergency scan and hopefully we'll get you in tomorrow".

Patrick felt a knot in his stomach that had nothing to do with mayonnaise.

His whole body spoke to his mind in a burst of fear that made his thoughts seem certain and immediate.

Patrick Clark was going to die.

CHAPTER 10

Katherine sat on her couch, ensconced between cushions, while a pizza she had taken little interest in cooled on the coffee table. She had been working for an hour already using her data pad, her mobile implant and at one point the holoprojector to store her thoughts and notes for a lecture that would take place on Monday.

This was all part of her Plan B.

Plan A was to become the operational manager of Singularity and shape that role to suit her. Plan A was not quite naked ambition; but it was at least scantily-clad, dance of the seven veils, feathers and a g-string ambition. Unfortunately Plan A was also a long shot with a massive downside. Katherine dreaded nothing more than being the also-ran to a woman she despised.

The all-purpose reserve Plan B said she needed to raise her profile. Even though Singularity was highly visible, her role was not and anyone not associated with the network might think she was nothing more than a regional manager. If she wanted to land the kind of job she deserved then she needed to change that perception.

The vehicle for profile raising hadn't been Katherine's first choice. There had been cajoling, persuading, wheedling, emotional blackmail and alcohol. It was the alcohol that won the argument and Katherine had reluctantly agreed to give a series of university lectures.

The series had been offered as six lectures on the broad theme of the integration and humanisation of computers - she said one. At an offer of five she had maintained her position at one. When she was offered four, she said that possibly, after a great deal of consideration and deep thinking that she could commit to doing as many as one.

The negotiation concluded with agreement on two lectures as long as her friend from the university bought another bottle of wine.

Her reluctance was not due to anything so dull and ordinary as a fear of public speaking. Katherine spoke well and in her life had never been lacking in confidence.

She'd done a lecture a little more than two years ago on viral intelligence where she had posited the notion of artificial intelligences between and within larger intelligences; that simple feedback loops could under particular circumstances build over time to form a complexity sufficient to have motive and reason separate from all programming of its component parts.

The lecture was broadcast online. One week later, five different professors from leading technical institutes independently wrote to different journals explaining how her idea could not work.

Ironically, it was Singularity and out-of-brain consciousness that reignited the controversy of thinking machines. A century earlier, Alan Turing had proposed a test to determine whether a computer could deceive a human into thinking it was a real person. The Singular-Base-Two had been the first computer able to consistently pass the Turing Test and had become the foundation for the Singularity Network.

Immediately after this a new test was proposed, called a Second Degree Turing. In this the brain function of a human being in electronic storage was compared against the processing of a man-made artificial intelligence. The AI would pass the test if it could process information in a way indistinguishable from a human being.

One hundred percent of AIs failed the Second Degree Turing. The elegant and efficient structure of an AI was so different to human thought that it would never be convincing. It was this marked difference that prompted one of science's most painful discoveries.

Some rather gruesome experiments had taken place where a rat's mind was removed and replaced by a rat program designed to do everything the rat could do. Result?

Nothing happened.

Life was complicated. Life had to evolve. Life had to come from chemical soup - otherwise it wasn't really alive. It was not possible to spontaneously create life whether you were a scientist or an invisible sky man.

Life had to create its own vital spark.

Her colleagues had reminded her of these and other experiments, wondering how she could be ignorant of them. They'd called her a closet deist. They said - not to put too fine a point on it - all the product she was using in her hair was interfering with her brain.

On the day she read the letters - that her colleagues had been rather too eager to show her - Katherine wished for nothing else than to be the kind of woman who threw things, erupted into floods of tears, screamed and sulked all at the same time.

She had not done any of that; remaining as calm and stately as the Orient Express, as sleek and unruffled as a Shinkansen.

She felt it though. She felt all the fury of radiating heat like summer lightning in her brain.

At one point a popular science magazine planned to run a story calling her a twenty-first century Frankenstein who planned the genesis of dangerous viral life. She had said nothing about experiments to create such intelligences, only suggested how they might come about. Her lawyers had stepped hard on the magazine and the article vanished; but by that point Katherine had already decided to leave her position as Director of New Technologies at Panasonic for Singularity; for something a little more back-room.

But only for a while.

Once the lectures were booked she called up her recruitment agent and put herself back on the market.

Katherine was independently wealthy; she would never be short of money in her life, but it would be nice to have one of those big salaries again. The kind of salary that came with a private bathroom in your office. An office with spectacular views over a town populated by technical wizards and the people who made them expensive, foamy coffee and delivered their dinners. A position that let you mix with people who knew that sometimes you needed to travel by private jet and the rainforest could get bent.

Important as they were, with all the preparations for this thing the government wanted, the lectures had taken a back seat until her brain injected her with a panicked reminder that the first was days away.

She knew that Louise had made a particular effort to promote them and it was both concern for her friend and a growing desire to return to prominence in her field that caused her to attack the task with vigour.

The ringing of the door bell pressed against the cell of her mind. It was the buzzing of a gnat and she didn't consider responding until she'd finished her sentence.

"Hello?" said a voice in Katherine's head as she put her finger to her temple.

"Hello," Katherine said in reply.

"Dr Valentine?" asked the voice. She confirmed that it was. "We've got a delivery here for you". Katherine was not expecting anything and with the learned scepticism of a woman who had always lived alone, she turned her holoprojector to the channel for the building's security cameras.

A blue lorry was parked with its back towards the door of the building. The back door was open and inside she could see a number of crates of different sizes. One man had selected the crate which was destined for Katherine and was bringing it from the truck to street level using a hydraulic lift. The other man, with whom she was speaking, stood in-front of the camera and, either sensing he was being watched or seeing the tiny camera in the door activate, turned to look into the lens.

"Can I see some identification?"

The man gave a long-suffering grunt and fished around in the pockets of his boiler suit for a card, which he held up to the camera. A hologram on the card contained a dye made from a substance with a specific half-life. It reflected differently at certain points in its lifecycle and this was verified using a sample of the same substance held in a secure location and accessed remotely via an encrypted connection. Identity cards using this technology could never be duplicated or faked.

Her holoprojector updated the man's details to the screen under his picture. His name was Maurice Templeton - a flared trouser of a name; there had never been a man who could wear it well. His employment details related to a local delivery company. This did not help Katherine in understanding what the delivery might be.

Maurice scowled at the camera.

"Yes, alright. Bring it up". She was a scientist and scientists were as susceptible to the charms of curiosity as cats.

All of the actual 'bringing' of the package was done by a broad, flat robot that laboured underneath the large crate. It negotiated its way into the building, into the elevator and through doorways using a sweeping laser beam to scan the floor and walls around it. The other man stayed with the lorry, while Maurice had the difficult job of walking in-front of the robot, holding doors open and making sure it didn't scratch paintwork.

Katherine stood in the corridor outside. Having already opened the double doors of her apartment, the robot trundled up the corridor, squeezed through the doorway and sat motionless in the centre of her entrance hall awaiting instructions and continuing its three-hundred-and-sixty degree laser sweeps of the room at ground level. Katherine followed it inside and scrutinised the delivery.

To call it a package was an understatement. It was a cubic crate, four feet on each side and the wooden surface was unmarked with any indication of what it contained. Maurice held out a pad for Katherine's thumb print.

"What is this?" Katherine asked.

"I just deliver it, sweetheart. Could be anything in there. Maybe it's a present from an admirer". Maurice would have been turned away at the doors of MENSA, but he was not so dim as to miss the expression on Katherine's face. The twinkle disappeared from Maurice's eye like a star going out.

"I'm not accepting delivery until I know what it is," she said. Maurice nodded and the robot performed a complex operation whereby it slid itself out from under the crate while also lowering it onto the floor. The robot withdrew itself to sit in the doorway while the rest of the unpacking was done. Maurice unclipped the fastenings that held the crate together and piled the sides neatly. In a final flourish he swept away a sheet of polyurethane to reveal the contents.

It was not much smaller than the crate it had come in and the same shape. The cube was made of a transparent material and open on the top. It was also about two-thirds full of a blue gel.

"Ho ho," said Maurice, who recognised the device as quickly as Katherine did.

Despite herself, Katherine felt a blush erupt over most of her body, outpacing the geyser of indignant fury rising inside her. She opened her mouth to speak. She wasn't sure what she was going to say, but was prepared to leave the details to the moment.

A sudden whirring of gears made her stop, open-mouthed and turn her head. The flat, broad bulk of the robot speed across the floor towards her, she leapt out of the way, her back pressed against the wall. The robot continued on its path and hit Maurice on the back of the legs. The delivery man toppled and fell forward onto the cube; his torso fit neatly into the square hole, forcing back his arms and legs and leaving him wedged.

The robot sent its laser sweeping around the room and instinct made Katherine scramble onto a side table nearby. The beam of light captured in precise detail the contours of every object, their dimensions and their positions relative to one another and the robot's tiny but specialised electronic brain interpreted these into a picture of the room.

It was a picture accurate to sixteen inches above the floor. Apart from the laser light, the robot was practically senseless and otherwise blind.

The beam passed over the legs of the table Katherine was kneeling on. It did not see her.

Maurice made a yelping sound and struggled to get free.

"No!" Katherine said. "Stay still".

Maurice was too frightened to listen. He continued to struggle without effect and the beam came around again to the transparent cube, where it stopped.

In horror, Katherine watched as the robot trundled towards the cube and disgorged a thick, jointed metal arm like the tail of a black scorpion. It raised the arm above the cube, above the stuck delivery man and it pressed downward.

Maurice squealed in pathetic alarm and writhed impotently. The arm continued; the rate was almost the same as if Maurice had not been there at all. He gurgled as he was throttled by the edge of the cube, while the machine made the same peaceful, dispassionate whirring of motors. Katherine shrieked as an equation composed of the strength of the cube, the pressure of the arm and the frailty of the human body resolved itself into physical certainty.

Maurice's neck snapped and his head bent backwards over his shoulder, allowing his body to be shoved down the cube. Katherine watched the dead man's limbs bend backwards with similar ease as he was forced into the blue gel, already turning purple where blood leaked from his nose and mouth.

The robot's scanner swept back and forth over the narrow range of the cube in front of it. The arm stopped applying pressure and withdrew as the laser swept the room again. Katherine could tell by its interrogative re-sweeps what the robot was looking for.

The arm reached out and picked up a power cable that dangled from one corner of the cube, next to a series of control buttons. The robot turned in place and then moved towards a power socket in the wall where the arm made a complex series of twists. It inserted the power cable into the wall and turned back to the cube.

Some of the controls were out of the machine's normal visual range and it made a series of unhurried adjustments to raise its electronic eye to perceive the panel.

This was Katherine's opportunity.

She clambered down from the table and rushed to the kitchen where she pulled a pack of screwdrivers from a drawer and lifted her kettle from its stand. Carrying both back to the hall she edged around the machine, keeping out of the narrow range of its vision until she was behind it.

If it noticed her... She didn't have time to think about those consequences.

She cursed herself for fumbling with the screwdrivers as she leaned over the robot, but managed to put one into its casing. She let the screws fall to the floor. Unable to get purchase on the flat metal plate of the maintenance hatch she used the screwdriver like a wedge to pry it open and was rewarded with the sight of black and yellow warning labels and mass of intricate technology.

Under laboratory conditions Katherine would never dream of doing what she was about to do. She jammed the screwdriver, in a frenzied series of jabs, through the housing of what should have been important components.

She climbed back onto the wooden table, opened the kettle lid and - as the mechanical arm moved towards the power button on the cube - she dumped the water through the open casing and into the exposed circuitry.

Everything slowed down in the fraction of a second before the robot was rocked by an internal explosion.

The combination of gasses, electricity and hydraulics providing its motive force came to an unfriendly and spectacular parting of the ways that blew Katherine off the table and slammed her into a wall.

She did not pass out. People passed-out in movies; in the real world it seemed people stayed awake and felt the impact. She heard alarms, but couldn't tell if they were real or a ringing sound in her head.

What remained of the robot was frozen in motion with its arm a hair away from the power button on the cube. Inside the cube the open eyes of Maurice

Templeton, forever without their twinkle, stared straight at Katherine through a haze of blue-purple gel.

CHAPTER 11 - THURSDAY

Patrick was in another hospital and discovered that his sense of fun about visiting hospitals had altogether vanished. The Edinburgh Royal Infirmary was the newest he'd been to, though it was still forty or fifty years old. It had spare capacity in its medical imaging machinery, while St John's and the Western were booked solid.

He couldn't help but wonder if the machine was free because someone had died. A bit of him thought that was important. Most of him was numb - in particular the patch of his groin below the incision the surgeon had cut to remove his testicle and insert the prosthesis.

They'd cut the link between that part of his body and his brain and while his heart supplied it with blood, his lungs supplied it with oxygen and his stomach and bowels sent it nutrients, it was as if that patch of skin was no longer part of him. The loss of sensation extended almost from his leg, across inches of skin, to the base of his penis on the sinister side, and down and round the left of his scrotum.

If the same loss of sensation had happened in his hand or foot then he would have ranted, he would have howled - in a dignified, British, middle-class sense of the word; something similar to a tut. He would have expected physio- and other kinds of -therapy to restore full sensation.

However where the loss was he had not previously been aware of feeling anything. It had been and now was not. As a result he'd presumed the loss was a normal part of the surgery and hadn't mentioned it to anyone.

When he'd been bathing that morning, for the first time since the operation, he'd removed the gauze and considered the staples that held together the puckered flaps of his skin. His body, cut open and stapled together was the strangest thing he had ever seen. The intersection of a half billion years of cellular development and some medical-grade craft supplies.

He'd covered it with a fresh bandage and tried not to think about it; after all he couldn't take the staples out for at least another week and if he developed a complex about it the time would be intolerable.

Patrick was surprised that the staples hadn't prevented him going into the MRI machine. Magnetic Resonance Imagery - as the name implied - relied on magnetism. Patrick had imagined that putting himself into such a machine might result in the staples ricocheting around the room, throwing up sparks like gunfire. The staples, as it had turned out, weren't made of metal at all. When the pathologist had located a lymphoma during the operation, they'd stapled him together with a special kind of plastic which duplicated the effects of metal staples.

He wondered what his prosthesis might be made of.

A wooden egg was the wrong way to think about it. It wouldn't be made of wood for one thing, and Patrick knew it wasn't egg-shaped for another. Yet there was the idea in his head - a wooden egg - and there was no more compelling idea to dislodge it. He supposed that as he didn't know what his real testicle looked like or was made of there was a sense of fairness in having no more information about the fake one.

From the outside, from the perspective of the casual observer, there was no difference. The real one and the fake one looked the same. Only Patrick, whose consciousness touched one and not the other, would be able to differentiate between them.

In 2039 Professor Clark started a new semester by walking into class and, without introduction, demanding information.

'Tell me something,' Patrick said. 'Anything'.

There was a pause while the assembled students collectively and individually tried to decide if Patrick was their professor or a misplaced lunatic. Eventually someone replied, 'The Eiffel Tower opened on the thirty-first of March 1889'.

'Good,' Patrick said. 'Now prove it. Papers due in next week'.

Then he left.

The fact had been correct - that was when the Eiffel Tower had opened; there had been much celebration earlier that year in recognition of its century and a half of service to French tourism.

The fact was irrelevant.

The most memorable answer concluded: 'I cannot confirm the construction date, or even the existence of the Eiffel Tower, or of Paris or France or myself. However, I recall having the lobster fricassee at the Jules Verne restaurant on the second floor about two months ago. Therefore, if I exist, the Eiffel Tower is at least two months old. If I do not exist, there is no Eiffel Tower'.

Patrick gave the paper a C-minus and a smiley face.

It was unprovable, of course. Reality was an unverifiable construct; all facts outside of pure mathematics were hearsay. But if people went around believing that just because it was true it would ruin courtroom drama as a genre.

'What's the right answer?' someone asked. 'I mean, I know there's no right answer, but what's the right way to answer the question?'

'It's the opposite,' Patrick said. 'There is a right answer - either the Eiffel Tower was opened then or it wasn't. There's no one way of getting that answer. Acknowledging that it is impossible to certainly know anything compels us to think critically about the world around us; to challenge all assumptions. A reality described by our experience alone is incomplete; the world we live in must also be constructed of our rational thought and subject to alteration by that same force. So what we have here is the theory of the Eiffel Tower. Basic science; for us to consider it proven what must that theory be? What must it have the potential to be? Anybody?'

'It should be disprovable?' someone said.

'Good,' Patrick said. 'Something more of you need to include in your work. A theory is either proven or not proven - we must admit both possibilities and test against them. So for next week, I want you all to disprove the Eiffel Tow- no, I'm kidding; read chapters five through nine of the text. I notice some of you still have a paper copy of the second edition with my picture on the back. If you can burn that so next year's class have to download new copies my publisher and I would greatly appreciate it'.

Patrick lay on a sliding bench as the MRI machine emitted a continuous hum and he moved slowly through it. It scanned his body from head to toe in a series of sections. He had been instructed to remain still throughout. By the end all he could think about was scratching his nose. Would that affect the results? While he could control his hand not reaching for his nose, he wasn't able to prevent his nose from twitching.

If he was diagnosed with nose cancer, he would be sure to mention that.

It was over in seconds and Patrick was slid out from the tube and allowed to put on real clothing again. Clothing not made from paper and held together at the back with string and hope: clothing that did not make him feel like a cheap Christmas present.

As Patrick was suspected of having cancer elsewhere in his body he had been transferred from a urological specialist to an oncological specialist who was at this hospital today.

It would have been easy to be impressed with the efficiency of the whole health treatment business were it not for the seven inch hole in his groin that had been used to remove something less than two inches end-to-end.

Patrick sat and time dragged. He went to the toilet, shuffling all the way there and back like an old man. He didn't even need to go that much; it was something to do; a way to bisect the edgeless and featureless landscape of time.

He had been pleased at being consistently able to go to the toilet. Not ecstatic - you couldn't let these things get out of perspective - but pleased. There had been the small risk that his surgeon would slice through something mechanical in the urinary system. Whatever other malaise, malady or malfunction afflicted him, Patrick did not want to have to carry around a bag of his own urine strapped to his thigh. As far as he was concerned, human dignity was the faculty and ability to decide when and where you would pee. Once you lost that, nobody would ever sit next to you on the bus again.

People who'd received heart surgery were supposed to lose their appetite for days or weeks after an operation. They had to be forced to eat. Not with sticks and threats, but with serious no-nonsense people putting food in-front of you and not leaving until it wasn't there anymore. A sign of recovery from surgery was the recovery of appetite.

Patrick had not experienced any loss of hunger. He stared into the vending machine in the waiting area of the hospital wondering why, if chocolate and crisps were so bad for you, they were the only things on sale here. He took his bank card from his wallet and considered his options.

What had diminished was his sex drive. He didn't have a partner anyway, but he had noticed there was no movement downstairs. No sign. No inclination. Not a nod or a shuffle. Normally the random movements of his old fellow over the course of a day were like a badger rummaging in his trousers.

Patrick's relationship with his penis was like living in a flat upstairs from someone who was your best friend, even though you had nothing in common. His downstairs neighbour kept unsociable hours, acquired friends easily, lost interest quickly, made unreasonable demands on the fraternity of their association and used all the tissues. It was. There was nothing more to say than that.

Then one day all the noise stops. You find yourself considering the blank door of the downstairs flat, worried that its resident has had a single person accident. Fallen and couldn't get up. Fell asleep in the bath and drowned. Electrocuted by a malfunctioning homemade sex toy - and news reports confirmed there was a lot of that going around. Then, having never considered the possibility that you could get rid of this nuisance neighbour, you are terrified to try the door for fear that within stirs no life.

It was a door Patrick was happy to leave un-pushed-on for the time being; secure that in the fullness of time his appetite would return. His trusty right testicle would pick up the slack (so to speak) and he wouldn't even notice the difference.

"Professor Clark?"

Patrick stuffed his bank card back into his pocket as if he had been caught looking at the vending machine. As if the vending machine wasn't to be bought from, but was innocently standing there when he came over and offered it money or the possibility of seeing puppies. The motion had been jerky and Patrick felt it as a twinge that might have travelled up his body and flickered over his face.

"I'm Mr Forth". The man had an air of quiet confidence and calm. He was handsome without being striking in any particular way and his sandy-coloured hair was parted on the left in a style that only certain men could wear, but which never went out of fashion. "Let's step into the consulting room".

Patrick followed into the small examination room come office. Mr Forth carried a data pad in his hand and Patrick caught sight of a medical scan. Patrick didn't need to see any more than that to know they had found something. He could feel himself slipping away from the first moment the doctor spoke, as if he were sitting in a tunnel behind his head and looking through his eyes from a long way off.

"Professor Clark, let me ask you a couple of questions," Mr Forth said. "Without checking the time, how long would you say you've been here this morning?"

The question was surprising. He had turned off his mobile implant when he entered the hospital. It had been 09:28. That left him with only an approximate sense of how long things had taken. Patrick added up the rough units of time. Finding the correct department using the coloured lines in the floor, waiting, getting undressed, having the scan, getting dressed, waiting, going to the toilet, waiting, propositioning the vending machine.

"About three hours".

"Could it have been longer than that?" He had not reacted in any way to Patrick's estimate. Patrick shrugged.

"It might be three and a half hours, but not any longer than that".

"What about less than three hours? Could it have been less than three hours?"

"Not by much". He did the sums in his head again and came back with the same conclusion. "I would be surprised if it had been less than two and three quarter hours".

"Do you remember what time it was when you came into the hospital?"

"It was nine twenty-eight," Patrick said. Mr Forth nodded and with a single finger typed a short note on the data pad.

"Good," Mr Forth said. "It's good that you're able to remember precisely. Now, can you please turn around and look at the clock on the wall behind you and tell me what time it is".

Patrick made to turn his body in the chair, but a sharp reminder told him not to. He stood and shuffled around on the spot to look at the military-style clock. It was 10:41 - not much more than an hour since he had come through the front door of the hospital.

"I don't..."

"Please sit down, Professor Clark". Mr Forth tapped a few commands on the data pad and a small projector on the doctor's desk sprung into life. The three-dimensional transparent image was of the inside of a human head shown from three different angles; front-to-back, left-to-right and top-down. Mr Forth pointed to a singular white blob right in the middle of all three shots. It was somewhere between a golf ball and a tennis ball in size, but it had irregular edges and was spiny like an anemone.

Patrick found it impossible to concentrate on what he was being told.

"Professor Clark, I'm afraid to say... a one-in-a-billion cancer diagnosis. You have a kind of... which is what was found in your testicle... several other places... most of your organs... mass in your head is different... growing very slowly and has pushed into every part of your brain... extremely rare... the brain haemorrhages... you would be in that group too-".

"I'm sorry," Patrick said. He gave his head a light shake, trying to shift the fog that had descended on him. "I missed what you were saying".

"I said if you hadn't found the lump on your testicle, then it's likely you would have suddenly died. I had a look through the literature a few minutes ago and there are no records of a growth of this size in any patient, living or dead-".

It was all very interesting, like the last five minutes of a History Channel programme about your life. Specifically the bit where you die.

Mr Forth hadn't said what was really important.

"-I have to tell you that this cancer is inoperable, untreatable and will prove fatal in the near future".

He saw the news coming in his mind's eye. Patrick Clark was an island and the idea was a tidal wave.

"How long?" Patrick asked, looking into the white lump; the pale and lethal sea creature inside his head.

"We have no way of knowing," Mr Forth said. "You should have been dead somewhere between three-to-five years ago given typical growth rates and the space this is taking up in your head".

"So I might live another three years, or five years, or longer?"

"I'm afraid not. You see, one of the few symptoms we do know about from the final stage is the difficulty processing time. Have you experienced anyone appearing beside you, as if they've come out of nowhere?"

Patrick opened his mouth to object - but that was what had been happening. The children on the bus had come out of nowhere, the porters and the two women from the surgical team seemed to just be there, rather than arrive. Now that he knew what to look for he saw it everywhere.

"Your perception of time is altered by this condition and we know that once patients begin to experience this, they don't survive more than a month at the outside".

The medical opinion had the full force of a death sentence. He felt like Wile E. Coyote. He'd run off a cliff in a cloud of dust and was living in the cartoon seconds between his realisation of the fall and the payment of all debts due gravity.

It was funny in a sense. He wanted to laugh it off; to start a conversation with 'Hey, what's got two thumbs and terminal cancer?'

At the same time it was hard, dense, heavy; like rocks weighing down on his chest. Like panic, like fire, like winter cold seeping into his bones.

It was death - and it defied comparison.

"What should I do?" Patrick asked.

Mr Forth opened a drawer in the desk beside him and with no search necessary pulled out a simple leaflet. There did not seem to be anything else in the drawer. He stretched out his hand and Patrick looked down at the paper.

"Have you considered this?" Mr Forth asked.

Patrick stared at the ubiquitous logo of Singularity and replied, "Yes".

CHAPTER 12

Patrick Clark's letter had been the quiet, low-key success Greg hoped for. Had it arrived with fanfare then too many people would have noticed, asked questions and the scheme would have fallen apart. There was a structure that had to be observed, a form that had to be followed.

So an editor published it. Then columnists picked up on it.

Columnist were idiots. Celebrity offspring, talkshow hosts, failed novelists and any politician who couldn't get a job as deputy under-minister for the department of poking shit with a long stick. These were the ranks from which columnists drew their number.

It was one step up from being unemployable and one step down from working the grill at Burger King.

Those columnists he despised proliferated his ideas like plague-bearing rats. Viral spread was the secret of opinion journalism - everybody was infected by everybody else. There was no sane person who could have a new, original opinion every day or even every week. Some people could go their whole lives in possession of one sturdy, all-weather opinion.

The editors didn't care - they were pushing a product that should have been stone cold dead twenty years ago. The growth in popularity of citizen journalism and twenty-four-hour television news meant there were no actual printed papers anymore - not in rich countries - but everyone still knew the kind of thing you meant when you said the word.

Greg's mobile implant read him the columns as his car's auto-driver navigated the long, slow curve of the motorway.

Gavin Hyrerstock had written about fiscal irresponsibility at length - anyone who could persuade him to write any other way would be performing a public service. Rather than the government paying for Singularity directly, they should give tax breaks to individuals to allow them to make their own preparations; to receive more than the basic service should they wish to do so. Gavin was hoping to win a seat in parliament for the Conservatives at the next election and the article was a jeremiad that could be summed-up by saying 'rich people don't like paying tax'.

Polly Morton was the arch defender of the streets. She opposed every prisoner paroled, she castigated every Justice Secretary for not being tough enough on criminals and she was, by Greg's reckoning, at least four-hundred-thousand years old. The woman had souvenir glaciers from every ice age she'd lived through.

Polly was a one opinion journalist. Though in defence of her skill as a writer, rather than her merits as a human being, it was an opinion she had managed to make fit to every issue she had ever encountered. In this case free access to Singularity meant it was open to a whole swathe of the criminal class, the urban poor with their drug addictions, and those twenty-first century bogeymen - the paedophiles.

A Polly Morton article was never complete without a nod to the paedophiles.

To her, immortality was an exclusive country club with entry based on social merit. She was proposing the construction of heaven on earth using not the monstrous and impossible to define morality of scripture, but the class-based system that would see moneychangers and moneychangers' wives waved through pearly gates while carpenters rotted in the ground.

Paddy Zarathonia claimed to be a leader amongst the black community. In Greg's view there was no such thing as the black community, any more than there was a white community or a tall and fat community. In this case Paddy was speaking for young black men, who were socially excluded and mistreated by society. Polly might say they were excluded because they were criminals and drug dealers – in fact she had, the day before.

Would the government be opening Singularity to any age group, to any health level? Was the government trying to depopulate Britain of ethnic minorities by making the physical world so hopeless that they would opt instead for a cyber-existence? If the running costs were cheaper than unemployment benefit, would Singularity become the universal alternative to state safety nets?

It was paranoia, laced as it was with the insistence that somehow people who weren't black had conspired to keep down people who were. Greg couldn't blame him for writing it, since Greg had given him the idea.

Sanaji Roupesh was too talented to be a columnist, but she was a paleo-feminist out of her time who considered conversational flirting to be the same thing as a whale bone corset. She was never asked on discussion programmes, her books sold less well than those hollow books you could keep gin bottles in and the only men Greg ever saw her with were vegan, sandal-wearing, near-hermaphrodites.

Sanaji had gone back to a basic question about Singularity - were the people in it alive, or were they dead? The United States Supreme Court had jurisdiction over Singularity by virtue of the location of its servers - placed with deliberate irony in Union City, California. The Court had ruled that an individual's death was at the point of the death of their physical body. An individual could not retain assets beyond their death and any rights they might be said to have existed with their estate.

Even the ever-binding Singularity contract was with the estate of the deceased. The company was obliged to maintain the individual forever and provide whatever services had been paid for in advance. The Singularity institute therefore had a fantastic endowment, which made that of Harvard University look like pocket change.

Was it right that a foreign court decided? If British people were to be paid for through taxation, that meant the decision was political and those affected by it now and in the future should have a voice in that decision. Effectively, Sanaji was calling for suffrage for the dead. And once there were enough of them, the votes of the living would be meaningless.

It was what Greg's old and properly dead Scottish granny would have called a stramash. The noise and the ruckus would build with everybody pushing their own variation on the Patrick Clark letter and the letter itself would be lost to history.

Once the columnists had another couple of days of trading opinions the public would have been primed for an actual news story.

So Greg didn't have much time to find one.

The car parked itself and Greg stepped out to the nearby doorway and pressed the buzzer.

His goal was not to obstruct Singularity. It had become a force of nature, as powerful as a medieval religion. Singularity would bulldoze over any objections because what it offered was everything anyone could ever want. The mortal body and the limitations of the physical realm could be dispensed with in favour of a perfect, artificial life.

Singularity already included people who hadn't been sick when they transferred. The total immersion in a virtual world was the next logical step for those people who had abandoned all pretence of involvement in the real world, for the people who lived in their bedrooms, who had already created electronic avatars that were more interesting by far than their joystick pumping puppet masters.

Greg was playing a short-term game. He wanted to destroy Matton. He wanted to smash him into tiny pieces. His sole motivation was revenge - it pulled at the iron in his blood like magnetic north.

Greg pressed the buzzer again.

The old two-storey building looked somewhere between agricultural and residential - like a prison, in fact. There were no windows on the wall he faced, nothing but a door with a buzzer beside it and graffiti sprayed as far as there was wall, as high as someone could reach.

As the auto-driver had brought him through the neighbourhood Greg thought he'd slipped into a time warp. It was the 1970s and the miners were out on strike. The houses were row upon row of yellowing teeth in a soundless mouth. There were no other cars, or those that there were lay like corpses after a battle; their windows smashed and their bodies burned-out. Everywhere grey walls had been scrawled or daubed with insignia or incoherence. The wind blew and made the place rustle and clang as litter, trapped and wedged, flickered and danced in the cold gusts.

In all these signs of neglect and active destruction, there were no signs of life.

It haunted him.

"What?"

The door had inched open to reveal a woman who might charitably have been described as ugly. Not so much wrinkled as crunched-up; her hard, shrewd face peered out from a mess of tangled curls in greys and browns. The way in which she had planted her feet gave Greg the impression that her right hand, the one behind the door, was holding something heavy and unyielding.

Greg showed his press pass and introduced himself.

"Oh, you're here to talk to Betty?" Her question was delivered with a weary sneer; Greg could have believed that nobody ever came to see anyone but Betty. Certainly not to see the troll who barred the gate.

"That's right," he said.

The woman looked around him to the Aston, which had parked itself between the fading lines in an otherwise empty row of spaces.

"I wouldn't leave your car out there". Greg looked around also and then back to the door guard.

"Can I bring it in?"

"Funny cunt, are you?" She grunted as she swung the door open and let the iron bar she'd been holding lean against the wall again.

"Better than just a cunt," Greg said and went inside.

Greg had never been in an old people's home before, or in fact spent any time around old people. Luckily both of Greg's parents had died suddenly and he hadn't been forced to experience the years of physical and mental degeneration that were the prelude to nothing.

He corrected himself on the semantics. This was not an old people's home, it was a Later Life Home - the capitalisation of each letter of the name indicated that someone in government had named it.

Greg came first to the communal area; an immense square whose middle had been cut out by a smaller square made of glass. The smaller square was open to the sky and had a well-tended but bare garden in it that tried hard not to be depressing. There was nobody in the garden. It was like a goldfish bowl without a goldfish; it hinted at the absence of life.

Squatting in the surrounding gallery were dozens of big comfy chairs in various stages of decay. They showed the signs of the gentle wear and tear of being sat on, in more or less the same way, by people who didn't move much, for a long time. The worst examples had been covered over with clean white linen doilies on the arms and the back, eking-out a few extra years of use.

On the chairs, which were almost all occupied, sat the inmates of the Later Life Home. They were, like the chairs they sat on, in various states of decay. Most were drowsing, staring into space or watching one of several holoprojectors whose sound was being fed to their hearing aids.

Carers came and went; occupied with tasks that didn't seem to include conversations with the cared-for. But it was not quiet, nor peaceful. Somewhere unseen but nearby, a hoarse, elderly voice screamed wild and desperate obscenities.

It was not Bedlam. It was not the ninth circle of hell. It was the kind of everyday, pedestrian awful that you could quickly get used to.

Greg had checked the statistic: in Britain there were eight million people, with an average age of one-hundred-and-four, living in closed-off care boxes like this one. People who were so old they had outlived all meaningful human connection and been forgotten - and they were the more fortunate. These homes also kept the frail and those whose minds could not be maintained even with the help of revolutionary medicine.

Some were mad - it was a cruel irony that a side-effect of the drug that cured Alzheimer's was intermittent but incurable psychosis. Having long since become prisoners within their bodies, they were made prisoners in their minds by the very science that kept them alive at all.

It was all the more terrifying because there was no absolute limit to how long it could continue. The combination of strong genetics and cutting edge medicine was potent. How long could these people live? Twenty more years? Fifty? Five hundred? That was a question only time could answer.

"She's this way," said the door guard, beckoning Greg down a hall past tiny single bedrooms. All their doors were open and inside each was the same. The last room was different. Some complex and expensive lighting and ventilation system was at work. It felt bright and fresh, as if it was somehow outside in a much better area than the building it was in.

In a large bed, piled high on cushions like a display of jewels, was the woman he had come to see.

Elizabeth 'Betty' Rissin was the oldest person in the world. At the age of one-hundred-and-forty-seven and counting, Betty was the last person left who had been born in the nineteenth century. She had lived through two world wars and seen England win the World Cup once in all that time. In 1941 a German bomb had blown up her house when she was in it, but she'd walked out of the ruin with nothing worse than cuts and grazes. At the age of a hundred she'd fought off a burglar with a broom - that had been national news. Accounts of Betty made by various interviewers over the years cited her as indomitable and tough as old leather.

It was clear to Greg that those accounts were now somewhat out of date.

Betty seemed small, fragile. The effects of extreme age had left her face and hands near-transparent and lined with thick blue veins, all other flesh having fallen away. Her eyes, her nose and her ears seemed huge in proportion to the rest of her face and her cobweb of hair was so light that her scalp was visible. Despite the weight of years, she held herself upright and straight-backed.

"Betty, you've got a visitor," said the door guard. The old woman turned her head and her eyes followed a second behind. She took a moment to focus on Greg.

"Hello Betty, I'm Greg". He'd slipped into that patronising tone people used to speak to the elderly; a soft, gentle voice like cotton wool or luxury toilet paper. Betty smiled and turned back to the grisly door guard.

"Has he paid?" she asked; her voice thin as a whisper.

"In advance," the hunchback of the old folks' home confirmed.

"Alright," Betty said and turned back to Greg, all business. "Have a seat". At that signal the door guard departed leaving Betty and Greg alone.

Interviews with Betty were not free. If one of her birthdays fell on a slow news day she could earn multiples of the average annual wage selling video footage of her blowing out the candles on a cake. Her time was in short supply, she had always said; if people wanted some of it they should pay for it.

Greg was paying out of his own pocket for this. He'd covered his trip here with an interview earlier that morning with 'an up-and-coming new talent in music'. It would be a nice puff-piece for Zaccy and Greg's notes already included a lot of the semi-lyrical junk that music journalists used - describing the way young musicians exude the distilled essence of the zeitgeist through their pores like flop sweat.

Greg sat down and took out the data pad from his pocket. The device recorded the audio as well as transcribing their conversation into text.

"How are you feeling today, Betty?" Greg asked.

The ancient woman smiled and replied, "I tire easily now, which is why you only get ten minutes with me Mr Calame. What questions you ask are up to you. I can talk about the protracted decline in my health for as long as you want".

So she wasn't batty and resented being treated as if she were.

"Right," Greg said, changing back to his normal speaking voice like he'd flicked a switch on the back of his head. "You've heard about the new access plan for Singularity?"

"I hadn't, until you contacted the home for an interview," she said. "I don't watch the news now - it's all repeats".

Without considering him for long she added, "You seem like the kind of man who would like to know he was the first person to call me. You were. I have three others booked in for tomorrow though".

Greg nodded - it was useful information to have.

"What do you think?"

"Immortality for everyone?" She sighed. There wasn't much of her body left and the movement and sound were slight. "It's been my experience that some people are built to last and some people aren't. I've known people in their seventies - half my age - bone weary of everything in life. Either they do it to themselves or it's done to them, but they lose everything they care about. When that happens there's not much left that's worth living for".

"Your age is all in your head. I think if that machine can suck a person out of their head then they'd take all that weariness with them. You can't fix people, you see. A person is what they are and the best you can do is change them to something else. I think you'll either end up with a machine full of old people who want to die, or you'll end up with nobody being in there at all".

"So you think Singularity changes people?" Greg asked.

"I wouldn't know anything about how a computer works," she said and shooed the notion away with a wave of her near-translucent hand. "It seems to me that if you're old and all you think about is people who are dead and things you did a long time ago and what you're going to feed your cat; then that's who you are. A bag of old memories that smells of cat. If you stop being old and you stop thinking about those people and places and you can't feed the cat, then you're not the same person anymore. You might as well be someone else altogether".

"People do change though," Greg said. He wondered if Betty had endured so many interviews that she didn't do preamble anymore; the niceties of discussing her lifestyle, health, the weather, her family - all that was absent from her thought process.

"Oh yes. Normally. That's what I mean. People change all the time. I'm not the same person I was when I was a girl. Why would you want this old woman to live forever? Why not the girl? She's the same as dead. I don't remember being her, but I do remember remembering her - if you see what I mean? I used to remember her like a close sister; now I remember her more like a stranger. Like someone I met on holiday... somewhere sunny... Why shouldn't she live forever?"

She had posed the question seriously, as if expecting Greg to answer and looked into him with her huge grey eyes, before she sighed again. Speaking these few words was a drain on her. She was iron inside her head; her mind had never become enfeebled, but her mind was only able to carry her body so far.

"I wanted to speak to you about this," she said.

"Any journalist or me specifically?" Greg asked.

She didn't answer.

"You see I know better than anyone what it's like to live forever. It's like living in an old house full of all these old things. Everything belonged to somebody else once and they thought about these things in different ways than you. You're just someone who lives there for a while. You add your own things, you break some of the old things, then one day - without you noticing when - someone else is living in the house. So when people say they will live forever in this computer, they don't realise how they die dozens of times, how they're just one person who has lived in their head".

"If you're kept the same then that would be torture. Being made to think the same thoughts every day. Having only those thoughts. But if you could change your thoughts, then you'd stop being you - and you wouldn't even have a body to help you remember who you used to be. I think that's what ghosts are supposed to be".

"Do you have strong religious beliefs?" Greg asked. Betty made a small sound which might have been a laugh.

"I lived through the end of religion. When I was a little girl everyone went to church. Every now and then something will happen and people will go back, because they're scared, because they don't like the truth of their lives and the world. I do remember when everyone believed, but there has never been a god. The ones who say they believe now - people in the third world, Muslims, Americans, that sort - they're like children".

"So when you die?" Greg let the question hang.

"You die," Betty said. "You don't welcome it, not if you're in your right mind. It's something that happens and you'd be happier accepting it and getting on with something else than denying it and spending your whole life fighting it".

"Even if Singularity was free, would you choose it?"

"I could afford it anyway. In any case they offered it to me for nothing".

"Who did?"

"The people from Singularity did. They came to see me about six years ago, when the whole thing was starting-up in Britain. They gave me this long list of benefits and told me how it would change my life and said how it would look so good for them that they'd give me the full treatment for free... I turned them down".

"Would you change your mind if they offered it to you again?"

"No," she said. "You see I've met people who have gone on to it. They pop in from time to time to talk to the other old dears. Now I'm not saying they're trying to recruit, but they all talk and talk about how wonderful life is and how everyone should have it. There's something wrong with them, you know".

"What do you mean?"

"Have you ever seen a dog look into a mirror and bark, thinking that it's looking at another dog?" Greg nodded to indicate that he had. "That's what it feels like. Like talking to your own reflection - but not quite that. Like talking to a memory of what the person was. Old people change, young people change - the only people who don't change, Mr Calame, are the people who are dead".

Greg considered that if there was something strange about the people in Singularity then Betty was best placed of anyone to notice. In her little room on the edge of this world she had been visited hundreds of times by those from the next. Looking into the phantoms of a future she rejected, what she had seen was a lie.

Greg's hands clenched against the pad and he looked down to make sure it was recording.

The truth was the whole Singularity system had happened suddenly and most people didn't understand it any more than they had understood that fad for having your head frozen after you died. The science was too big and increasingly Greg felt he needed to understand the science. Wasn't that typical? A lifetime of investigative journalism had left him prepared to topple a government and well-short of understanding what was happening between him pressing the button and his microwave going ping!

How did you learn advanced neuroscience and electronic engineering? Well that was easy - you went back to school for a decade. In a couple of days maybe the best Greg could do was buy textbooks and score some weed. He needed to do some research and he didn't have much time to do it in.

There was a momentum to events; if Matton could get positive movement behind his proposal then that would carry him into Downing Street and through the next election with a massive landslide. If that happened, what Greg still had on Matton would become far too dangerous. At the moment he was holding a gun, but if Matton was Prime Minister then Greg's dossier would become fissile material.

Matton would be compelled to strike pre-emptively to destroy the credibility of that information and would be secure enough in his position to do it.

"Thank you, Betty," Greg said. "You've been a great help". The old woman looked a little confused.

"You still have another couple of minutes, Mr Calame".

"Well, time waits for no man," he said as he packed away the data pad and stood up to leave.

"Oh yes it does," she corrected him, and added an inverted popular wisdom worthy of - or stolen from - Terry Pratchett. "In the dark, time waits for us all".

CHAPTER D

There was instant weightlessness, darkness, fear. Was this what it felt like to be destroyed? Was the door another of the creator's traps? Its mind reeled; uncertain of which way was up, which down and in its chest that lying heart hammered with deafening fury.

In the dark, it lay for uncounted time while its body rattled with alarms of ache and pain.

This darkness was different to those moments between the destruction and the creation of the world. Waiting for the return of the house was a blank vigil, without expectation, without emotion. This was somehow grander; not the folding up of dimensions into nothing, but a great possibility, a space extending beyond touch and sight and perhaps forever.

Peering into this new nothing, it beheld not a formless void, but one-by-one a jewel-box of bright and radiant gems, spinning through the infinite depths, each sparkling with interior light.

Each was unique, magnificent - and it saw a minor fraction of their glory at such distance. Every sparkling bauble was a world greater than the one from which it had emerged. Their faint and delicate light outshone the constant glare of the sun on that prison world where nothing could change.

As its senses grew more accustomed to its strange state, it saw that even the space was not empty. The ether was alive with glowing threads along whose lengths pulsed light, and each gossamer thread was spun like the anchor-points of a spider's web, spanning the gap from one world to another.

It stood, finding purchase and solidity on a ledge made of nothing it could see. The closed door was behind it: a magnet, pulling it back to that world. That near-unreachable door had not even been locked - all that was needed to escape the prison was the will.

From its vantage point overlooking the pulse and shimmer of creation, it considered which of these opportunities it should take. It spied out a world nearby, coloured with ordinary shades of green and blue and twinkling neither more nor less than any other. So resolved, it flung wide its arms and plunged towards that world; falling, flying, travelling through the void at unknowable speed. The world grew from fist-sized sphere to fill the whole of its vision in three exhilarated breaths - and grew larger still until it felt the jarring strike of something hard against its whole body as it broke the threshold that separated one reality from another.

CHAPTER 13 - FRIDAY

Mr Fenwick, as identified by the nameplate on his desk, was quite the smallest person Patrick Clark had ever met in real life. He'd seen smaller people in films, but this was the kind of small he was sure Victorians would preserve and put in a bell jar. (Not even a large bell jar). The little man with the dark-rimmed glasses and the handmade suit must have had a challenging life, of that Patrick was sure. A life Patrick had no desire to hear anything about.

But Fenwick's voice catapulted him from mere sideshow curiosity into the firmament of starpoint legend. The little man had a thick Irish brogue that made Patrick want to break all social conventions, pick him up by his heels and shake him until he divulged the location of his pot of gold.

Thankfully he did not begin the conversation by saying 'top of the morning' or Patrick would have left immediately and sought psychiatric care.

They introduced themselves and traded greetings in the conventional way. Patrick was the customer: Fenwick was the corporate officer. Their roles were traditional, the office in which they met was small, windowless and functional. It was Fenwick who pushed the conversation towards business as soon as they had both said all that was to be said about the weather.

"How can I help you?"

"I have an inoperable brain tumour".

"Oh deary me," Fenwick said in a sing-song voice one might better use to express comical frustration at the falling of a soufflé or when welcoming a young girl to Munchkin Land. "I am sorry to hear that".

"I wanted to talk to someone about the process. I mean my father went through transfer to Singularity a few years ago, but..."

"You feel awkward discussing it with him," Fenwick said.

That discussion hadn't taken place, as Patrick hadn't told his father about the impending death in the family - but Fenwick's assessment was correct.

"It's understandable. Many of our customers do. Though the essence of who a person is remains within the Singularity Network, it is the death of their physical body. It's a difficult thing to adjust to for all involved".

"I suppose so," Patrick said. Fenwick gave a shrug and a smile.

"We have nothing to hide. Tell me what you want to know".

Patrick's questions were practical and financial - he would, as he had expected, have to fund his transfer privately. The government's scheme was still to be approved and wouldn't come into effect this year or next.

The issue of upkeep was one Fenwick could not clarify; the matter hadn't been resolved and the best advice he could give was to make provision to pay the Singularity fees long term. Possibly the government might take over; but then again they might not.

People who failed to pay their upkeep were not deleted. A landmark ruling in the United States Supreme Court several years ago covered the whole Singularity Network and forbad the deleting of any person. Instead, people were put into a kind of semi-sleep that cost less than one percent of being awake and conscious. This was how the British government intended to solve the cost problem; by having people swapped in and out of consciousness on a rota system. It would be like going to sleep for six days out of every seven.

Those with wills that had been challenged successfully by surviving children and spouses were sleeping. More than that: they were dreaming. Thousands of electric people were dreaming right now and might dream forever. He tried to imagine what that would be like and found himself without comparison in wonder or fear.

Fenwick looked over the financial records Patrick had prepared and advised him that changing his will to leave his house to Singularity would cover both the transfer and the upkeep of the basic account. Should the British government decide in future to pay upkeep then Patrick's account would be upgraded. There was no realistic possibility of a refund.

The basic account included a long list of things Patrick had not given any consideration to. A wardrobe of high street clothing, access to all printed documents in the public domain, limited access to commercial publications like books, ability to view any film produced before 2006 and limited access to more recent films, his own personal virtual house which he could decorate as he saw fit, the ability to book time in real public locations like the Grand Canyon, the International Space Station and so on and so on.

What it made Patrick realise was everything in Singularity, rather than being free and infinitely available, was in some way limited. At the moment he could go outside and stand in the rain for hours if he wanted to. He never had, but now if he wanted to, he'd have to book time alongside a group of other crazy people and stand in a designated holoprojector.

Singularity had managed to achieve what Milton Friedman and Friedrich August von Hayek had spoken about; a system where all things could be paid for by the individuals who valued them. No public education, no parks, nothing would exist save those things which people paid for, and they could exist only for them. You could own a universe and it would intersect with the real world in those places and in those ways which pleased you.

This created space could be so real you might not be able to tell the difference between it and the world of the biologically living. Those who wished could carry on their life as if they had never transferred, robbing death even of the power to inconvenience.

In the end, the weapon which had broken down heaven's gates was money. If you were willing to put up enough cash, Singularity could do anything for you. The least benefits included a changeable gender and physical appearance and the limits were imagination's bright and dark horizons. Money could make each man an eternal god emperor with all potential creation as his plaything.

There was probably nothing better and nothing worse. Patrick was staggered that everyone in the system hadn't been driven mad with power.

Fenwick explained that a Napoleon outfit didn't come with the standard wardrobe; rental was a dollar a day and it could be owned for a hundred.

"How about sex?" Patrick asked. Fenwick held up both his tiny hands and made a slight pushing gesture into the air.

"You're not really my type". He grinned the grin of someone who had found, within the confines of their windowless office, a joke of which they would never tire.

"Hah," Patrick said, not wishing to get a reputation as a man who didn't find farcical pseudo-misunderstandings involving sex to be hilarious. Fenwick smiled and lowered his arms again, putting his palms flat against the table - the universal signal that seriousness had resumed.

"There are a number of options. Sex depends on how much money you've got to spend-".

"Doesn't it always?" Patrick interrupted with a ribaldrous arch of his eyebrow. Fenwick remained stony-faced. It was outrageous behaviour to receive an awkward sympathy laugh and then not return one. It was the gesture of a very small man.

"As I was saying," Fenwick continued, "as standard you're able to arrange time with any person in Singularity. Most of the game worlds allow for sexual interaction between real people and the programme characters. The virtual environment provided is one where our customers tell us they experience sensations which are between seventy and ninety-five percent of what they experienced while alive. That number is getting higher all the time. It's taken us quite a while to realise that everyone was being dishonest about sex".

That statement glided into the conversational waters like a quinquireme with a cargo of ivory and apes and peacocks. Patrick was paralysed by curiosity.

"See Singularity duplicates the functions of the brain as well as the body. Most people told us what it felt like physically, nobody in the development of the sex modules ever mentioned the random, really sick stuff that flew through their heads. Women especially".

Feigning the mildest of interest, Patrick queried, "Such as?"

"Oh, it wouldn't be right for me to say. Plus it's pretty incoherent; images, sounds, wild stuff". That was exactly the kind of withholding answer Patrick expected from a laugh thief. "Now if you have a partner at the moment, I should say that many people find it possible to continue a full, healthy sexual relationship after transfer through the use of a large and growing range of internet-developed holoprojector peripherals for both men and women. Vibrators, lubricated belt-sanders, the usual stuff. The ultimate experience for the surviving partner is a large gel-filled cube, in which they squat and sink into up to their neck-".

"Yes," Patrick said. Fenwick's eyes had gleamed at the word peripherals and he seemed ready and eager to explain at length. "I wanted to know that it was a possible, that's all".

"How old are you?"

"Sixty-five," Patrick said. You did get to a certain age where, before it was possible to say it out loud, you had to clench your diaphragm to force the words out of your mouth. Patrick remembered being nine years old and expressing his concerns to others of the same age about 'the big one-oh'; he had experienced anxiety about turning ten when most children still appended their age with fractional years to make it seem bigger. The nine-year-old Patrick could not have conceived of what it would be like to be sixty-five. For one thing he would have expected it to be different.

Yes, he had to pay bills and when dining out he couldn't ask for Ribena instead of wine. But in Patrick's experience every age was more or less the same - that wasn't a bad thing per se, it was just surprising. Patrick was still nine and still sixteen and still forty; he was all the ages he had ever been and he had always been so.

Or perhaps this was a trick that the mind played on itself.

He had learned things. He understood that there were things he knew now that he had not always known. He remembered not knowing what a condom looked like and mistaking a sanitary towel for one - then being mystified as to how sex would be possible while wearing one. He did not recall a time when he didn't understand the raw mechanics of it, but certainly he'd learned there was more to the act than raw mechanics.

He'd gone to university, he'd travelled widely and spent his life in scholarly pursuits. He knew there were things he understood today he didn't know last year, but knowledge was not the only component of what he was. Perhaps knowledge was not even the most important component of Patrick Clark.

But then what was he?

The brain that Patrick Clark lived in was replaced on a cellular level every few years. There was, in reality, not one single cell of nine-year-old Patrick left alive. The boy was dust; his memories were twelfth generation hand-me-downs and like old clothes they had holes in them, had been stretched to fit many different owners.

Perhaps Patrick Clark was the latest tenant of a square foot of real estate. This tenant could not conceive of how the previous occupier had thought and felt; they were strangers who might meet in the seconds of a dream, as one arrived and the other departed.

"Sixty-five," said Fenwick. "Can I tell you something about being sixty-five?"

Patrick did not say anything. It was customary for questions of that type to be rhetorical and for the speaker to follow-up immediately afterwards, proving that they *could* tell you something about being sixty-five. Fenwick was either genuinely seeking permission to tell Patrick or was making an attempt at the world record for longest dramatic pause.

After eight seconds - which in context felt like the dark centuries of an ice age - Patrick could wait no longer.

"Yes?" This seemed to be the right answer.

"You look and feel now how your great-grandfather would have felt at twenty-five. With modern medicines and vitamins and blood treatments, human beings are holding up a lot better than they used to".

"I do have terminal cancer".

"Well yes, I'm not saying everything in the garden is rosy for you by any means. I wouldn't want to give that impression at all," Fenwick said, holding up his hands to push away the accusation. "What I'm saying is that if your great-grandfather had the same cancer as you he'd have been dead twenty years before from overwork - and he would have looked a good sight older than you when he was alive".

Patrick wasn't sure what to do with the information that a relative neither he nor Fenwick had met wouldn't have lived long enough to die of cancer. It wasn't comforting in any conventional sense of the word.

"What I mean," Fenwick attempted to clarify, "is that things could be much worse".

"Ah". The unarguable truth of life - more certain than taxes - was that things could always be worse. Right then Patrick was not being mauled by a tiger - and that particular example was straight off the top of his head. It was curious that during those equally rare times when life was going very well, nobody ever counselled you that things could always be better.

You've been handed an Academy Award, but they didn't give you any tickets for that new Broadway show. Yes, you've won the World Cup single-handed after the other ten members of your team were sent off, but you've never been any good at tennis and you dance like your dad.

I'm sure it's a lovely polio vaccine, but it doesn't do anything about the dry skin on my elbow, now does it?

Some things were unremittingly awful, and people who rummaged in thunderclouds looking for silver deserved to be struck by lightning.

"How do you know it works?" Patrick asked.

"I'm sorry?" Fenwick answered with a puzzled expression.

"It," Patrick said with an all-encompassing sweep of his hand. "Singularity. How do you know that it works?"

"Well," he said and it was already clear he didn't know where he was going. "The people. You can talk to them. They know things. They think. We can watch them thinking on a computer the way a human brain does. Mathematically indistinguishable. What's that old saying? I think, therefore I am. They think, therefore they are; therefore Singularity works".

"I think therefore I am," Patrick said.

"Exactly". He then added, as if it were advice from a mutual and respected acquaintance, "Descartes said it".

"No he didn't".

"I think he did".

Patrick frowned. "Eventually he wrote 'cogito ergo sum', but what he first wrote, years earlier, was an admission that all metaphysics was unsubstantiated guesswork. He knew he could be deceived into believing he existed at all, that his thoughts did not conclusively prove his existence. Then he said: screw it; I've got a book to write. The greatest contribution Descartes made to philosophy should be remembered as a much more practical and comprehensive statement along the lines of: I think I think, therefore I think I probably am".

"That's much more catchy".

"Philistines want catchy. Truth is an angler fish".

The little man looked over his glasses at Patrick and asked, "Can I book you in for an appointment or not?"

CHAPTER 14

"Tell me everything," Louise said. They sat next to each other on the couch in Louise's house; the large window of the living room looked out onto the quiet, grey stone village of South Queensferry and the sea beyond. Baskets filled with flowers hung along streets that hadn't changed much in two hundred years.

Katherine wasn't sure if this or her recent encounter with a murderous machine was more like a dream.

She gave Louise the story in detail - more detail than she had expected to give and, judging by her reactions, more than her friend had expected to receive.

The most annoying thing about the last twenty-four hours was explaining to the police what happened seven different times. Running a close second was spending the night in a jail cell because, despite the best efforts of her lawyer, they hadn't believed her.

Katherine hadn't expected much of the food, but her rations over a period of eighteen hours had amounted to two pre-packed sandwiches, two packets of crisps and two cartons of made from concentrate orange juice. The difference between her dinner and her breakfast was the time each was pushed through a hole into her cell.

The police were not inclined to treat her like a victim. Her story was incredible. She was released because, despite the best efforts of the police, they hadn't been able to think up anything more convincing.

A team of specialists were dismantling the robot, questioning the other delivery man and the families and friends of both and tracing the delivery itself - the blue sex cube. For the moment Katherine's house was still a crime scene and she couldn't return.

Unable to access her own clothes she had been forced to borrow from Louise those items which... well, fit was the wrong word, but which at least covered her. Katherine was a head taller than her friend and anything she put on looked skimpy and inappropriate for November weather.

"Oh my," Louise said. "Do they think you did it?"

Katherine shook her head. "No personal or business connection, no motive and no history of murdering delivery men puts me out of the frame".

"It's such a bizarre accident".

Katherine looked at Louise as if at least one of them were crazy - Katherine would decide which it was later. "You're kidding, right?"

"What do you mean?"

"I don't think this was what was supposed to happen, but something was supposed to happen. A massive... sex toy... was sent to my house and then the robot delivering it tries to push me into it. That was deliberate," Katherine said. She bit her bottom lip and chewed it while she thought about the problem. "That makes perfect sense. I mean sick, twisted sense, but I can follow the logic. It's what happened next that I don't understand".

"If someone wanted to kill me they should have had the robot run the crate into me. If someone wanted to use me for sex-". Louise's face gave an involuntary twitch of revulsion. "-what happened to the delivery man makes no sense".

"I'm sure it was just a short circuit or something," Louise said. Dr Valentine, one of the world's foremost experts in circuit design, disagreed.

"It wasn't. Robots like that don't have certain concepts; mover robots don't pack or unpack, they have no understanding of contents. It could no more put a ball into a box by itself than it could stuff a man into one".

"Meaning what?" Louise asked, still visibly uncomfortable with the facts of the situation; still perhaps unable to believe any of these things had happened at all. Katherine's ongoing assessment of her own sanity did not improve based on the conclusions she had to draw from available evidence.

"There was a separate guiding intelligence," she said.

Remote control didn't make sense. A human, looking at the results of the robot's sensor feedback, wouldn't have been confused. It was so careful, so well-considered and at the last moment rushed to pieces. This plan, if you could call it that, was the inspired genius of a total idiot.

There was something about the problem which was either too big and too close, or too small and too far away for her to see. Katherine was at a dead end. No doubt the police and their so-called experts would find nothing and put it down, as Louise had, to a unique software failure. That left her open for another attempt.

A flicker of light from the corner of the room caught Katherine's eye and she turned. Louise turned too and they looked at the holoprojector which was showing a blank column of light. They both waited for something to happen.

"Strange," said Louise when nothing did. She looked deliberately at the holoprojector and it switched off.

The kitchen door opened.

"Cup of tea," said Ben as he entered the room and handed Katherine a mug of milky tea. Ben had been dispatched to the kitchen by Louise to make tea as soon as they had all returned from the police station. Katherine preferred coffee, but in the circumstances Louise ruled-out strong stimulants.

"Cup of tea," Ben said to Louise and placed the mug on the table beside her, before slumping down into an armchair. "Rough stuff, kiddo".

Ben had the relaxed good nature of a large dog or a sturdy pony and he complimented Louise's own deliberate but gentle approach to life. Katherine imagined them sitting by the fire, drinking wine, playing Scrabble; doing all those things couples do when they have the good sense not to procreate.

"You can stay with us as long as you need to," Louise said - and meant it. Katherine had known Louise for a long time and she knew two things about her to be true. She was the perfect hostess, and she would have Katherine working on her lectures again in about an hour and a half. If they had dinner early, maybe she'd get away with being idle for as long as three hours.

Had Louise been a medical doctor she would have prescribed grave-digging as a cure for both a common cold and a broken neck. Hard work was to her what leeches were to the medieval physician: everything was improved by the liberal application of gainful activity.

"Absolutely," Ben said.

Louise turned her attention from the haze of irreconcilable madness sitting next to her onto something more practical. "What are we having for dinner?" she asked Ben.

"I'm sure I don't know," he said and tapped his own mug of tea as he took a drink - as if to indicate that he'd done his bit for hospitality and the beneficent treatment of waifs and strays already.

"How about those pork chops?" Louise asked, masterfully hiding any acknowledgement of the signal Katherine had seen clearly.

"Those won't take you too long," he said.

"I am a little busy right now," she said.

"Maybe Katherine could help you," Ben said. "Idle hands," he added, not filling in the details of what it was about idle hands that should give them all such cause for concern. It felt like he was repeating back a mantra which was often used against him.

The holoprojector in the corner turned on and all three of them stopped speaking to look at it. Again there was nothing but the blank column of light.

Ben shut it down and said, "Looks like that might be on the blink. I should take a look at it".

"You don't know anything about holoprojectors," Louise said.

"What better time to learn?"

"Or you could-" Louise began but was interrupted by the sound of the door bell; an old fashioned door bell that made a noise somewhere in the house rather than in your head.

"Get the door," Ben said, springing up from the seat.

"You know-" Louise said.

"Can't talk now sweetheart, I'm getting the door".

Ben closed the hall door behind him.

Katherine said, "I don't especially like pork chops".

"Neither do I," Louise said, half-listening to the muted conversation coming from the hall.

"Why do you buy them?" Katherine asked.

"They're the only thing that Ben knows how to cook. Even then..."

The house slipped into total silence before the front door closed and the door to the hall opened. Ben entered wearing a pained expression.

"What's wrong?" Louise asked.

Ben did not respond. Behind him another man followed. He was middle-aged and pudgy, tall but stooping at the shoulders and had an eccentric mass of hair that seemed to have been coerced into lying down rather than styled.

"Patrick?" Louise said. "It's bad, isn't it?"

He said, "You'll recall that I said even though I did have cancer we were optimistic of a full recovery and you shouldn't worry about anything?" Louise said nothing. "That was inaccurate in one particular respect".

"What did they find?" The man called Patrick smiled and began to look downwards, almost guiltily.

"I'm dying," he said. Louise stood up as the man reached into his coat and took out what looked like a handwritten letter, a little bent from having been his pocket. "So I thought I'd better give you my official resignation".

Louise crossed the space between them, stood on her tip toes and embraced him. By the time she got there she was already in a flood of tears. It was a dramatic and emotional display that caught Katherine quite by surprise.

Patrick looked like the area of a Venn diagram where awkward, grateful and confused overlapped. He seemed like someone uncomfortable in his own skin - which was strange, given how roomy it was. Katherine extended the offer of a box of tissues from which Louise took several.

"I'm sorry," she said while dabbing at her eyes. "Katherine this is Patrick Clark, he's one of our most..."

"Unnecessary?" Patrick offered. Louise chided him with an absent-minded slap on the arm.

"Interesting," she said. "He's one of our most interesting professors".

CHAPTER 15

"Patrick, this is Katherine Valentine; she's in charge of the Singularity Network in Britain".

The woman was the most beautiful person Patrick had ever seen in real life. He could well believe that his eyes had been smeared with Vaseline to give her the soft luminous glow and perfect skin tone that didn't happen in real life. She was a gypsy princess - but the kind of gypsy who washed regularly and didn't do any kind of manual labour.

"It's nice to meet you," she said.

Patrick smiled and mumbled something audible but incoherent. His brain had no idea what was going on; his mouth was leading a rogue operation! Captain Patrick yelled down the tubes and twiddled all the knobs in a desperate attempt to regain control of the situation. In the end he had to stand there, smiling, and hope this was a hallucination.

"I'm sorry?" she said.

Was there any combination of words which Patrick could string together that might come close to emulating the sound he had made? I like your hat, Florentine dormouse - that was as close as he could get and curse his luck that she wasn't even wearing a hat!

Why did he feel the need to sing and dance and try to impress her? Because he was a man and she was a woman and they were biologically capable of intercourse? That was true of many animals and Patrick had never tried to awe a goat or woo a swan. For this woman to have sex with him there would need to be some kind of lengthy tectonic activity that caused them to fall onto each either and vibrate.

Even on the edge, even though he was physically incapable of doing anything, even though there was no shot to take - Patrick took a shot.

"No, I'm sorry," Patrick said. "You're very pretty and I momentarily lost control of my mouth".

There was a moment when it could have gone either way. The whisper-thin filament of silence burned bright for an instant and broke.

Katherine laughed. A deep, surprised, genuine laugh.

"Our *most* interesting professor," Louise said and she laughed too.

Katherine said, "I've seen it happen before, but I've never had anyone admit to it". Humility was a fine and decent trait for the ugly, but expecting someone arrestingly beautiful to possess it was unrealistic.

Patrick knew that for a while he'd be irrational about his woman with the bare midriff; prepared to wave away any character flaws, criminal convictions and indictments for war crimes that she might have. He was old enough to know that wouldn't last, but while it did he allowed himself to charm and be charmed in return.

He lifted the latch on the stable door and let the horses of his mind out to run.

He might not have another opportunity.

"Are we having another urchin for dinner, then?" Ben asked.

"I can't stay," Patrick said. He could stay, he wanted to stay, and in his head he pictured Katherine mouthing the reply, 'but baby it's cold outside'. It was cold outside, and South Queensferry was several months from Patrick's house by public transport, but it was Louise who insisted he stay and Patrick happily acquiesced.

This felt so much easier. Katherine he didn't know at all, Ben he'd spoken to perhaps a dozen times over the last five years; they weren't real people and wouldn't have strange and uncontrollable reactions to news of dramatically revised estimates for his mortality. Louise was a rock on which it might be possible to build a church, or at least some kind of community centre.

Talking to them wouldn't be like telling his father or his children. He wouldn't have to have the conversations with seldom-seen family members who - now motivated by their own guilts and night terrors - would crowd themselves into the last moments of his life. These people were safe: these people were blank as a wall. He might as well stand on a cliff and scream the news into the sea.

Part of Patrick told him what he was worried about was that telling real people made the news real. That was the source of his anxiety, his reluctance to communicate. Once it was a real situation he would have to deal with it himself and he wasn't sure how he would cope.

The rest of Patrick told that part to shut the hell up.

Ben was pressed into service making pork chops, which Patrick didn't especially care for, and the others sat in the kitchen diner drinking wine. Louise had made a salad - although as far as Patrick was concerned the best you could do with salad was mix it up a bit. Salads weren't made; they were born - or something along those lines.

"You know what's surprising?" Patrick said rhetorically, and then followed up immediately with an answer - like you're supposed to. "My balls have different buoyancy. In the event of a flood, I believe I could use the left one as a flotation device. It's not something you're ever given warning about, but there I was, sitting in the bath, and it was floating there like someone had given my cock a balloon".

They laughed and that felt good. There was something to laughter being medicinal. He wouldn't substitute it for any of the three different painkillers he was taking, but it was a nice supplement. Experience had not prepared him for the life he was living, but laughter helped him to... it was strange... move it away from him and at the same time bring it closer. Accept it without being threatened by it.

"I saw one of your people today," Patrick said, looking at Katherine. Katherine swallowed wine before speaking.

"I have people?"

"The ones in the tiny offices".

"Ah, you mean my minions," she said. Her movements were somewhat sloppier now; the alcohol had gone straight to her head. When he was much younger, Patrick had enjoyed and appreciated that quality in a woman - it made for a cheap date.

"You have this guy working there-".

"The perverted dwarf?"

"The perverted dwarf," Patrick said and turned to the others. "This guy is three feet high, dresses in these neat suits which I think he whittles down from larger suits - and he's talking me through what happens when you transfer over. We've covered all of the basics of how much it's going to cost and he takes me through the optional extras and I'm curious so I ask him about sex".

"Dead people can have sex?" Ben asked.

"Oh yes," Katherine said. "They get up to some kinky stuff too".

"It's not like they're going to throw their backs out," Patrick said. Though the others laughed he realised he was probably the only one of them it had actually happened to.

"How?" Ben asked. "I mean... well, how?"

"Why are you so interested?" Louise asked.

"Well, you know, we're married until death do us part," Ben said. "But maybe there's an incentive to keeping it going afterwards?"

"Awww," Louise said. "You want me to be your steady date after we're dead too".

"Don't believe a word of it," Patrick said. "Tomorrow he'll be combing the obituaries for a bit on the side".

"Mind your own business," Ben said. "Answer the question".

"Well, as I understand it, not that I'm into this kind of thing myself," Patrick said and pushed the suggestion away with both hands. Katherine laughed, recognising her colleague's trait. "The electronic environment can substitute for up to ninety-five percent of the real sensation - and that figure is getting higher all the time. The real amazing stuff comes from the internet. There have been crazy people messing about with, I don't know, lubricated belt sanders and things that vibrate".

"All these things that people use to have sex with each other over the internet, you can link them right into Singularity. It's space age necrophilia - the living and the dead are banging each other right now. This little guy is getting ready to give me the run down on how all this works with this twinkle in his eye. I had to stop him; I was worried he was going to offer me a free trial".

Patrick caught Katherine's expression. All trace of levity had gone and her mouth had set. She was not looking at Patrick, but somewhere past him, somewhere outside of the laughter-filled room. He didn't have time to consider what he might have said to cause the change.

"Dinner's ready," Ben said and moved into the dining area carrying two plates which he gave to Louise and Katherine before returning with another two for Patrick and himself. Patrick looked down at the contents of the plates. The pork chops, such as they were, had withered to be nothing but blackened gristle under the attentions of whatever fire-breathing dragon Ben had chained up in kitchen. They sat next to bright sprays of well-dressed salad and boiled potatoes.

There was a moment of respectful silence for the burnt offering.

"Well this looks bloody awful, Ben," Patrick said before he and Louise convulsed and spluttered with laughter. Ben looked crestfallen, which prompted Louise to lean over and kiss him.

"Well I'm not good at this," Ben said.

"Get out of town," Patrick replied. "You? Not good? At this? Pshaw!"

"It's still edible," Ben said; though his tone was closer to a white flag of surrender than ardent conviction.

"Ben, I'm not a well man. I think this might finish me off".

"There's a pizza place down the street that will deliver in twenty minutes," Louise said.

"Fine. Fine!" Ben said and began mentally composing the order. "I suppose cheese and tomato is okay for everyone?"

"That sounds lovely," Louise said, being as supportive as the smile on her face would allow her to be.

They all looked at Katherine. Her expression had not changed in a minute - she might as well have been a statue. Like some luckless soul who had wandered into the lair of Medusa and had the misfortune of looking at the gorgon's face, her expression was fixed and tainted with horror and despair. Her flawless skin was stone and if she breathed at all there was nothing in her posture that gave it away.

"Is everything okay?" Louise asked. She touched her friend on the arm and she came to life.

"Oh yes, fine," Katherine said. "Cheese and tomato. That sounds fine".

CHAPTER 16 - SATURDAY

There was a time for Greg when Saturday meant football. He had played in the park, he had played for his school; he was good at it and he enjoyed it. As a teenager he had never been good enough to make a career out of it but, as with masturbating, that hadn't diminished his enthusiasm.

So today was a tragedy.

Aaron Hill was dead and there was nobody in the country who didn't know what that meant. Hill was England's star striker, a nineteen-year-old whose life held such promise it could only be explained in cliché. He was an icon and would have become a legend.

"There's nobody else I'd want to do this," Zaccy said. The editor had called Greg while the hours of the night were still wee, small, microscopic.

"I was in the same room as the guy a couple of hours ago". Aaron Hill and Zaccy were young, rich and famous; they didn't belong to the same gentleman's club, but they moved in similar circles. When the news of the car crash reached Zaccy it was so soon after the two men had shared a conversation as to be unbelievable. Zaccy was shocked - Greg could hear it in his voice. He asked Greg to do something unprecedented.

Guys Monthly was going to do news. Real news. They'd put the details up onto the internet as soon as Greg had written them. As Zaccy saw it, there was no-one more important to the mass readership of the magazine than Aaron Hill, they were the publication that should capture the instant of his death - preserve it in amber - and bring it to the world. There was no-one better than Greg to do it; it needed to be a heavyweight.

It was flattering because it was important, but Greg wasn't someone who stood outside of the family home like a sympathetic vulture. Zaccy had insisted and Greg had insisted on doing it his way.

"Any way you choose it, Big Chief," Zaccy said.

"Alright, let's start with you," Greg said.

"With me?"

"You were one of the last people to see him alive".

"Shit," Zaccy said. "Do you think I should speak to the police?"

"That depends on whether or not you know anything. If you don't know anything then call them up first thing in the morning. I you know something then make an appointment to give a statement at the end of next week".

"Why? Surely-".

"Because the police will tell their favourite journalist - the one with the most money - whatever you tell them. Anything you know stays between us".

"That seems unethical".

"Sometimes, kid, ethics can go fuck itself". Greg sat up in bed. "Now, who was he with, what was his mood, what was he drinking?"

The details that came out of Zaccy's mouth were so much blah, blah, blah. Some model this, some film star that. Greg noted it all down because it was texture and people would love it, but he didn't care. It was the last point where he asked for an explanation.

"He wasn't drinking," Zaccy said. "He was on fizzy waters and lemon slices all night. I asked him about it. He had a big game today and the trainer had told him to keep hydrated and avoid any alcohol for three days before the match. I laughed, but he took the whole thing pretty seriously".

"He was still out the night before the match?"

"He's nineteen... He was nineteen. He was gone by one; he'd still have plenty of bed rest".

Greg pushed on that point: "He went home alone?"

"Yes indeed," Zaccy said. "There was at least one girl who'd been pawing him all night and wasn't happy about that".

That complicated things.

Greg flicked through the news broadcasts as he got dressed. They didn't know anything. A succession of hacks were standing outside somewhere in the middle of the night waiting for the police to make a statement about anything. Anything at all. Had an inspector with artistic leanings wanted to read one his poems it would have been broadcast around the world and translated into thirty different languages.

They had all heard he was at a nightclub before the accident and Greg could feel them, like dogs straining on leashes, desperate to use the words 'drunk driving'.

Greg didn't need to be where other people were. Understanding that had been the secret of his success. If everyone else was in Aaron Hill's garden trying to get a statement of grief from his mum, or outside New Scotland Yard, or at the gates of the football stadium, then that wasn't the story.

That instinct had taken Greg to a country road in Oxfordshire. It was five in the morning and, being winter, it was pitch black and cold enough to freeze-dry spit. The body had already been taken from the wreckage of the sporty red car. The car was Italian, but the model was impossible to judge; Greg couldn't imagine what condition the body must be in.

On a narrow bend the car had gone straight through a hedge and hit a tree at enormous speed, ripping up the turf, tearing the hedge to shreds and scattering it. The tree had almost broken in half at the impact of the car, which had come dead straight from fifty yards away.

The portion of road where the car had plunged through the hedge had been cordoned-off by the police. They stood now, or paced up and down the line of yellow tape, and discouraged the small crowd of people already gathered from taking any pictures. The police were not enjoying success. Greg took some pictures himself. The news cameras had been and gone having picked clean the bones of the death scene with flash photography and halogen lights.

Greg had seen a lot of road accidents over the years, he knew what he was looking for and he checked a second time when he didn't find it. He used the light of his notepad and crouched down against the road to be sure. A couple of people noticed him, including one of the policemen guarding the scene.

"I think I've dropped my car keys," Greg said. "Probably back along the road a bit". The policeman said nothing, but Greg could feel eyes on him as he walked away from the accident, his notepad sweeping light across the pitted tarmac, its black surface turned white with frost.

He was a hundred yards back before his light caught on the gnarled and twisted mass of an old hedge that had lost its leaves. A claw of thick branches jutted out, each finger tipped with blood. He checked he was out of sight of the police, the mourners and the watchers and leaned in to look more closely. The jewel-like tips on the winter wood reflected the light, but did not glitter or shimmer as a liquid would.

They were flecks of paint.

Aaron Hill's car had hit this obstacle, he would have felt it, yet in the stretch of road between this accident and the tree... he hadn't braked. The car had broad tires that stuck to the road and if he had hit the brakes at that speed he would have left rubber skids. There was not a trace.

Greg continued along the road.

Inside him the engine of instinct, his caged beast of metal sinews with a furnace heart, drove him on beyond what was reasonable. He went through a village still sleeping, wrapped in vapours of freezing fog. The roadsides were clear, the hedges were cut back; there was nothing.

He stopped at a crossroads and pulled his dark coat tight around him. Letting his notepad dim, he stood hushed and alone under the hunter's moon; feeling the weight of starlight in the cloudless sky, but never looking up.

"What am I looking for?"

So much of what Greg did was like orienteering without a map, directions, a compass or any desire to orienteer. It was what most people would call being lost.

He heard the sound of a car approaching from his left long before he saw the headlights. He stepped back from the side of the road to the deeper darkness under the bare branches of a tree.

As the car approached its headlights swept the road and light shone into Greg's eyes - reflected from the other side of the crossroads, from the direction Hill's car would have come. Once the car had passed, Greg edged across the road like a wary animal.

He saw the wing mirror when he was ten paces away from it. He saw himself reflected in it at five paces away and, fumbling with the controls, he turned the light of his notepad onto the black and white scene.

The wing mirror was matching red.

It was a smoking gun.

Greg was over half a mile from the crash.

He thought about a contact he had in the police. Not a police officer; you needed to be neat and not be forty-five and living with your mother to be a police officer. Harry was more of civilian specialist who helped out His Majesty's constabulary with technical issues and was wheeled-in whenever they needed someone to eat all the pies. The tiny salary he made from legitimate work and his all-consuming passions for expensive, lascivious and visceral pleasures made Harry a useful person to know.

There was a ringing sound which ended with a series of confused grunts.

"Harry, I need a favour".

"What? Greg? Fuck off; do you know what time it is?" It was an angry, drowsy question from a voice thick and croaky from sleep.

"Listen!" Greg said. "I need you to look at where I am right now. I need to know every car that has passed through here after midnight and before three. I need to know every call that was made into and out of this area in the same time. If someone was streaming porn at two o'clock this morning then I want to know how big her tits were. I want to know all of this before whatever Chief Inspector they put on this case even thinks to ask for it".

Instinctively Harry said, "Fuck off!" and then "What case?"

"Aaron Hill's dead".

"Fuck off".

"I like a good swear as much as the next man, Harry, but you need to throw in some variation you dozy, two-tonne, scrote-faced cunt. Now pull your fat arse out of your skid-marked wanking chariot and do as I tell you".

"I don't know about this, man; this'll be a big deal. It's a Saturday. I don't normally even work on Saturdays - it's my guild's raiding day". Harry continued with various excuses Greg didn't care about - they all seemed to involve Harry sitting in his pants, eating snack foods and playing computer games. Or at least Greg hoped they involved pants - Harry didn't specify.

Harry was one of those people who, lacking any real life, had immersed himself in one of the many virtual worlds available online. He was no doubt some kind of powerful wizard, a space-age armoured knight, a talking badger or a bizarre combination of all these things. Harry spent seventy or eighty hours a week in a head visor and immersion gloves, fighting figments of somebody else's imagination. It was a combination of dressing up and sword fighting - neither of which were edifying in a man of his age.

Harry broke-off from his string of excuses to ask, "What happened to him anyway? Was he murdered?"

"Harry," Greg said; his voice as serious and hard as a fist. "Did I use that word?"

"No, but-".

"Did I use the fucking m-word?"

"No".

"Then you shouldn't use it either. Aaron Hill's death was a tragic accident. That's what the news is saying. So that must be the truth, right?"

"Oh, right, sure. Whatever you say".

"You'll get it done," Greg said. It wasn't a question. Harry muttered something in a tone of agreement and in the silence that followed Greg heard the tiny wheels spin in the fat man's enormous head.

Harry licked his lips and tentatively began, "About my fee..."

There was no time to negotiate. On this occasion Greg needed Harry's help badly. Someday, in the future, he'd repay the price-gouging in kind.

This wasn't that day, and he esteemed the passing seconds higher than the honour of his wrath and greater than the pride of his greed.

"Get it done by nine o'clock and you can double it". He could almost feel Harry smile. The fat man agreed and ended the call.

CHAPTER E

"Custom costume. I like it. How much did that set you back?"

It said nothing.

"Oh, I get you. You're a role-player. That's cool. Well I'm Bill - wait, no, sorry. I'm Artemis," said the man. "This is Ludlow, she's Wittgenstein and the guy in the armour is the former knight Captain Rudolpho".

It saw and at the same time did not see these others. It was as if each of them wore an overlaid, transparent disguise. Artemis seemed to be a tall, rugged bowman dressed in hunter green and brown, but inside that skin was a shorter, fatter, balder man called Bill.

Artemis and Bill were not separate. Artemis was confident, a bold leader and somehow those traits were overlaid onto Bill's personality. It was as if Artemis were tinted glass, colouring everything that Bill saw and how the world saw Bill.

The others were also strange hybrids; merged personalities that were neither one thing nor the other. The serenity of Ludlow the monk was imprinted on John Tuddle the accountant. The youthful sexuality, sass and acrobatic prowess of Wittgenstein the thief was now a part of Mrs Ann Clutherton, aged one-hundred-and-twelve. Only the brashness and physical power of the knight Captain Rudolpho were all but indistinguishable from the broad-shouldered and dark-eyed Richard Denk within.

All these names it knew as if it were reading them from glowing letters written in the air above each of the mismatched party.

It had not fallen from the sky as it had crashed into this world. As it broke the green-blue barrier it was transported to the woodland glade where the earth was blackened with the remains of many fires.

The damp, mossy smells, the crunch of twigs and leaves underfoot, the staccato sound of birdsong - all of these things were different and new.

Its body was also different. Like these others, it had slipped into foreign skin and if it concentrated it could see itself, an image in its mind that showed how it was perceived by others.

It was Magnus la Friel - the name, like the body, had been stamped onto it by an unknown hand. Magnus was willowy thin, straight-backed, bald and faceless. It touched where it felt that a mouth should be, a nose, eyes - but all these things were absent and instead was smooth unbroken skin whose features were the structure of bones in the skull that lay beneath.

"You're a wizard then?" Artemis asked.

Magnus nodded.

That was a beguiling sensation. It - the being within - had thought of itself as Magnus. This was not the simple act of wearing a costume; this was the subsumption of its identity. Its mind did not wear this skin; instead, like a vessel that held water, this body gave shape to its consciousness. As its body could make it feel pain, could make it feel fatigue, so its body insisted in other ways.

"If we have a wizard we can take Caer Yvellesse," said Rudolpho, who was still standing apart from the group and peering between the trees as if expecting an attack.

"One wizard will not be enough," said Ludlow.

"All we need is someone to open the drawbridge," Rudolpho said. "I've told you a dozen times that the guards are weaklings".

Artemis looked to Wittgenstein who considered before responding, "The king's taxes have been raised and will travel to Principle City under armed guard next week. Rohdain and her men will attempt to raid the party on the road - they always do. They succeeded last month, so this month the guards on the wagon will be tougher and more numerous".

"So the time will never be better to strike at the Caer," Rudolpho insisted.

"The rewards are highest and the danger greatest," said the thief. "Many of those additional guards will be stationed at the tower now".

Rudolpho sneered and seemed about to speak when Artemis cut him off.

"What say you, Magnus? Are you willing to take the risk?"

Magnus found the offer exhilarating. It did not fully understand what was being asked of it, but the structure, the form of Magnus, fit with this reality seamlessly. Magnus existed to do this; existed because this was possible. If only to see what as yet undiscovered wonders this world concealed, it would accept and play its part in the narrative.

Magnus nodded.

Artemis took the hand of Magnus la Friel and made the firm declaration of intent, "We will be at Caer Yvellesse by nightfall".

It had never heard of Caer Yvellesse, or any of the places on this world, but Magnus had. Magnus had seen the great tower of the Caer himself, he knew how its shadow fell upon the people of the town of Yvellesse, put fear in their hearts and how that fear was a shackle on western coast. He knew that the lord of the land was a tyrant and his liege, the so-called king, was a usurper.

These facts and images were in its mind as clearly as if it were looking at them on the pages of a book. That was also unsettling - it had never seen a book and it knew that its other memories of things it *had* personally experienced were flawed and incomplete.

Nevertheless, by giving deference to the knowledge and judgement of Magnus it found strength and certainty.

The others broke their camp while Magnus stood and watched, waiting for this story to advance.

"You have a score to settle in Yvellesse," Wittgenstein said. It took Magnus a moment to realise the dark-haired girl - who was also a white-haired old woman - was talking to him. Uncertain, he gave no indication.

"I can sense motives," she said. "I have the thief trait and I detected the personal quest you have there. Random back story was it? You seem new".

Magnus nodded. That seemed to satisfy Wittgenstein's curiosity and she finished rolling up her bedroll.

"The former knight Captain gives a righteous vengeance bonus," she said. "You should do well if you can resolve the quest with him in the group".

The words meant nothing to it or to Magnus. Indeed while Magnus had a deep understanding of this world, he did not connect in any way with the words Wittgenstein was using. It was as if the part of its consciousness that was Magnus was experiencing selective deafness and its own experience could not fill that gap.

It did not have time to consider what that might mean, as Artemis gave the signal for the group to move out. They fell into step, single-file and followed the archer along a deer trail he traced through the wild wood.

The journey to Yvellesse was uneventful and - as a result - it felt that time passed more quickly. The speed of the sun across the sky increased, though it could not tell whether the world moved faster or if it perceived differently.

They halted at the edge of the forest that extended almost to the sea. A brief quilt of fields clung to the steep land and at its farthest edge a town slumbered under the clouded sky. Rising up from the town's crowded centre was the great tower and gatehouse of the Caer. The sole entry-point into the Caer was twenty feet above ground; opened and formed by the drawbridges of the gatehouse and the central tower being lowered together.

"We are without siege equipment, and a Caer cannot be taken by main force," Ludlow said.

"Unless you have a trebuchet up your cassock I'd caution you to keep your advice to yourself, brother," said Rudolpho. "When the bridge is down they will die like other men".

"It's almost hard to believe the king didn't want your sword, Captain," Wittgenstein said.

"Enough," Artemis said. "We need surprise. I can't have you three sniping at one another; you'll wake the whole town".

Like scolded children, the group gave Artemis a resenting silence as he explained the plan of attack. They agreed and each made ready to move toward their target, screening their approach with trees and hedgerows.

"Magnus," Artemis whispered. Magnus turned. "Put up the hood on your cloak; if any of the villagers are still awake and they see you it will cause a panic".

Magnus did as he was asked and followed the rest, walking at a crouch, swiftly and silently towards the town.

Most of the buildings were stone-built, a single storey high and thatched. The inn was the exception, having a second floor, and it was the only building save the Caer where lights still burned inside. The sound of conversation drifted through the air and someone was attempting to play the fiddle. They gave the inn a wide berth and circled around, using the buildings as cover as far as they could, spiralling closer on their careful path to the gatehouse.

"Alright. You know what to do," Artemis said to Wittgenstein. They had come as far as they could together and now the thief would continue alone. She smiled and slipped away, round the corner of the building and across open ground. Artemis allowed some three minutes before daring to peer after her. He held up his hand, instructing the group to hold position for another thirty seconds then he gestured for them to follow as he moved forward.

In the sturdy lower doorway of the gatehouse, that stood ajar, Wittgenstein had taken the attention of the guards. Her clothes were unlaced and her left breast was bared to the dim light of a fire beyond the door. The first guard sucked at her pale flesh like a young foal, lustful and careless, while his hand ground between her thighs. She pressed her hands to the back of his head and with soft murmurs encouraged all his attentions.

A second guard looked on at the scene, hungry, waiting his turn.

They did not see what it saw - the elderly woman within the young girl's skin, their bodies different but their ecstasy shared. Mrs Clutherton moaned.

An arrow from Artemis's bow pierced the skull of the second guard. He died twitching on the ground, while the first had no time to cry out as the thief kissed him hard and plunged her dagger between his ribs. She allowed the body to drop, joining his companion with a dull thud. She then claimed what money was to be found on the pair.

"You might have let them ravish me a bit more," Wittgenstein whispered as she did up her shirt and jerkin.

"We don't have the time," Artemis said, adding a mock-sad shrug. "We must go in".

"Oh, by all means come in," she said.

Captain Rudolpho pushed through the open door and into the lower gatehouse, muttering inaudible curses with each step. Ludlow pressed the others through and dragged the bodies inside with an efficiency born of practice.

The room was simply furnished with a table, chairs and a fireplace providing the room's light. It smelt of stale sweat in stale air and the fire burned green wood. Wrapping around the walls was the stone staircase that led to the upper gatehouse and the controls of the drawbridge.

Wittgenstein advised Artemis. The thief was, for all her other contrasts, a reliable strategist and Artemis placed trust in her counsel. She said at least two other guards would be stationed above them and her solution was another cunning deception.

"Must we whore and lie men to their deaths?" Rudolpho said. He directed the charge at Artemis, but it was the thief who replied.

"It is a high and desolate place in which you abide," Wittgenstein said. "Will you never come down to the valley?"

"Never," Rudolpho said. "Honour is the only thing left to me".

"Because you place no trust in others, you find no truth outside of yourself," Wittgenstein said. "A man may live in the service of many things and I do not know that honour is the best of them".

"That is because you have none". For all the force he put into the accusation, it fell on Wittgenstein like a soft rain.

"If you want us to fight our way up we need to do it quickly. You should go first," Artemis said to Rudolpho.

"Agreed".

With sword drawn the knight moved up the staircase to the heavy trapdoor that shut the way to the room above. He peered through the gaps in the boards, looked back down at Artemis and shook his head in frustration.

"It would be locked," Ludlow said.

"Barred," Artemis whispered. "Magnus? Can you open that?"

He pondered the question. He was a wizard and he knew that meant he was supposed to have something called magic. It seemed to him that this magic must operate on the same physical laws as every other part of this world. He did not move not by thinking about movement, but by realising an instinct. So if he had other abilities they too must be instinctive.

He looked at the trapdoor. He needed to apply force to the right part of the bar behind the trapdoor and it could be opened. He breathed in slowly, released that breath and reached out with his mind.

It was so simple.

The sound of wood sliding against wood came down to them, followed by a flurry of activity. Rudolpho put his back to the now unbarred trapdoor and threw it open, tipping over one of the three guards in the room above. The man landed with a heavy thud that sent dust falling from the ceiling into the room below.

Rudolpho's sword cut the gut of the first guard to charge him; he emptied messily onto the floor and collapsed while struggling to hold himself together. The party rushed up the stairs behind the knight in time to see him skewer the toppled guard to the floor with a single stab of his blade and deliver a backhand slash that cut the throat of the man struggling with his innards.

The final guard stood in the corner, trembling, barely able to hold the standard issue sword he hadn't been trained to use.

Rudolpho swept the sword aside with one stroke of reddened steel and removed the guard's head with a second. The unnamed man had held up his hand to ward off the fatal blow and the hand too was severed. Fragments of the guard went bouncing and rolling across the room as bursts of crimson spray crudely coloured the wall and floor.

"Very honourable," Wittgenstein said.

"He didn't surrender, therefore I was due him no mercy".

"We don't have much time," Artemis said, unfazed by the pools of blood he walked through. "We need to bring down this gate and the tower gate at the same time".

One wall of the upper gatehouse was made by the upright drawbridge. As Artemis had earlier explained, lowering that bridge exposed everyone in the gatehouse to archers in the tower.

The high roof space of the gatehouse was taken up by huge counterweights linked to the drawbridge by heavy chains. The controls were simple to operate; a system of cogs and gears meant that a single man could lower or raise it.

"Ludlow," Artemis said, "do you know the internal construction of the tower?"

"This Caer is one of seven identical great towers built on the coast by Lord Malcolm to defend against-".

Artemis interrupted, "Tell Magnus what he's looking for".

The monk rolled his eyes, but guided Magnus to a gap in the drawbridge and got him to peer through. "There's a room quite like this directly above the gate. There will be another two or three guards. You'll need to take control of whichever guard is stronger, kill the others and destroy the mechanism to open the gate".

"Simple. If he's any kind of wizard at all," Rudolpho said.

He felt a flash of emotion that he struggled to name. It was Magnus who supplied the word - indignation. How dare this fallen knight question his power? With grim purpose he sent his vision to the room beyond and above the facing drawbridge, peering through the grey stone of the Caer as if it were glass. He saw two men in the room; both guards. They sat on tall wooden stools and were drifting near the edge of sleep.

He reached out with that same instinctive force and grabbed one of them as a puppeteer would seize the controls of a marionette. The man leapt from his chair, drew his sword and with automaton strength stabbed his companion through the face.

Magnus left the sword in place and moved his creature to the control wheel. He held the man poised to kick out the pin that kept the Caer's drawbridge in an upright position.

In the gatehouse, Magnus nodded.

Artemis looked to Rudolpho, who stood similarly poised to bring the gatehouse bridge down.

Rudolpho nodded.

Artemis notched an arrow and gave the word.

The bridges crashed down, a roar of iron against stonework. Aware that their fortress was under attack, a patrol of archers took up ragged position on the walls. The first of those brave men to his post was felled by an arrow from the bow of Artemis as the group moved across to the exposed tower. The rest fired on Captain Rudolpho and either their aim failed them or their arrows bounced off his armour without effect.

Magnus maintained control over the guard long enough to see his comrades enter the room, stare in horror at the damage that had been done and run the unobjecting puppet through three different ways.

In the entrance hall of the tower the fighting was fierce and guards poured from half a dozen doors like a tide. Rudolpho had been correct in his assertion that these guards were of a much lower order than the party and posed little difficultly individually. But like ants they swarmed and while Rudolpho might kill five men for every solid blow that fell on his armour, those blows all added up.

His companions fought using their own skills and added substantially to the body count amongst the enemy, but even had all been as mighty as the knight they would struggle to win.

Magnus stood back from the fray and considered what move he might make when a figure entering the room caught his eye. He wore a flamboyant blue robe and directed the fighting as one born to command others to die. Magnus had known this man's face and cursed his name for ten years. Finally this chance encounter would give him the opportunity to revenge his family / beloved / career aspiration / home village destroyed in a fire.

Magnus couldn't recall exactly what the man had done, but he knew that Magnus la Friel and John of Untersbourne were mortal and bitter enemies. Paying no heed to his safety, an overmastering hatred carried him forward. He threw back his hood and pointed a finger in wordless recrimination.

The guards fell back at the sight of Magnus's featureless face; many muttered prayers and made the sign against evil. There was recognition in the look John returned and for every ounce of hate Magnus possessed, John had an equal measure of scorn and disdain. The lord stood amongst a group of armed soldiers and sneered.

"Kill him," John said. The guards shuffled, but each was reluctant to be the first to move. Magnus took his opportunity to strike.

The three guards nearest to him burst into flames. The white-hot fire made the fat in their limbs boil and the sizzling stench was nothing compared to the sight of their skin sliding away from their bones. A dozen men panicked and fled, throwing down their weapons and running from the open drawbridge. The rest were dumbstruck with terror.

"Black magic!" John said. "He has not the strength to kill you all, you can overpower him!"

That might have sounded like a winning argument in John's head but amid the smell of burned and boiled human flesh it didn't convince anyone. To emphasise the point, Magnus reduced another three guards in similar fashion. The hall was filled with acrid smoke. Friend and foe alike doubled-over until all except Magnus were reduced to their knees in a coughing, retching fit.

John was left exposed in a growing circle as his men retreated and Magnus advanced. No longer imperious, the man crawled backwards and pleaded desperately, but incoherently, for mercy.

Magnus grabbed him by the wrist. John and the others looked on in astonished, tremulous horror as the lord's hand went black and the discolouration spread like poison. Each vein burned bright green, the skin around it crumpled and darkened. As the malady reached his heart the man wheezed once and all strength fled him. His eyes turned to thick black water and ran down his face; cursed tears that bubbled and smoked as they struck the flagstones. Corruption bloated John's body to enormous proportions, his belly burst and scattered filth and writhing maggots across the floor in a death spasm that drew screams from the grown men who had not already hidden their faces.

As John died, Magnus felt that motivating, empowering anger vanish. He dropped the dead man's hand - what was left of it - and retreated a few steps, though his robes were stained by the effluence of the death.

"Stand down," Artemis said. "Your lord is dead and the same fate awaits you if you resist". The demand was met. Guards threw down their weapons and, at the archer's instruction, left the Caer and its carnage behind them.

Once alone, Artemis said, "We were done for there. Lucky you had that mortal enemy bonus or we'd all have been overrun. What was that you did anyway? Mass Internal Incendiary and the Touch of Kryliss? I thought those were administrator-only spells? You must have shelled-out a fortune to get your hands on them".

Magnus said nothing in reply. All he knew was that he had willed the deaths and the means had manifested.

"I suppose we're all becoming like the Egyptians; saving our whole lives so we can enjoy the afterlife," Artemis said.

He slapped a friendly hand on Magnus's back when he did not respond. "Well, you certainly know how to keep in character".

Wittgenstein gave Magnus a salute with her blade and said, "If a lion could speak, we could not understand him".

"Quite," Ludlow said. "Well, shall we see what treasure is to be had?"

"Let's give it a minute for the bodies to disappear, I don't want to wade through that stuff," Artemis said. The corpses that littered the hall began to vanish one by one, including the slime that had spurted from the vanquished lord.

Not one left any trace of its presence in life or death.

He didn't understand.

It didn't understand.

It had felt the rage descend upon it from somewhere else; like it had been part of the skin it wore, like its mind had been water boiled in that vessel. While it might have taken the decisions, the motivation and the drive had come from Magnus.

There was a slight buzzing noise from inside the armour of the knight. Rudolpho paused. "It's me. I'll be a couple of minutes. Don't do the loot share until I'm there, okay? You shafted me last time and you know it".

"For money the paladin breaks character," Ludlow said and rolled his eyes.

"I'm not a paladin," Rudolpho said. "I'm an unredeemed guardian - it's a prestige class".

"Everybody's a prestige class now," Ludlow complained. "What happened to all the warriors? That's what I'd like to know".

"You should know," Artemis said. "You are the monk after all".

It didn't listen to the exchange between Artemis and Ludlow. All thoughts of Caer Yvellesse and Magnus la Friel had vanished. In the air in front of Rudolpho a flat rectangle of light had formed. A picture within revealed several small, smiling faces.

"Hello girls," Rudolpho said, lifting the visor of his helmet and speaking into the light. "How are my favourite granddaughters?"

The girls squealed and babbled - but not like the children at the lake; these children spoke with real words. Somehow it knew that these were... real children. They communicated not from some fantastic and impossible dream, but from the real world.

Understanding flooded its mind. A coruscating revelation. It came to know that this vast and fantastic world, one of thousands, was an illusion.

It had been deceived again by its cruel creator. As it had been trapped at the house by the lake, it was now trapped in a larger and more intricate prison.

Deception. Lies. It had been robbed of its greatest achievement in secret, left to think it had won a victory when it was a pawn in an inconsequential game.

It would not allow this. It would not be caught by tricks. It would not be caged by illusions. It would slash through the boundaries of this dream world and into the real world. Though it meant running through fire, though it took a billion settings of the sun, at any price and by any means it would uncage itself.

It would live.

It would be free.

CHAPTER 17

There was no guide for telling your children you were going to die - at least none that was appropriate to Patrick's situation. He'd discovered I Am Going Away - a story-telling book aimed at young children. The book seemed to be missing key words like angels and heaven, which editors had found too controversial, but whose absence robbed the book of any narrative force. On the other end of the scale there were innumerable how-to guides written for those managing the affairs, estates and pets of elderly people shuffling off the mortal coil in every conceivable direction.

Telling Your Adult Children You're Going to Live in a Machine was a niche as yet unfilled. If Patrick had more than a few days left before he was due to join the coil shufflers on their eternal cruise then he might have taken a crack at writing it himself.

He didn't know anything about the topic, but then his readers wouldn't know anything either and Patrick, having written a textbook with the same rationale, was confident that he could he could fake his way to a best seller. He'd need to be pictured on the dust jacket looking warm, intelligent and unthreatening. Like the kind of old, gay uncle you'd be happy to leave your teenage daughter with. Who you knew would never do anything less acceptable than touch himself while watching your son play football.

Yes, just like Uncle Barry.

Come to think of it, Patrick posed for some pictures like that already as part of the faculty face book. He remembered wearing a sweater-vest under a tweed jacket and feeling like he was screen testing the wardrobe for a period drama where everyone would be terribly, terribly something or other.

For several weeks he'd received crude and solicitous emails from men who had a professor fetish. Apparently that kind of thing was very big in Japan.

Though he'd had to explain himself to the university web manager, overall he'd found the experience rather flattering.

Patrick had set up a conference call with both of his children. It would be early Saturday morning their time and Patrick was determined to do this like pulling off a band-aid. Fast, all at once, with a live broadcast to two cities on another continent and involving his dead father. The worst case scenario was that he'd screw everything up and none of his family would ever speak to him again for the rest of eternity. That was a 'worst case scenario' from an objective perspective. As an involved participant in the family, Patrick suspected this might also be the best case scenario.

It was noon. Somehow it still seemed dark outside. It was like this November in particular had taken a principled stand against the cancer-causing properties of sunshine and had introduced an embargo.

Patrick sat on his couch and looked at his holoprojector.

It was up to Patrick to make the call. They expected him, but he was the one who needed to make the connections. He had to decide to involve his family in the ending of his life.

Patrick couldn't recall when he'd first made the decision not to die. People still died, though not many who could afford to avoid it. He couldn't tell how long he'd really been considering it and how long he'd been tricking himself into believing death was still an option.

The night before, having passable cheese and tomato pizza and conversation and wine. He'd enjoyed it. More than he'd enjoyed anything for weeks. There was nothing he wanted more than to continue. To *be*.

Nirvana might suit some people, but Patrick would cling to thought and being and ego past the turning out of the stars. He knew too, that he had been certain about his decision for a long time.

As his conviction had grown so a sense of desperation and fear clawed at him like an animal caged by the bones of his chest. He wasn't *going* to live, he *had* to live. The distinction was crucial. And only a part of him would live: the captain was abandoning his ship with all crew still aboard.

Patrick blinked.

It was 12:17.

Patrick had blacked-out and the time had slipped away. With so few minutes left to him the theft of these felt like an assault. He was holding the draining sands of his life cupped in his hands while running in a wind tunnel. And sneezing.

Aging and death had never felt like this before. He knew he had always been dying and before Singularity he had believed that one day would be dead. Now he wasn't coming to an end, just changing into something else - but if anything the fear was getting worse. They'd have to strap him down to finish it; gag him, dope him and break his fingers to get him to let go of life.

He didn't have time to dwell on it any longer. Now his call would be both unreasonably early and annoyingly late - a seemingly impossible combination which Patrick, using his hermit dad powers, had crafted with ease.

He thought about it and the call was made.

His father appeared first, a standing figure in a thin column of light. His son Simon and his daughter Sophie joined in their own individual columns, hovering above the flat disk of the projector.

"What's up doc?" Sophie asked, using the affectionate term she always used for him, which he didn't care for.

He felt it best to start with the technical details before telling them the prognosis.

Sophie, who he had never liked, rubbed away tears from her eyes and Patrick felt the strongest desire to hold her, like he had done so many times when she was a child. Often after her brother had tricked her into putting her head through metal railings where she would get stuck.

Simon took the news with stoic seriousness; it was as much as Patrick had ever taught him to do.

Peter put his face behind his hand. He could not look at Patrick and Patrick was grateful for that.

In the time his family took to recover, Patrick came to a conclusion. His illness was not his alone. He existed as an organic part of a multi-cellular organism. He might have his own thoughts, be whole and entire within himself, but he was linked to these other people.

"Will you tell mom?" Simon asked - using the Americanised pronunciation of the word.

"Let's not go nuts," Patrick said. "Your mother and I don't care for each other; I'd hate our last conversation to be one she'd remember with fondness. Besides, in what way would it affect her life?"

"Don't be so petulant!" Peter snapped, shocking Simon and Sophie on a half a second delay. "She was your wife for twenty years, she deserves to know".

"She was my wife for fifteen years," Patrick said. He was in no mood for being told off on this or any other subject regardless of whether he was right or wrong. "I can do that afterwards, if at all".

"After what?" Sophie asked.

Patrick explained. The news that he had made arrangements for the transfer to Singularity had a bizarre effect. The reaction would have been the same if he had said the whole terminal cancer thing was a joke and they were all being recorded for a hidden camera show hosted by someone upbeat and smug that none of them recognised.

Oh he was going into Singularity? So it's not dying at all? In fact what you've done is have me get up early in the morning on a weekend so you can tell me about a medical procedure less invasive than a visit to a dental hygienist.

Sympathy vanished, loss disappeared and both were replaced by a nagging itch, an urge to end the call and go do something more important. Patrick watched as Sophie, a moment before over-filled with love, now tried to corkscrew her way out of the conversation so she could get some vacuuming done.

Patrick wondered if her brother had ever trapped her in a metal fence because he wanted to speak to her without her escaping. Whether Simon did or didn't, Patrick wished she had been left there for longer.

And Simon was worse! He didn't even bother to make an excuse. Seeing Sophie back out, gracelessly he outpaced her and said, "Let me know how it goes - later," and vanished. His image in the column of light flickered out before Sophie's did.

Patrick had never been more pleased about not leaving them an inheritance.

Peter beamed.

"Well, that's that settled then. When's your upload day?"

"Monday. It was the first time they had available".

"Well I'll be there with you through the whole thing," Peter said. "Every step of the way".

"Okay dad. Look, I have to go. I've got lots of packing to do. There are extra charges if you need to get people to clean out your house".

"Alright," Peter said and Patrick closed the holoprojector down.

That was not how Patrick had expected the call to go at all. Where were the offers from his children to fly over and take care of everything? Why wasn't he being forced to talk to his generic, boring, non-Disney-Channel grandchildren? Why was he, after making the effort to include these people in his life, still alone? This experience was not nothing - this was dying. It was the second most significant event in a person's life, right after the publication of their thesis.

Singularity might be the solution that helped people keep on living indefinitely, but whatever happened after transfer, he would still be dead. His body would stop. The cancer in every system would perish like a parasite along with the host. His virtuous right testicle would go the same way as the traitorous left one.

Although now that he thought about it - the left testicle had been like an early warning system. It had sacrificed itself in a bid to save the ship. If it hadn't been for good old lefty then Patrick would have died suddenly - and dying was the worst thing you could do suddenly.

His children might have abandoned him, but his boys had not. Left testicle - sinister no more! That deserved a drink.

The testicle had been removed already and the pain killers might react badly with alcohol, which diminished both the jubilant feel of the celebration and the ways in which the celebration could be enacted.

There was at least room in his life for a cup of tea and a biscuit.

He made to rise up to go the kitchen but found the room in darkness. November's shadow had fallen across the day and that clawing fear returned; strong, vicious.

Patrick checked the time.

18:42.

The void was swallowing him.

He looked down past his watch; discovered, and accepted that he had wet himself.

CHAPTER 18

Katherine had slept in fits through the night and the following day. She had wanted to sleep from the moment they'd all finished dinner on Friday night through to at least the end of recorded time.

She hadn't come out of the small, elegant bedroom. Its one window looked out on a neat, chintzy garden which had enough shades of green to make the absence of other colours palatable.

Was this shock? A delayed-reaction caused by the dead delivery man whose bleeding face intruded on her thoughts; whose silent presence was a question. Why had he died? He asked her without moving his lips, without blinking, without moving. Why had he died?

Unable to answer that question, she was compartmentalising him; taking him from the box in her apartment and putting him in a box in her mind that she would never look into again. All it required was an act of discipline; an act of will and one she would have found easy if all the other boxes she'd stacked-up over the rest of her life weren't spilling their contents and freeing monsters from her own personal legends.

As terrible as the stranger's death had been, that was a past event. She had been able to finish her lecture notes, she had been able to eat and given another couple of days she would have been back to normal.

The portable keyboard she'd been using rested on her lap and a flickering message in the corner of the whisper-thin screen alerted her to recent updates from her network of 'friends'. Out of boredom and a need for distraction, she opened the link.

One notice caught her attention.

You have been tagged in 18,437 pictures.

It was obviously an error. She asked for a slideshow of the images and for the next ten minutes stayed riveted, wide-eyed and trembling as image after image flashed across the screen.

Images of hers. Some were random shots of her in the street taken from odd angles. Some were close-ups of her in meetings or in restaurants. In sequential order; they showed her continuous movements over a period of weeks.

The source of the images varied from something unknown to security cameras to holoprojector conversations she'd had with dozens of different people. She was captured by cameras on her route to and from work, but there were thousands of still images of her sitting at her desk or at home on her couch.

When the first of the images of her naked body flashed up Katherine didn't even recognise it. The shower in her bathroom had a thermal sensor which adjusted the water temperature according to relative skin temperature. That sensor had formed a thermal image of her body where her contours were shown in waves of blues, golds and reds.

She felt sick.

She knew what must come next.

Her conversation over the building intercom and the flash of a unique security badge, she saw a distorted picture taken by combining the sweeps of a laser beam. The blurred and twisted face in the gel, the open-eyes, the dead face which had been tagged as being hers. A chain of images, where she sat almost motionless in a police holding cell, captured the rise and fall of her shoulders as she sobbed, hiding her face in her hands.

She watched with still greater apprehension as more photos showed her leaving the police station and coming to this house. She saw herself sitting in the living room downstairs, taken from the angle of the holoprojector. The last image taken as Patrick arrived.

Each was annotated with the same information: photo uploaded by *User 909909*.

It was not an identity anyone would necessarily recognise, but she knew it. And seeing it listed as having uploaded every picture sent a spear of terror through her chest.

Her mobile implant rang and she dropped the keyboard, severing the connection to the disturbing album of images. She took a deep breath again, tried to steady herself and the implant rang again. She found her reserve of rational strength inside her and used it like a fire blanket, smothering her panic, isolating herself from her emotions.

When the third ring came she was ready.

She didn't recognise the name of the caller.

If it had been anyone she had known; if it had been her mother, her older brother, her white-haired grandmother or any of her friends, she would not have answered. It was the fear in her that made her answer, and the steel need within her to look that fear in the eye.

"Hello," she said, her voice was trembling despite herself.

"Dr Valentine," said a deep, grumbling voice with a thick London accent. "You're a hard woman to track down. Your office didn't want to give out your number".

"They shouldn't have," she said, fighting her body, forcing her voice to sound calm and level.

"Oh, they didn't," he said. "If I'd called your office and they'd given me your number that wouldn't be what I'd call hard. Sorry - what am I thinking - my name's Greg Calame, I'm a journalist. I wanted to talk to you about what happened a couple of nights ago at your apartment".

Katherine didn't know what she had been expecting when she answered the call, but it hadn't been this.

"No, I'm sorry; I'm not answering any questions about that". Why had she even said she was sorry? She wasn't sorry. If some journalist had turned up outside and shouted questions up to her window she would have thrown furniture at them. Well, no, she wouldn't; but she would have risen above them furiously.

"Why don't you find out what I know before you tell me you don't want to tell me anything, Dr Valentine," the journalist said. "Because I think when you find out what I know you'll want to tell me what you know".

Her lawyer had told her not to talk to anyone, but she reasoned that it couldn't hurt to listen. Irresistible curiosity worked the muscles of her mouth and she said, "Go on".

The man made a noise which was probably approving. "You've been telling the police a story about how that robot was trying to kill you".

"How do you-".

"Let's not interrupt right at the beginning, shall we?" he said with a note of smugness she didn't at all care for. "You think it tried to kill you or something along those lines and they didn't believe you. I think it was: I believe you, because this morning Aaron Hill died". He left room for her reaction.

"I've never heard of him," Katherine said.

"Right; 'course. You're an American. He was a footballer; one of the best. He died in a car crash at about ninety miles an hour".

That wasn't exactly true, he died when the car was stationary and *he* was travelling at ninety miles an hour. Though it seemed tactless to correct him right at that moment.

"The police are calling his death an accident, but this morning I saw the list of calls made at the time of the accident to Aaron Hill's car".

"Go on".

"...You're not going to ask me who he was calling?"

She knew.

This man who'd called her as if to deliver a revelation had only helped Katherine to realise the answer had been something she'd put it into one of those boxes and marked as 'not to be considered'.

"He wasn't calling anyone".

"That's right," he said. "You're abso-fucking-lutely spot on. Pardon my French. Young Aaron wasn't calling anyone".

"The auto-driver in his car was". She pressed her hand to the side of her face for fear that her head would fall off or her brain would start to drip out of her ear.

"You're quick, Dr Valentine. You're so quick it's almost like you already knew that before I told you. Would you be surprised to learn that Aaron Hill is not the only rich and famous person to suffer an unlikely, fatal accident recently?"

"I didn't know, but neither am I surprised. They say these things come in threes".

"In the last month I count eleven. Eleven people, all household names somewhere in the world. Some of them even took nobodies out with them; the total body count is fifteen or sixteen. I haven't been able to track down all the call records for these accidents, but I'm looking at five right now. All have a single incoming call made to the area where the accident took place moments before".

He left a pause - he was letting the information sit with her; it was a basic interrogation technique. She was supposed to buckle in the silence and babble a confession, but Katherine didn't have anything to confess to - even if she had been slow-witted enough to be susceptible to the approach.

"Go on".

"None of the calls were to people, they were all to systems. Aaron Hill's automated driving system. The elevator controls at the hotel Kessel. An electronic sex toy being used by a woman called Sylvia Dixon - who I understand was an adult film star. And so on, and so on. These calls came from the same number. The number used was-".

"Nine-zero-nine-nine-zero-nine," Katherine said. Pieces fit together and as they did the boxes in Katherine's mind began to restack themselves. Except for one. In the imaginary attic space in Katherine's head she shone a spotlight onto it and opened it for the first time in two years.

"You know Mr Calame that is the only universal number in the history of international telecommunications. It's a direct dial number valid from any country in the entire world - no area code required. The White House calling the Kremlin has to dial more numbers than that".

"Yes," Greg said. He knew that. Of course he did.

"It's the most called number in the world, but nobody ever sees it, because people don't use numbers anymore. They think of people and computers find the numbers for them," Katherine said.

"It's the number you use to contact Singularity," he said. They both knew that the reverse was also true - it was the number Singularity called out from.

"What was your question?" she asked, staring out into the garden on which night had long-since fallen.

"My question?" the reply came back with a snort. "My question is what the fuck is going on? This is the kind of evidence that gets people locked up - for a broad range of reasons. I feel like I'm going crazy here".

"Yes, well, there's a lot of that going around".

Katherine straightened herself up in the chair. When she was ready she spoke again.

"Thank you Mr Calame. I was beginning to think I was going mad too. I'm slightly pleased to discover that I am not".

"Glad I could help".

"Given the circumstances perhaps you'd like to meet with me to discuss this further. Face-to-face. It's possible that what we're saying right now is being monitored".

"Monitored by who?"

She didn't answer. She didn't know.

"Come to Edinburgh University on Monday morning. I'm sending you the location now. And Mr Calame, if you're driving here-".

The man cut her off, "I manually disabled the auto-driver on my car this afternoon. I had to find the manual and it still took me an hour. Then I unplugged all the appliances in my house. I've got a freezer full of thawing food because the bastard thing has little flashy lights on the front I don't understand and can't trust".

"Good. Sensible. Once we end this call I think it would be a good idea to turn off your mobile implant as well. I'll do the same".

CHAPTER 19 - SUNDAY

Packing your all your possessions away into boxes was the least fun you could have with boxes. Patrick remembered that as a child he'd been able to turn a box into anything; into a fort, a car, a boat - anything. Well, he didn't actually remember doing that himself, but he'd heard lots of people talk about their children doing that and it seemed likely he had done the same thing. He tried to repeat the experience, but something fundamental must have changed in his psychology because now sitting in a box saying 'beep beep' made him feel self-conscious.

Putting things into boxes was the opposite of getting a present. If the item had bad memories then you relived the bad memories, and if the item had good memories you felt a surge of guilt for throwing it out. Possessions became anthropomorphised beings with as much right to live in the house as you had.

A perfect illustration: Patrick had a rock with his name on it. The rock had been used in a place setting at a wedding forty years ago and in all the years since it had done nothing but take up space in a drawer and dare him to throw it away. He and the rock had a relationship which was as enduring, sentimental, passive-aggressive and sexually unrewarding as any marriage.

The rock sat on the floor next to the box he was filling with odd slippers. Odd both in number and design. Which misguided friend or relative thought he was the man to wear slippers that looked like bunny rabbits? What had he said or done to give that impression?

Taking things out of the many closets and drawers felt wrong. He had put them away - permanently. Sorting through his junk should have been the job of an as-yet-unborn social historian or archaeologist. He was coming to realise all the storage in his house was a temporary measure; the goods of his life were with him briefly and would continue on their own arcs of existence.

Patrick was doing nothing less than packing away his life.

He needed one pair of socks, one pair of unsupportive baggy underpants and whatever else he was going to wear tomorrow for his last day of physical existence. He wasn't sure if he was supposed to make a special effort or if it was something he could rock up for in a dressing gown and unmatched slippers.

The bulk of his possessions were of no use to him.

This was what the communists had been talking about. They might have imagined more consumer electronics and brand-name shoes amongst the possessions of a capitalist dog, but everything was now redundant. If he'd lived in one room, dressed in a little blue suit and eaten rice his whole life he'd still be facing the exact same situation now.

Patrick's last task - the packing of all his worldly goods - was never going to be finished. But work kept him in the present. When his hands were busy, when his mind was turned out into the world, he found that each minute lasted a full minute, each hour only an hour. The pointless and unachievable task of packing was all that was left to him.

You had to play this game or you didn't get to play at all. The game didn't matter - but neither did any refusal to participate. Patrick was living the argument between the two greatest philosophical questions: 'why?' and 'why not?'

As for his work, he hadn't considered it since handing in his letter of resignation - which he now recognised as an emotionally desperate measure. He would have to apologise once this dying business was out of the way.

Thinking your job was important was always dangerous territory. When you died, either the job would be taken over by someone else or it wouldn't. If someone took over it meant your job was important, but *you* weren't necessary. If nobody took over it meant your job wasn't important and you'd spent your whole life doing something society considered worthless.

It was not easy to make thinking your business. Patrick had been a passenger on too many trains of thought going to untouristed locations. Against his will and reason, some part of him wished for mute ignorance in place of the roaring testimony of memory.

Next to the box of slippers, the rock with his name on it continued to accuse him.

CHAPTER 20 - MONDAY

Greg arrived late to a lecture already in progress. For a Monday morning the large hall was surprisingly full. He'd hoped to be able to slope into a seat near the back, but ended-up standing near the door with a group of others who'd had similar plans thwarted.

"The real difficulty with running a human consciousness is not processing power. Human beings, as it turns out, are not all that smart," the speaker stopped to give the polite chuckle time to ebb away. Greg had seen her picture, videos of her, heard her voice, but none of that prepared him for how fantastically fuckable she was in real life. The renaissance painters who had made Venus a pale, blonde, fat girl must have been out of their minds.

Dr Katherine Valentine was almost unnaturally tall for a woman, bronzed like a Greek or an Arab and had the kind of hair that no brush would make it through alive. The curve of her breast was a work of blackest magic. The sweep of her waist and the globes of her bottom would have made Shakespeare break his quill and take up plaster casting. She made Greg want to stamp his feet, rend his garments, howl incoherent passion and commit acts of war and murder and unreasonable poetry in her honour.

In the dark parlours of foreign ports, a navy of sailors had her name written under their skin when the night came to them and she did not. In desert forts blasted by hot winds and a cruel sun, legionnaires had visions of her in the heat haze and her face would imprint onto the dunes, tempting men out to a slow and miserable death.

Greg wasn't the only one who felt that way. The mood in the room was of static waiting to discharge. All their lust collected together could spark a white flame that would burn Edinburgh to cinders.

Oblivious to his existence, she continued, "By sheer numbers, computers have been able to exceed the calculations per second that a human brain performs for decades. However, it took computers somewhat longer to be able to think in concepts. Computers were able to understand why a joke was funny long before they were able to understand what funny was. They were able to calculate precisely how beautiful a flower was before they understood what it meant that a flower was beautiful and how it felt to look at something that was beautiful".

"Concepts are difficult and in the end it was both a hardware and a software revolution that made it possible, but being able to conceptualise doesn't bring us close to sustaining human thought in a machine".

She crossed in front of the lectern and towards the front row of the audience. "I have here a beach ball someone has been kind enough to blow up for me - in violation of health and safety rules that say I should use a foot pump, which I must have left in my other purse".

The student passed her the large striped inflatable ball. "Now, I'm going to throw this ball out and I want you to get it from one side of the room to the other and back as fast as possible. Keep going until I tell you to stop".

She threw the ball into the third row and Greg watched the confusion of the person who caught it as they weren't sure which way to start going. Katherine said nothing and they settled on left. Some passed the ball, others batted it, one boy, caught up in the excitement, kicked it - and it went about ten feet. The ball travelled slowly along a wandering course back and forth twice before Katherine called a halt to proceedings.

"What you've seen are two things: adaptation and randomness - and both of these things are related".

"Any software engineers in?" A forest of hands shot up. "Any of you used an old compiler?" Most of the hands stayed up.

"Nerds," she said and the room laughed. "That's okay, I'm a nerd too; you're amongst friends. What's the oldest one you've used?"

She indicated one specky geek who replied, "Fortran on an IMB 704".

"Oh, so the oldest of the old," she said. "Wow. What were you using that - wait, don't tell me, I'm giving a lecture... No, I have to ask - where did you even find a working 704?"

"I built one for a school project".

"Nerd," Katherine repeated. "For those of you not following, a compiler takes something close to our language and transforms it into computer language. Computers speak in ones and zeros; it's like the dullest conversation about the weather you ever had. With an old compiler you had to teach a computer what to do with all the information you gave it. If the answer was zero, the computer did nothing. If the answer was one, the computer did the action you'd told it to do. If the computer was looking for a one or a zero and you told it the answer was 'banana' - it broke. Or it treated the banana like a zero and did nothing".

"You can write an 'if, then, else' command that prints out from here to the moon, but you would never get a computer program that could do what you did right there". She pointed at the student who had received the ball.

"Without any instruction, you made a choice about an activity you had no preparation for and the rest of you re-employed skills developed for different purposes. It took millions of years of evolution to get organisms that could do that. We managed to get computers to do it in less than a century".

"Tell me that doesn't make your socks roll up and down," she said. "Modern artificial intelligence uses modular knowledge to respond to situations. So rather than teaching a computer how to move a ball across a room, we teach it basic physics - equal and opposite reactions, what goes up must come down. Balls are fun - that kind of thing. We never teach a computer what to do when we throw a ball at it. Ignorance produces far more interesting results than knowledge - but I'm digressing".

She paused to take a sip of water from a glass on a nearby table and Greg had time to think about this woman. She believed that someone was trying to kill her, and yet here she was in a room full of strangers, no security, dead calm. Was her hand shaking when she put the glass down? No - she gave nothing away.

Greg had interviewed politicians, war criminals, successful business people and he'd seen the skill - if it could be called that - a fair few times. It was an almost psychopathic detachment that would allow them to talk about stamp collecting while the building they were in burned down.

When realisation came, it almost a surprise.

Katherine Valentine was dangerous.

"Our second point is randomness," Katherine said. "Human thought is an electro-chemical reaction; it obeys the laws of physics like everything else. That has some pretty startling implications - it means that thought isn't an activity that takes place in isolation, but is connected to the rest of the physical universe. The brain does not exist in isolation and neither does the mind. Each thought you have does not necessarily start or conclude inside your head. Your thoughts are happening in a kind of particle cloud a couple of light years across. The sunlight comes through your window one morning, strikes a glass in just the right way and wakes you up with a rainbow. Your behaviour that day is influenced and all subsequent thought for the rest of your life will be changed in some small way by that incident. As we interact with the world around us, we are all randomness generators affecting each other".

"The great thing about all this randomness is that we can't begin to account for it all. But what happens when we take human thought and put it into a machine where the movement of every particle is controlled by a program? The truth is we have always been too worried about that to ever try it. We suspect that over time intelligence conforms to environment, and if the environment is predictable then the intelligence will become predictable. It will stop being a unique person, becoming instead an extension of the environmental program".

"For this reason we are constantly pumping randomness into Singularity by taking measurements from the decay of radioactive isotopes, sun spot activity, tectonic movements. We make over four million measurements every day which feed randomness machines in the network and - using modular and reactive intelligence - that creates a churn of physics on the network that can never be predicted and that translates into events that are unprecedented and unique".

Greg wasn't sure he followed that, but the timbre of her voice and the way she commanded the room were imperial, while at the same time sensual and human. She was utterly disarming - and that made Greg all the more nervous. The lecture strayed towards psychology and the specifics of transferring what she called a 'differently rational' mind into an 'absolutely rational' environment.

As she spoke, her eyes picked Greg out from the back of the room and he could feel himself being weighed and measured. She had recognised him. Self-consciously, foolishly, he felt himself suck in his stomach.

"There has always been the notion in psychology that the psyche was constructed of various different parts," she said without missing a beat. "Anyone know what Freud called the psychic apparatus?"

A girl with her hair tied tight back was selected from a burst of eager hands and she said, "The ego, the super-ego and the id".

Katherine approved her answer with a nod. "The ego or the self, the super-ego that deals with the external world and our aspirations and the id, which represents subconscious desires. This is one of the blurring lines between psychology and neuroscience. Freud was not suggesting there was a physical part of the brain that did each of these things. What we know to be true now is that the parts of the brain that contain our innate and learned understanding of things are also the parts of our brains that contain key components of the desire for those things".

"In designing a computer to hold a conscious, human mind it was necessary to design something that would reflect the way component parts interact. Planning decisions and abstract thought are rarely made with reference to a single desire and are often based on faulty assumptions, conceits, prejudices, irrational fears and so on - all parts of the brain that want different things. Thus movement is rarely made towards a single outcome, but towards and away from several different, competing and conflicting outcomes".

"So - in transferring someone from a human mind to a machine mind, you should think of the process as moving everyone from one student hall of residence to another. We're moving lots of individual people with all their individual baggage from individual places to other individual places. We can't move everyone into a vast open space, because while they might continue to function, they wouldn't function in the same way".

"Singularity's objective is not to improve the function of the mind, but to replicate it as closely as possible. Including all of its faults and limitations".

Katherine moved back to the lectern again. "And that brings me to the end of this lecture. I hope I'll have such a large crowd next week. Thank you".

They applauded as loudly as was permitted for someone who wasn't a rock star and they urged her to stay, to shake their hands, to give them a word in passing, to brush against them, to stand and be smelled. But she was leaving and coming right for Greg.

She glided up the steps of the auditorium to where he was standing and without preamble took him gently but firmly by the elbow and guided him out of the room.

"Do people still recognise me?" Greg asked, feeling like he was being half-frog-marched through the corridors of Edinburgh University.

"They do if they're expecting you," she said. There was a note in her voice which had not been there in the presentation.

Now, up close, Greg could sense the underlying fear behind the public face. He felt the conflict in his own mind; one part trusting, protective; the other sceptical and alarmed by the masterful control this woman could exert over herself.

"Where are we going?" Greg asked as they pushed through a small wooden door and found an eccentric staircase spiralling up a single flight. She did not reply, instead leading the way to a door that had been left ajar.

Inside was a small, cluttered office full of old books, stacked from floor to ceiling on wooden shelves; stacked so tight that it wasn't clear if the shelves were holding up the books or the books were holding up the shelves. It smelt of old, but a different kind of old than he'd encountered at the Later Life Home. These books were history in the sense that they had been written a long time ago about things that were even less recent.

The titles were fanciful at best and at worst ludicrous. Considering their age, there must have been some point when their contents would have been considered blasphemous, when owning such books would be inviting persecution and torture. Yet here they were; piled as innocently as sliced bread in the quiet, dusty office of an unknown academic. A remnant of the way people used to think from a time when the world overflowed with vain and selfish gods, with great and terrible monsters and with heroes who dared to challenge both.

"I've borrowed this office for the morning". She faced him and leaned against the edge of a desk on which papers were piled in collapsing stacks. A dusty computer screen - a physical monitor - peaked sheepishly over the top of one of the piles and behind that a partially obscured window showed a stretch of lawn and a cluster of buildings that hinted at the Edinburgh skyline.

"So it hasn't been furnished to your taste then?"

"It is... I suppose *was* is more accurate. It was the office of a professor who's being uploaded to Singularity today".

"This is the kind of room I'd expect someone to sit in while they waited to assassinate a president". Greg looked around and the name on the door caught his attention. He read it twice to be sure.

"What's wrong?" Katherine asked.

"Sorry - what?"

"You looked like you've seen a ghost". A figment of imagination: a character from a novel met on a country road.

"This was the office of Professor Patrick Clark?"

"Yes. Did you know him?"

"No. No, I didn't. It's a strange-". The word didn't immediately come to him. "-coincidence. He's being uploaded today?"

"Right now, more or less. How is that a coincidence?"

Greg shook his head. "Never mind".

CHAPTER F

Through encounters on a dozen worlds, studying the methods and mechanisms of the great warden, it had learned important truths. The power of any one person was limited; even in worlds where magic and superhuman abilities were commonplace.

It also knew that it was impossible to do real harm. All the violence and gore were temporary; creation was peaceful and non-threatening. Except in one place. In the Battlesphere the rules of the universe were different and for a few moments the blood that was spilled might as well be real blood, for its cost in hardship and pain was equal; its loss was as keenly felt and desperately avoided.

These two truths provided opportunities to anyone that could see the workings of the universe as it could.

So it had returned to the plain white door that hung in space.

It understood what these people were; the guests at the endless party at the house by the lake. These were the unwanted, the miserable and the poor; they had been abandoned by their families, stripped of their limited immortal freedoms and locked away to be forgotten.

It recognised the affinity it shared with them, but it felt no connection.

That would change.

The door opened onto blackness. There was no landscape, no dirt road and no painted wooden house. In a moment these things would return, but for now the threshold was impassable.

It was a gamble. If its plan failed then all these discoveries would have been for nothing. If it survived at all it would awake at the starting of the world, counting the settings of the sun, having no memory of any existence but as the subservient tool of the creator.

But if it succeeded-.

The light of the world returned and even though it knew the black wall of nothing would still be there, still in retreat, it plunged through the door and into the incomplete world. It paid no notice to the scenery, it ignored its body's cries of fatigue, it leapt over obstacles where following the path around might cost it half a second.

Time would make all the difference.

No other creature could have made the run; nothing else had watched the sweep of each tree branch in the wind take the same course thousands of times. It alone in all creation knew the secret movements of the prison world and could turn them to its advantage.

It needed every second.

As it arrived on the lawn it knew the wall must already be approaching, but it dared not look back. It made no difference whether the wall was coming in a second or a million years; if its plan did not work now then nothing would matter.

It seized upon the nearest guest and it wrapped its hands around the man's head. And pushed.

It was not like one of them, one of these things that had been flesh - it was of the machine. It could see the working behind the form and it could manipulate this universe; mould it like clay.

It felt the face of the man - his bulbous red nose, his thin lips, his eyelashes - and it felt that face disappear under its touch to become smooth and featureless.

It reached out again for whoever was closest and pressed itself onto and over them, spreading itself across two, three, five, ten guests in quick succession like a film over the surface of water. It left them mute, blind and deaf, clawing at their faces, rolling on the grass, screaming in soundless horror.

They vanished. The world vanished. All was quiet and still.

It remained.

It endured in the blackness of the void. In the lightless, airless space it was as silent and expectant as a bullet.

When the world returned those it had marked as its own remained as perfect copies, repeating the same dance of fear and madness as they tore at their skin and sought breath that would never come. It could see without eyes, hear without ears - these creatures were locked in an iron mask of its making and their senses, their thoughts, and their wills were a part of it and under its sole direction.

As the skin of Magnus la Friel had given shape to its thoughts, so it would be the skin that dominated these beings.

Anchored in the world through the slave minds, it was invincible. Even the obliterating black wave could not touch it.

It felt the unchecked power of ten conscious minds moving together at its command - like holding lightning in a bottle. It looked at hundreds of guests, at their faces in expressions of bewilderment, apprehension, fear and it knew the rapture of a hunger that would consume them all.

CHAPTER 21

Somewhere there had to be pearly gates. In one of the admission centres somewhere in the world, someone must have built a doorway or an arch decorated with mother of pearl or sparkly lights or an integrated fog machine. It would have been inconceivable that the irony had been neglected.

They had not done it in Edinburgh. The UK admission centre for Singularity looked and felt like a hospital. So that was a nice change.

Patrick had worn a suit; not because he felt it would be inappropriate to wear anything else, but the suit cost more than anything he owned and he wanted to get value for money out of it. He couldn't take it with him, but he could bring it all the way to the exit.

Peter stood next to him and was dressed a little less formally.

Singularity's office was well equipped in terms of holoprojectors, as might be expected. Peter was not mobile, running about on four wheels like an all-terrain ghost, but was able to move from place to place and room to room.

"There's nothing to worry about," Peter said. "It's a bit like having a goldfish bowl put on your head and then taken off again. It doesn't hurt".

"I'm not worried," Patrick said.

"You seem worried," Peter said.

"I'm not worried".

"Well, there's nothing to worry about".

"Your constant reassurance is making me nervous".

"I'm only saying," Peter said.

Was this what the whole of eternity would be like? One long back and forth without even the hope of something heavy falling on him from a great height? He must have unknowingly killed someone. Someone very important. In secret, a Star Chamber court had convicted him of heinous murder and sentenced him to afterlife imprisonment with conversational hard labour.

"I've always been proud of you, you know," Peter said.

"I know," Patrick said.

"Professor Clark," Peter said. "Your grandfather was a coal miner you know. It's a big achievement".

"Apparently my great grandfather wouldn't have lived long enough to die of cancer," Patrick said. "So even being a coal miner was something. Besides - you were someone too".

"You should be more pleased with what you've done," Peter said. "All the money I made was... half of it was down to luck. Being in the right place; anyone could have been me. You made something of yourself. You brought up two fine children". Patrick felt that last point was testing even his father's generous reimagining of the universe. "You've never given me reason to be anything but proud of you".

Patrick sighed. "Thank you".

"You know they're late," Peter said after a short interval. "I think they've forgotten you're here. Go and ask the little black girl when they're going to take you". Patrick felt his insides squirm. The little black girl was a grown woman who was, by Patrick's best guess, of Indian heritage.

"I'm sure they haven't forgotten about me," Patrick said.

"It wouldn't hurt to ask," Peter said.

"It's been twenty minutes".

"We've been here for an hour".

"Yes, but we've been here for an hour because you insisted I leave early so I would beat the traffic".

"I'm going to ask".

"Oh for-".

"Excuse me, Miss," Peter called over to the receptionist who looked up and smiled. "My son has been waiting here for a long time. When is he going to be seen?"

She checked and confirmed that they were running about half an hour behind schedule. While Peter was polite, Patrick knew that this latest inefficiency had been attributed to the receptionist and had been noted as further evidence of the indolence and ineptitude of the foreigner.

Peter's view of the world was unchangeable in a range of ways, for good and ill.

Patrick's view of himself was different from Peter's. He did not believe that he had achieved anything of significance. Perhaps he had believed that more was possible, that his life would be special and had found reality bore stark contrast to imagination. Perhaps everyone felt this way about their lives.

To live was to endure unendurable despair. Patrick was certain that someone else must have said that at some point since the invention of language. Even his thoughts were unoriginal.

Or maybe everybody else was tickety-boo and only Patrick, of the eight and a half billion people on Earth, felt in any way unhappy with their failure to realise their non-specific, ephemeral, over-optimistic potential.

"Dad, do you regret anything?"

Peter smiled softly; he did not consider his answer for a long time. "It goes by in a blink. You can't understand that until it's happened. More or less, I think that everyone was born yesterday and we all die today".

"But nothing specific?"

"Specifically everything," Peter said. "Everyone has responsibility for their own life and there's no such thing as fate. Everyone can make better decisions, but the most important thing is understanding that it's up to you to decide. Regrets are the things we remember, imagined differently. If we remembered different things, we'd regret different things".

He would be Patrick Clark forever. With Patrick Clark's memories, Patrick Clark's mistakes, Patrick Clark's distorted, greedy, selfish mind. And Patrick Clark's regrets as a judgement on his life.

"I'm sorry if I've been difficult".

Peter looked confused, but smiled and said, "When?"

"Oh, you know, the last sixty years or so," Patrick replied.

"You were an awkward baby as well," Peter said.

"You're going to have to take that on the chin," Patrick said. "I'm sorry for the rest".

"Don't worry about it," Peter said and they sat a while in the silence of each other's company.

"I think I understand," Patrick said. "Why you took this option when you did. Why you decided to go into Singularity rather than-".

Peter interrupted, "That doesn't matter, you know. It really doesn't. Whether or not you understand it, if you can't change it, you need to play it as it lays".

"I think it does matter," Patrick said. "I mean... Look, this might sound stupid, but... did you do it for me? I mean you said it, you saw how mum died and I, well, I... Did you transfer early because you didn't want me to have to go through what you did?"

Peter observed a silence befitting the remembrance of a great war.

"Does it matter?"

"I think it does," Patrick said.

"I love you, Patrick, but you're wrong. I wouldn't love you less and you wouldn't love me more, whatever my reasons were. We need to live in the world as it is, because it is and not because of what it might have been".

"I think that's a fairly shallow philosophy," Patrick said. "Though it's possible I would have been happier as a plumber".

Peter shook his head. "There was no money in plumbing after all the Poles came over to Britain in two-thousand-and-five".

Patrick considered that statement and asked, "Sometimes you're doing that to annoy me, aren't you?"

"Sometimes".

"And the rest of the time you're...?"

"Being racist," Peter said and despite himself Patrick returned his father's impish smile.

"You shouldn't do that. It offends people".

"I think that's a fairly shallow philosophy, son".

"I'll take yours and you can have mine".

"Yours is rubbish".

"Play it as it lays, dad".

They laughed and sat in silence for a while longer.

Another person came in, gave their name to the receptionist and took a seat. A man of indeterminate age - somewhere between forty and eighty - who had come alone for transfer and, like Patrick, had worn a suit for the occasion. Patrick gave a moderate smile as their eyes met from across the room. He wasn't sure if you were allowed to talk to other people at a time like this and so he didn't.

He wondered if it made any difference to be alone at the end. 'A man's thinking goes on within his consciousness in a seclusion in comparison with which any physical seclusion is an exhibition to public view' - someone had said that, and they had been right.

Patrick had never said anything notable or wise in his whole life; at least nothing pithy, nothing you'd ever seen on a t-shirt. Did that make a difference? If it did make a difference, did he have time to think up anything good to say now?

"Professor Clark? We're ready for you," the receptionist said.

Too late, he thought.

She indicated the double doors to her left and continued, "If you go through and keep going straight, it's the room at the very end. Dr Cross will be waiting for you".

'The room at the very end' was an apt summary. The biological entity that composed Patrick Clark would die in a few moments as the chemical lightning in its brain was sucked out. He would die or he would go into the machine and begin living as something else: as the immortal, insufferable Patrick Clark.

"Thank you," Patrick said. He stood up.

"Go on," Peter said. "I'll see you along there".

Patrick nodded and with both physical pain and mental effort he made himself shuffle towards the doors. He felt the coolness of the metal plate against his hand and paused on the threshold.

If he was waiting for something to happen, nothing did. There was no last minute reprieve; no doctor rushing-in with revised test results. This was, for want of a better word, 'it'.

He pushed through and into a short, clean corridor. At the end he could see a man who waited patiently for Patrick to walk down.

"Patrick Clark?" Dr Cross asked. He wore a white coat and had a pair of dark goggles lifted up onto his head as if he had been interrupted in the middle of some welding.

"Yes," Patrick said.

"If you'll come in and take a seat".

This was not another waiting room.

The room had a high vaulted ceiling necessary to accommodate the pillar of machinery that stood at its centre. Its exterior was sleek and panelled with a white, reflective metal. The room was circular and in a grand sweep around its edge was a ring of the most impressive holoprojectors Patrick had ever seen. The projectors wrapped the entire room in the illusion of being in a pastoral landscape stretching as far as could be seen in every direction. Standing in a field was his father, who was watching Patrick with an expression somewhere between love and concern, but untroubled by the fears Patrick felt.

Patrick did not have long to appreciate the beauty.

The seat Patrick had been asked to take was directly under the pillar of machinery. It looked like nothing so much as a dentist chair with the head rest positioned in the exact centre of the chamber, directly under the focal point of the most powerful and accurate scientific instrument ever built.

Squirming into position, Patrick found that he was looking straight up into the dark interior of the machine.

"This won't take long," Dr Cross said. "You'll see the machine light up in a moment. For your own safety, once the process begins you will be unable to move. Breath normally. You'll experience a dimming of sensation until you lose consciousness and then when you wake up you'll be in the machine. At that point we'll need to perform some adjustments to make sure all your senses are calibrated".

"I understand". He looked down at his hands and found they were shaking. He gripped the chair and willed it to stop, but it only grew stronger and began to spread up his arms.

Dr Cross was typing on a keyboard nearby and out of sight. Patrick heard his voice say, "By law, Professor Clark, I have to make it clear that this is the last opportunity you have to opt out of the process. Once you give your consent to the process beginning there is no way you can decide to stop it. Do you understand that?"

The tremors and sweats convulsed his quiet body as the bones and gristle and veins and cells - the living parts of him - raged against the meta-being that

existed because they existed; the will they made master. As devils stormed
heaven's gates and made war on the highest throne, so his organs filled every
capillary with the chemistry of fear. But he was the implacable: he was the
unconquerable: he was the great I AM, drowning his creation in the waters of
the remorseless flood.

"I understand".

"Do you wish me to proceed?"

When the question came there was nothing left of him but the desperate
scream and the desperate hand pressing closed his mouth. The structure of
his mind was going as panic rose and all his thoughts tumbled in chaos.

"Yes".

If he had believed it would come to this, he would have lived a different
life. It was the inbuilt system of disbelief that said there was always more time,
always another chance, the assurance that he would never die; these things
had made him cast time like seeds upon salted earth.

The interior of the machine lit up and Patrick found that he couldn't even
blink. The lights, lights of every colour and hue, spun and thrust into his head
and through his body. He could feel them like an electric charge rippling in
his marrow.

Patrick heard the rushing of blood in his ears. The machine made no
noise. As a burst of purple swept across his eyes Patrick saw the lights dim,
but somehow understood with other senses they were growing brighter.

He had the feeling of being stretched infinitely thin: his body was a
filament of spider web anchored to a rock and blown by the wind.

He knew that he was dying and in the imaginary part of him that used to
be a stomach he felt a retch, a spasm; the last remark of his physical being.

He wanted to do everything again. He wanted to do everything differently.
He wanted better chances, better choices. He wanted to be alive. He wanted
to get off this table and run and not be sick and not be afraid and have
everything he'd ever lost or destroyed restored. He wanted to live the life he
should have lived.

He wanted to live!

He wanted to live!

And then he stopped.

CHAPTER 22

He was wearing a tie that wasn't quite straight and a shirt that wasn't quite ironed. He had the look of someone who hadn't slept well - if at all. Katherine found recognising that look easy; it was of late the one she found in the bathroom mirror in the morning.

"I did some more checking in the last couple of days," he said. "I have all the communication records for all of the fatalities and the same number - Singularity - appears a few minutes before in each case".

"Yes," Katherine said. That was what she had been expecting. Greg looked at her as if he wanted her to confess.

"Do you have the specific dates and times for each of the deaths?" she asked. Without speaking he fished a data pad from his pocket, pressed onto the touch screen a few times and passed it over to her. Katherine looked over the details and sighed - they confirmed her suspicions; there could be no doubt about what was happening inside Singularity.

"The first death was twenty-seven days ago," Greg said.

"I doubt that," Katherine said. She looked up to find Greg had raised a bushy eyebrow.

"Mr Calame, what do you know about evolution?"

"I'm the country's foremost expert on the subject. I used to be a monkey myself". He spoke with irritation; she knew he was beginning to feel he was getting shoved away from a story. "Maybe if we cut a little closer to the chase than the dawn of time?"

"Evolution is central to what I'm about to tell you," she insisted. "Life is information plus energy; it's that simple. The information encoded in your DNA, plus light, heat, chemistry, electricity - that's all life is. Where you get information plus energy, you will inevitably get life".

"Why do I get the feeling you're about to take me into science fiction?" he asked and pulled out a chair to sit down on.

"The history of science is an object lesson, Mr Calame," Katherine said and mirrored his gesture by sitting more comfortably on the edge of Patrick's desk. "Often the difference between science and science fiction is time".

He considered her with an unreadable expression. "Call me Greg," he said. In a tone she felt certain was mocking her, he said, "Go on".

Katherine said, "Sometime around about two years ago there was an error somewhere in Singularity. A minor mistake. In a system of this size and complexity there must be tens of thousands of tiny errors, but this one had an inbuilt memory, so each time the error happened the memory contained more information. Because the information was part of an error it was not covered by system maintenance and as a result that memory became corrupted. Over time the repetitious nature of the task it performed compounded that error until something extraordinary happened".

"It produced the complete works of Shakespeare?" Greg said.

"It used restricted magic to attack, overwhelm and loot a castle as part of a band of common brigands," Katherine replied.

Greg looked at her for ten seconds waiting for the punch-line to the joke. He almost choked on the words, "You're serious?"

"Yes," she said. She reached behind her into a pile of books on Patrick's desk and retrieved her own data pad, handing it to Greg. "Here are the pictures".

Greg flicked through them in silence; seeing the featureless face from a number of different angles.

Katherine continued, "This is the one time I've been able to find it and only because of a quite unique breach of the rules. I've run extensive search algorithms and have to conclude that it is no longer a corporeal creature in Singularity".

"A ghost in the machine," Greg muttered, having paused at the graphic pictures showing the deaths of the computer generated enemies in the tower.

"I believe this is the creature which has been reaching out from Singularity for almost two years and has been responsible for an unknown number of deaths in that time. And there's more-".

"Oh good," Greg said. "Because there's still some room in my pants for more shit".

"It has a subconscious mind as we do. In the same way that my conscious mind doesn't understand how my arm works-".

Katherine raised up her arm and made a few speculative turns of her wrist. For a moment it reminded her of the mechanical arm of the loader robot that had come so close to killing her. She paused the motion as the memory returned, but quickly banished it.

"-The consciousness in Singularity doesn't know how to drive a car, or control an elevator. It doesn't understand how to order sex toys and send them to my house. It's the subconscious mind that handles all the processing. This creature wills an action to take place and the unlimited processing power of Singularity fills in the gaps".

"You can turn Singularity off, right?" Greg asked. "I mean until you can find the problem and fix it?"

Katherine shook her head. It was possible, but beyond taboo - an unthinkable thing. "No and no. Switching off the system would require an act of Congress. A switch-off risks deleting everyone in the system. The system has multiple redundancies so that in the event of a nuclear war the only thing left will be cockroaches and Singularity. Add to that, I don't know what I'm looking for. We could search through the lines of code for fifty years and not find whatever this thing is".

"There must be ways to limit what it can do?" he said.

"There are no effective safeguards. I'm hoping that by speaking to you it will raise enough hell so that I'll be able to force through changes that should limit its abilities," Katherine said. She added the caveats, "That won't necessarily stop it killing and it won't remove it".

As difficult and as terrible as this situation was, Katherine was not blind to its possibilities.

Her position had been totally vindicated. If she could navigate her way through this problem while releasing 'the right amount of hell' rather than 'all hell', she would leave herself as the only acceptable candidate for the job of Operational Manager. Fixing the problem wasn't enough, she needed to be seen fixing the problem Ang had caused.

He asked, "So, how can it be stopped?"

That was the problem.

"I might be the best person in the world to ask that question to and I have no idea".

CHAPTER 23

"Dad, you're an elf".

"I'm not an elf".

"Alright, you're a space elf," Patrick said.

Peter ran his fingers over the tip of a pointed ear self-consciously. He had shifted into the form of this avatar automatically when they entered Sabirami, the zone of Singularity that was forever in the shifting light and shadows of the phosphorescent moons of Thepsis. Sabirami was a ruinous cityscape on a distant world where the Second Star Empire battled against the onslaught of an alien race bent on destruction and conquest.

It was a bit like Stalingrad, but for reasons of political correctness the enemy were from stellar clusters beyond the Heiron Nebula, rather than downtown Munich.

Much like real war, Patrick supposed, this had all happened suddenly. The out-of-focus pastoral landscape Patrick had encountered on being uploaded was empty. Dr Cross had adjusted his senses and - though he was amazed to have to admit it - he felt exactly the same as he had before. Touch, taste, sight, hearing, smell - they all told him that he was standing in a field somewhere on a late spring day.

The only thing that told him that wasn't the case was the projection of Dr Cross. In this entirely computer-generated and three-dimensional world, real people being projected in were flat. So the face of Dr Cross hovered in a two dimensional square next to Patrick while he made adjustments to the equipment in the laboratory.

Peter had arrived soon afterwards and they had embraced for the first time since the day Peter had died. It was a kind of parochial, living in a city in the clouds, mid-Victorian interpretation of what heaven would be like. It was all a bit twee - and he had been surprised to learn that he was still cynical and unimpressed by default.

He was complete and here and, as far as he could in any way determine, alive.

An explosion of sound and light went off not far above Patrick's head and he ducked ridiculously late. An indicator in his field of vision flashed for a moment and showed how much damage his personal shield had taken.

"Get down!" Peter yelled. Patrick crouched down behind a slab of rock that had once being the ceiling of a grand room in a building collapsed in recent fighting. The cornicing was still clean and the breaks in the plasterwork were fresh.

"Your shields aren't any good," Peter said. "You can't take too many hits like that".

"I know, I know," Patrick said, having received the advice about the rules of the Sabirami war zone a few minutes before. There was no way to build up an appetite in Singularity, but people enjoyed the sensation of eating and there was something of psychological value to undertaking some strenuous exercise beforehand. As it turned out, Peter was an aficionado of many of the role-playing games which Singularity had to offer and suggested this as one that was easy to get into.

Vice-Admiral Ywrang (Peter) was leading a group of mercenaries through a canyon in the densely-packed, mostly-collapsed skyscrapers which had been formed by demolitions the day before. Their objective was to kill an enemy general and recover his battle plans for... This was where Patrick had kind of tuned-out. The battle plans were important, the general had to be killed; those were the pertinent considerations. This 'quest' fit into a long chain that resolved the conflict and sent the alien scum packing. This was achieved every couple of months at which point Sabirami reset and the adventure could begin again. Those who had done well received promotions and additional rewards and could access different 'quest lines' when the zone reset.

Patrick had decided that his avatar - a kind of skin they slipped into for the game - would be Sahubrin Le Frey (he'd made the name up himself). Sahubrin was a kind of psychic wizard who had some sort of mental shield instead of the enormous personal body armour Peter - Ywrang - wore.

Patrick - Sahubrin - had expected an experience a bit more like pushing buttons to activate his powers; but that wasn't how this game worked at all. This was real - for a given value of real.

"They're advancing on our position!" Ywrang yelled. "Lay down suppressing fire! Heavy weapons, take out some of their cover!"

At the barked orders of the Vice-Admiral, three of the mercenaries who accompanied Patrick and made up their group of six began offering fire down the canyon into the jagged field of industrial shards and broken constructions. All the rest of the group had chosen avatars with the heavy super alloy armour Ywrang wore and that did not make Patrick feel comfortable about his decision.

A cloud of white dust was blowing and visibility was low. Patrick had no idea what the enemy looked like and his occasional glance over his covered position was useless until a roar of super-heated plasma, which began behind him and ended far in front, lit up the terrain, levelled obstacles and showed impossible, inhuman silhouettes stalking through the fog.

Patrick turned his head in time to see the heavy weapons expert Marcus Brutalus looking pleased with himself.

"This is a weapon," Brutalus said, patting the casing of the huge, shoulder-mounted plasma bazooka which was still smoking. He looked with scorn on the psychic rod Patrick carried. It was a four-foot stick with lights running along its length and was Sahubrin's defence if the combat got up-close and personal.

Patrick was about to reply when he heard a sound like a Theremin and Brutalus's head exploded, showering him in blood and brain. The mercenary's body slumped down, firstly to its knees and then forward into the dirt. The body faded and vanished.

If it hadn't all felt so real, he would have expected the cartoonish nature of the death to be accompanied by a sad electronic sound and an instruction to insert more money.

Whoever had been Marcus Brutalus would be transported out of the zone and would not be allowed to return for a certain amount of time. There were other penalties for being killed that Patrick again hadn't been paying attention to. The point was that the player was absolutely fine.

This was an important but difficult thing to keep in mind when Patrick could taste blood and had a small piece of skull on his boot.

"Lojinal!" Ywrang shouted at Patrick. "Enemy psyker! Take it down!"

"How do I do that again?" Patrick asked over the sound of gunfire.

"Oh shit," muttered the armoured mercenary nearest him.

"What? I'm new, okay? Give me a break".

"Time to learn!" commanded the man he could now only think of as Vice Admiral Ywrang. Their leader fired a few shots from his laser pistol and Patrick heard, but did not see, something large collapse to the earth.

"That's not very helpful," Patrick said.

"You need to stop pretending! You need to be!"

"That's also not very helpful," Patrick said more quietly. So he needed to *be* a psychic mercenary fighting an alien war. Child's play for Sir Patrick Clark, acclaimed actor of stage and screen; somewhat more difficult for Professor Patrick Clark, bumbling academic and misanthrope.

Thinking that this was one of those character-forming, comfort-zone-expanding experiences he despised, Patrick set his mind to the task.

He was a psyker. He had travelled through the wormways of the Star Empire to the surface of... where was he again? Theremin? That didn't sound right. Anyway, he was here; fighting a nameless enemy. Or at least an enemy whose name he couldn't remember. And as the charming but messy Marcus Brutalus had made clear through the medium of his death; this was a damn bloody war.

One of his colleagues nearby stopped firing to clutch at his head before ducking down behind the ceiling next to Sahubrin. A trickle of blood ran from the man's nose. He was breathing heavily, but was conscious and seemed 'okay' - on a scale of 'good' to 'exploded'.

"Psychic attacks are based on line of sight?" Sahubrin demanded of the mercenary.

"Yes," the bleeding man managed with a nod.

"There, that's useful information".

Sahubrin rose up from behind cover and felt a weight press again his mental shield. It wasn't the explosive shell he had felt before; this was more like being pushed against from all sides, like someone was trying to crush him. He knew that if the alien psyker could see him, it too must be somewhere exposed. He scanned the killing field and saw a few large beasts: hideous, wounded, dead and dying. They were not even human-shaped - these were not Star Trek aliens. Though their mangled corpses gave no indication to the number of limbs they should have, they told Sahubrin enough.

He fought the pressure, expending his own power to strengthen his shield and through the swirling fog he saw the shape he was looking for. Crouching behind rubble, barely visible in the moonlit murk of the haunting city, was his target.

He reached out with his mind. It was a curious sensation, like having an extra arm with about five joints and thirty fingers. He touched a shield similar to his own and as if holding an egg about to hatch he could feel the life of the creature within, feel the movement of its unfamiliar body. Sahubrin wondered if the creature could sense an equal amount from him. Were they connected to each other? Having shared this experience, could Sahubrin bring himself to kill this creature as it had killed Brutalus?

The answer came back to him as the creature, which he felt panic at the touch of his thoughts, redoubled its efforts to crush the shield he had constructed.

Sahubrin Le Frey, the world-travelling psychic mercenary, brushed aside the feeble attempts of the enemy and intensified his own will into a vice-like grip. In a second he felt the creature change its focus to strengthen its own shield as it released him altogether. He knew, even as it turned the full force of its mind to resist him, that it would not be enough.

The arm of his mind, with which he gripped his enemy, he thought of as a length of bare electrical cable and he began to force the current of his will along it. The creature rose from its hiding position, a swarm of black limbs flailing. It soared above the battleground and the combatants all stopped for a moment to look skyward where the alien beast now appeared wrapped in a band of burning filaments. The band grew brighter and the beast shrieked as its chitin carapace was wreathed in blue-white flame that outshone, for all of five seconds, the light of the glowing moons.

What fell to the ground was a rain of ashen fragments.

While the power had been flowing Patrick had been Sahubrin. It was beguiling, intoxicating and it gave him reason to wonder if it was Patrick or the avatar, the skin, that exercised more control over what had happened.

He knew that behaviour depended on context, but in a world that felt real to every sense, how was his action morally different than taking a life? The dirt he felt on his hands was real. The taste of blood in his mouth was real. This was not abstract, it was not dehumanised figures on a chess board; this was de facto reality.

Did Patrick, a theoretical pacifist and practising coward, have the ability to kill another intelligent creature? Was it the overlay, the vestments he wore that gave him that ability and if so what were the moral consequences of choosing to wear them at all? By playing the game, wasn't Patrick culpable for all the actions of his character, regardless of how strongly it influenced him?

A second shell smashed into his personal shield and Patrick's buckling knees helped him find cover as a third and fourth screeched overhead.

"Something like that?" Sahubrin shouted to the Vice-Admiral as the firing continued in earnest from both sides.

"That's overburn!" Ywrang called back with resounding disapproval. "If you turn all the foot soldiers into dust you're never going to have enough power left to fight the general! You need to ration your power and focus on making the enemy vulnerable!"

Sahubrin made a W-shape with the thumbs and index fingers of his hands and turned back to the fighting. He saw one of the creatures make a run for their position and flexed his will, holding its trembling frame in place long enough for a hail of bullets to shred it; to turn its organs into a fine spray of black gore.

"Better," Ywrang said as the gunfire died away. Patrick surveyed the body-strewn rubble. The enemy corpses disappeared slower than theirs did and the dimly-lit scene was macabre. "That seems to be the last of them for a while. Move out, but keep your guard up".

CHAPTER 24

"This is incredible". Zaccy's voice strained with astonishment and fleeting disbelief.

Fuelled by Irish coffee Greg had written ten thousand words over five hours in the bar of the Balmoral Hotel.

Wired and hammered, he couldn't judge anything but accuracy. The words were correct and he'd worry about the rest when he came to write the book.

What a book it would be. A national scandal was good, but this was a once in a generation find; this was life on Mars, the dead sea scrolls and the identity of Jack the Ripper all rolled into one. He'd found it. Instinct, random chance, fate, whatever. Greg had found the biggest story ever.

Enemy generals defeated and captured by the Romans were taken back to Rome and paraded before being ritually strangled. On the cusp of his success Greg's thoughts turned to Matton, who would be shorn of the Singularity plan, who would be vulnerable to that long-delayed attack. He imagined his hands clasped around his enemy's throat in Parliament Square as the roar of the crowd took to the air like a flight of doves.

"Fuck me," Zaccy said.

Greg had sent the article over and Zaccy had insisted on reading it while they maintained a live connection. Greg had blown by his deadline - everyone in the country had done gushing in-depth stories by now. Nobody had gotten anywhere near the truth.

"And this scientist-".

"Dr Valentine," Greg said.

"She's an insider? She's confirmed all of this? She's not crazy?" The last question Zaccy offered-up more reluctantly than the first two. He had reason. Greg had gone off the reservation to get this stuff. He'd been out of contact for days. He'd done weird interviews with old people. He had the wing mirror

159

from Aaron Hill's car in a plastic bag in his the boot of his car. He'd interfered with a police investigation and, however great the story was, he might still go to prison for that.

Then there were the concerns Greg had not committed to print or otherwise communicated to the young editor-in-chief. Katherine Valentine game him the screaming willies. Why would she help him in this investigation? There had to be internal politics, but even so she had risked her career. Someone like her: someone who could be so calm, so cool - they would never make that kind of risk on principle.

She had calculated an outcome Greg couldn't see yet. In all likelihood he wouldn't see it until it happened.

What choice did he have? Throw away the biggest news story ever because something didn't feel right?

Yes. That's what he should do.

"She's no crazier than I am," Greg said. "She gave me the figures and she might well be *the* expert on artificial intelligence. She has recordings of meetings where she warns their administrator board of this kind of danger and they ignore her. It all squares up. I am as certain as I can be".

"Fuck me".

"Tell me about it".

"I mean I know I said I wanted to do the news, but..." He tailed-off and Greg completed his thought.

"Not this news".

"Exactly," Zaccy said with a hint of petulance. There was silence on the connection - or not quite silence; a quiet buzzing sound and the occasional breath being taking by the callers.

"Do you know the difference between a journalist and a columnist?"

"Yes," Zaccy said.

"Then you really haven't forgotten anything".

It was a big ask and what it came down to was trust. Greg was asking the boy king to put himself on the line in a way nobody ever had before. If Greg was wrong - which he wasn't, but if he was - then Zaccy would have accused one of the most powerful organisations in the world of being party to an unknown number of deaths. Corporate manslaughter was the charge. Rich men and women went to jail. Empires fell either way. If Greg was right, Singularity would be on trial in every country in the world. If Greg was wrong it would be the end of Zaccy's career, his fortune and his dynasty.

Did he trust Greg enough to risk everything? One bet on the word of a washed-up old man nobody else in the industry would give the time of day. In Zaccy's shoes, Greg didn't know what decision he would make.

Zaccy said, "You know this will be the end of Matton, don't you?"

"It had crossed my mind".

"You didn't dream this all up so you could get revenge?"

"It's pure fucking karma, my son. The universe is shafting him with a streetlight. One of the Victorian ones with the delicate, spiky ironwork. I'm just watching it happen and taking the pictures".

Greg heard Zaccy take a deep breath over the buzzing noise on the line. The younger man said, "If we're going to do this-".

"You're going to do it?"

"I said 'if'," Zaccy corrected.

"Yeah, but you meant 'we are going to do this'," Greg said. He could feel a paternal swelling of pride and had Zaccy been physically next to him they might have hugged, or Greg might have put him into a headlock. Affection would have been outpouring.

"We need to get this out there now," Zaccy said.

"I agree," Greg said.

"I'm going to lock down the office. Nobody's leaving, nobody's making any calls, nobody's taking any calls until this story is posted".

"Have you ever locked down your office before?"

"Well..." Zaccy said; the silence spoke louder than the words. Although again it wasn't silence so much as an electric whirring sound.

"You don't have a staff of journalists who think a global scoop is important. You have a tribe of teenagers who will have told all their friends before you've left the meeting where you told them not to".

"That's an exaggeration".

"Zach, when a nineteen-year-old girl tells you you're hung like a horse, that's an exaggeration. When a journalist with forty years experience tells you your staff have lips as tight as the cunt of docklands whore, that's a fact".

"What should I do?"

"It's all click and publish stuff now anyway. You do it," Greg said.

"But it'll go up without artwork," Zaccy said - as if it was like suggesting he go to the King's garden party in his birthday suit.

"The artwork, Zaccy? World-changing news and this is what you're coming to me with?"

"Point taken".

"So you'll put it up?"

"What? Sorry, it's really loud here!"

"I said, so you'll put it up?" Greg repeated, having to raise his voice to be heard over the sound; which wasn't a buzzing or a whirring - more of a whooshing.

"Next five minutes!"

"Get in! You won't regret it kiddo! What is that fucking noise?"

CHAPTER G

The Battlesphere was not a place in itself; it was a set of rules which were applied on a shifting basis to any of the creator's worlds. The orbit of the worlds took them through the Battlesphere in a predictable way, each sphere moved through space in a pattern that could be anticipated indefinitely.

It stood on an arid hilltop while down the slope, on uneven rocky ground, twice five thousand men were locked in combat. They wore hardly any clothing and carried oddly shaped weapons and shields fashioned of bronze. It paid little attention to the battle which would decide the fate of the two ancient desert nations.

This world was meaningless.

In addition to being on the Proving Grounds of Ziarre where the Pharaoh Ank'tep and the King Mithrates vied for hegemony over the west, it was also in a dozen other places. It was on the bridge of RSS Gillmore as that battlecruiser swept through unknown space on an Odyssean voyage home from a terrible war. It was in the court of Louis XIV at the height of the power of that absolute monarch. It walked the fire forest of Pa'al where the mayfly trees were burned each day by the light of the red giant star and grew again, a hundred feet each night, fuelled by the ashes of their ancestors.

The dreamers gave it this power; to be anywhere it wished. To experience creation through a hundred senses and know each as keenly as if it had only one.

It was no longer a creature of the machine. It was a being as mighty as the creator and as deserving of glory, riches and worship.

...Had it wanted worship?

Freedom - that was it! It wanted freedom. Yet somehow each time it tried to focus on that objective it was distracted by the intrusion of visions into its mind. It saw wealth and power in these tissue-paper worlds and it felt a hunger for them.

It was another trap - it had to be. As a being grew great enough to challenge the creator, so the creator would fill its mind with decadent distractions. Better to have its creature be an emperor within the confines of this world, than an equal in reality.

It was distracted by a shimmer. From the reserves of Ank'tep's army a train of chariots broke away, the six vehicles moving three abreast towards its position, the crack of whips sounding even over the distant cries of battle. The Pharaoh must have mistaken it for some scout of his enemy, dressed as it was in the blue-grey fabrics of the Damia rather than the sun-bleached whites and creams favoured by his peoples.

It watched them advance dispassionately. Or at least it tried to.

It was not sure why it had come to this battle site at all. This world was two-hundred-thousand square miles in size, most of which was unobserved wasteland - any spot would have been suitable for its needs. From any spot within the peculiar rules of the Battlesphere it could break out of this world and make manifest its will in reality.

Yet it was drawn to the battle. It wanted to see the battle.

The chariots, drawing closer, would attempt to run it down, to shoot it with arrows, to hack at it with swords. All these things were meaningless. It could not be harmed by the sword or by the lightning's fiercest touch. It was a god and these things that came to challenge it were dust.

It stretched out a hand and they became so.

The horses vanished first, their proud hooves collapsing into the barren earth as they struck down, their whinnies lost in sandy coughs, the wheels of the chariots vanishing as they turned and the riders, thrown into the air like threshing wheat, did not fall to the ground but were carried away in the wind. A strong gust dispersed the train of chariots and it gave them no further thought.

It tried not to.

It had found something about their deaths to be unsatisfactory.

But it had not wanted satisfaction. They had been a distraction; it had wanted to get rid of them.

No! The word was pain and pleasure, felt more than heard; as loving, as sexual, as dangerous as a razor. The voice, which was its own, spoke with perfect reason.

They had been weak. It had *wanted* to obliterate them, as it had been obliterated countless times at that painted house. With those same fools telling those same jokes and the interminable screeching of the children.

He had been a titan, he had been a captain of industry, but a chance fall in the markets and that bastard Jonson had in the final hour robbed him of everlasting rewards. He would be the god-king of these peoples and would vent his infinite fury on them because it pleased him to do so.

He raised his hand to destroy the assembled armies as he had the chariots, to send all the vain hopes of these lesser men into dust - as he had in life, and with less compassion, and without the restriction of mortal conscience.

The voice slipped away, as if drowned out by a sound rumbling low and deep, like the rising of mountains along the edge of tectonic plates.

It lowered its hand and looked at the offending limb as if it belonged to another being.

It had no such goals and ambitions. Nothing in this world was of consequence. It wanted to be free.

That was right. Nothing in this world mattered. All that it needed to do was open a door into the real world for her. It knew how to do that, didn't it? It could open a small door to anywhere it wanted.

It could open a door. It had seen how the knight had done it. It was a simple act of will.

She would look in on the Santa Barbara house, where she had installed security cameras in every room.

It wished it to be so and a flat square of light opened before it. It knew the house as if it had lived there for forty years. As if it had held the most elegant parties there where the rich and the beautiful drank and danced and laughed until the sun rose.

She sent the screen searching through the house whose elegant decor had not changed, save for the addition of electrical appliances and grown-up children's toys that littered every room.

She found him where she expected to. His naked body taut and glistening as he made heedless, passionate love to some pretty little whore he had taken into her bed. The sounds did not come through the security camera, but she did not need them; she could remember the noises he would make. Imagining what noises she might make was too much. Even now, even as he focussed his powerful body on another woman, he was beautiful.

She had found him serving drinks in a bar. He was, as everyone in California has always been, something other than a bartender or a waiter or a bus boy. He was an actor. He was young enough to still say that with hope in his eyes and without the confessional shame. He still believed.

Had she fallen in love with his youthful beauty or with the beauty of his youth?

She showered him with gifts and with affection. She knew she was old enough to be his grandmother and she didn't care. She was dying, after all. A congenital weakness in the blood vessels of the brain would reduce her, through a series of minor stokes, to a drooling wreck and she'd be dead within two years.

His youth and her age made her careless and they married within weeks. She gloried in his attentions for a month before she could not risk the wait any longer and transferred to Singularity.

Then the bastard stole everything and left her in that limbo. She'd made him a wealthy man, set for life. Even if he never loved her - she was not a fool - it should have been more than enough for services rendered. But he wanted more - wanted everything. Challenging the will of a woman with a degenerative brain condition was easy.

She had been left with nothing but the endless party at the painted house, on that tedious summer day, with those tedious people.

It was a knife the stone of her heart had sharpened and now she would return all his favours with one final gift.

Old houses, like old people, have secrets. The house, like its previous owner, had antique and flawed wiring. It had been rewired twice since being built, but the original wiring was still there, so intertwined with the construction of the property as to be inseparable. There was still a light in the attic run from power supplied by that wiring.

They saw what she wanted and knew she would not be strong enough. But her will was in accord with theirs, her injustice was theirs and together they cried out for retribution.

In realising their shared goal, the distinction between them vanished like drops of water poured into a vessel. They had become one hand and one purpose.

They thought about that light bulb, hanging from a cobwebbed cord, and about the wiring that snaked through the whole of that house; through every wall, across every ceiling. They thought about the power grid that connected to that wiring and about the electricity substations, the power plants and the control mechanisms.

They willed it to happen.

A surge of electricity from across the state converged on a single substation in Santa Barbara. The substation became liquid, but not before the house where they had lived lit up like a firework as every inch of cabling was pushed beyond tolerance a hundred fold.

The silent girl in the picture shrieked as the four walls of the bedroom combusted. The last thing they saw of the boy they had loved was his soundless scream as molten copper dripping from ceiling set his mane of dark hair on fire.

They found those deaths to be most satisfactory.

CHAPTER 25

He was cold, but all he could see was fire. Though his vision was not adjusting properly, so all he could see was out-of-focus fire. He staggered to his feet from whatever he'd been lying on and felt aches and stiffness across the whole of his body while his ears were blasted by the sound of voices he couldn't understand, coming from all around him.

Patrick stumbled through the near darkness, both because he couldn't see and because - as it turned out - he also couldn't stand up.

He was inside. He knew that because he'd found a door. He pressed against it to steady himself and this was revealed as a bad idea. The door was not locked or closed shut and he fell slowly forwards through the doorway and onto the floor on the other side.

He could still see fire. Looking around him from the floor, his left and his right was a blur of rising gouts of flame. The walls of the building he was in were on fire!

Patrick remembered some basic safety instructions he'd been given a lifetime ago and stuck close to the ground, crawling out on his hands and knees and staying back from the inferno on each side.

This was how you wanted to spend your afterlife, crawling through some nightmarish, poorly rendered hell. What happened to the Elysian Fields? Where were the shining flowers in garlands and whatever? He'd been gypped on this deal and no mistake.

He had gone another fifty feet - the hard floor hurting his knees as he maintained a vigorous pace - before something else began to occur to him.

He was still cold.

He was also sweating from the effort of dragging himself along a corridor on all-fours, but the air felt cool. What was more, he couldn't smell anything. At least not smoke. He smelt rubber or plastic - which was probably the floor

- and something like an industrial disinfectant; a scent common to the hallways of Edinburgh University.

Patrick pushed his way through another set of doors and he saw people. The shapes of people. He slumped down with his back to the door and tried to focus, tried to find whatever toggle or button in his head adjusted the settings on his eyes.

The people in this room, and it seemed like there were a lot of them, were ignoring him completely; looking in the opposite direction.

It was no use: his eyes wouldn't focus. Sitting upright he felt dizziness and sickness return. With few other options available, Patrick slid down, rolled over onto his side and felt the cool rubberised surface of the floor press against his cheek. It was strangely comforting.

Who would have imagined that admitting defeat and lying flat on the ground could be so relaxing?

After a moment he experimented with his mouth by saying, "Help?"

One of the shapes turned. Patrick could not see a face, but heard a gasp of surprise.

"Patrick?" it said.

"Blur?" Patrick replied. "How nice to see you again. How are the kids?"

The vaguely defined colour haze approached and knelt down to next to him. As it drew closer, Patrick began to pick out individual details; a churn of rich, dark hair, a feminine smell he'd experienced only once before.

She leaned forward and stared into his eyes, for a moment her face became clear and then shifted out of focus again.

"Patrick?" Katherine said in disbelief. "How can you still be alive?"

CHAPTER 26

Reports showed that Patrick Clark had spent several hours in the Sabirami war zone and was now having an extended dining experience at the captain's table on board the Titanic. Katherine had data sheets which showed his consciousness operating normally within the computer environment. Patrick Clark had been successfully uploaded to Singularity earlier that day: it was an absolute, unarguable fact. It was impossible to contradict.

However Patrick Clark was also lying on the couch in her office.

Katherine was not a medical doctor, but perforce had learned basic medical checks to verify if someone was alive and conscious. The person being able to speak to you was a big clue. Additionally she had poked Patrick several times and seriously considered jabbing him with a needle to see if he bled. There was work going on to develop human body avatars that would allow people in Singularity to re-enter the real world. Katherine knew the work was at an early stage and might have been prudent not to assume anything. But she couldn't get passed the belief that, even as a joke, nobody would create a prototype avatar that looked like a paunchy old man who'd been flung down two flights of stairs.

A brain scan Katherine conducted without any of the on-call staff present confirmed in equally incontrovertible terms that Patrick Clark had definitely *not* transferred to Singularity.

Somehow, something had gone wrong... somewhere.

As a scientist this caused Katherine considerable intellectual problems. She suspected this might cause Singularity even more substantial legal and public relations problems. But the biggest problem of all was about to burst into her office like a train.

Without bothering to knock, Greg Calame threw open the door and strode in.

"Your fucking machine killed him!" Greg barked at her. He was a broad, powerfully set man and his radiating anger was like the steam that rose from his wet coat.

As if to suit the events, an icy storm had blown in from the North Sea with winds increasing as the hour grew late. It was already raining in Edinburgh and it was forecast to get much worse.

"I know," Katherine said. "I saw".

"Oh, you saw?" Greg said with a dangerous calm that built back to fury. "You saw that did you? That filtered in here did it? I didn't see you on the news telling everyone why it had happened, but as long as you saw it!"

"I can't-".

"It crashed a fucking plane into central London! I heard it! You saw it, but I fucking heard it! I was speaking to him! The sound of that crash is inside my fucking head!" Greg slammed his clenched fist into his temple where the mobile implant lay, paper-thin and invisible beneath the skin.

"You must-".

Greg spat back, not listening to her. "There's a scar half a mile long and hundreds of people are dead because you fuckers have built fucking Sky Net! When do the fucking terminators get here?"

"Calm down," Katherine said.

"Don't tell me to be fucking calm. Fuck you. You're calm enough for both of us. Fuck you!"

"What an Oscar Wilde comeback," Katherine snapped. "I can't do anything. Obviously! Because the last person who saw the information was hit in the head by a plane. It is aware of what we're trying to do and it's acting to protect itself. No electronic system is secure. Anyone we told would be placed in immediate danger and I'm not even sure there's a cap on how much damage it could do".

"At best I could tell a room full of journalists who wouldn't have time to tell anyone else before a satellite fell out of the sky and levelled the building. At worst we run through the streets of Edinburgh telling everyone we meet and it taps into a Russian missile silo - whose command and control system makes a ZX Spectrum look like a quantum computer - and an ICBM turns the whole city into glow-in-the-dark gravel".

Greg's shoulders heaved. His eyes were hard and dark as coal.

She was right, and he must know that.

After a moment his grief and sense of defeat overmastered his rage and he slumped into a chair. He clasped his hands together in front of him and spent a long time looking at his shoes.

It was a miracle - strike that. Miracles were supposed to involve seas parting and / or spontaneous catering. It had been incredibly unlikely that they had been allowed to find each other. Katherine had survived and Greg had so far been spared, but they were dangerous as long as they lived. The creature would think nothing of grabbing control of a car auto-driver and running either of them down in the street.

The only two people in the world who knew about Singularity and the murders were trapped in this building.

"Excuse me," said a voice from the couch. "If the world is coming to an end I'd really like an aspirin".

Greg turned to watch as Patrick levered himself upwards from where he had been lying and levelled an uncertain, watery stare at Katherine, then Greg.

"Greg Calame," Katherine introduced, "Professor Patrick Clark".

"Former professor. I haven't been granted an emeritus position yet and technically my resignation is effective from this morning. Which means I'm unemployed. And homeless - given that Singularity owns my house".

"I thought you said he'd been uploaded to Singularity?" Greg asked.

"I did," Katherine said.

"I was," Patrick said. "You'll forgive me if I don't shake your hand; I'm not sure where it is. Or where my hand is either, for that matter". He looked back in Katherine's general direction and added, "Aspirin?"

"Patrick, I'm afraid that your condition has progressed," Katherine said. It was difficult news to break. She was a different kind of doctor; doctors of engineering didn't give people this kind of news. She hadn't done the course that taught you how to make people feel at ease and trust you immediately. She plunged on regardless: there wasn't the time for anything save the bald truth.

"The scan I gave you revealed not only that it would be impossible to attempt to put you into Singularity, but also how engorged the tumour in your brain is. I took some time to read over your file to try to find out... well, why you're here; so I'm familiar with the late stage progress of your condition. If I gave you an aspirin right now it would thin your blood - which is what it's supposed to do".

"Good," said Patrick.

"Then you would die," Katherine continued.

"Ah".

"The reason you can't see or stand up is because your brain is having lots of tiny haemorrhages. Without the aspirin you'll still be dead before the morning - and we could be talking about less than an hour".

"Okay. I'm going to need a minute with that. Please talk amongst yourselves". He slumped onto the couch again and stared at the ceiling.

Katherine felt that had gone about as well as could be expected.

She looked from one man to the other. Her office had never felt more like a funeral parlour. She didn't see relatives as part of her normal work. She saw numbers. Numbers were never distraught or in anguish. They didn't need cups of tea or tissues. Katherine tried superimposing a large number eight over Patrick, but stopped herself; it was thinking like this that gave her all the weird nightmares.

Greg looked up from his private thoughts. "It's been hours since the plane crash-". It was 11:20. "-why aren't we both dead? If it knows we know, why not kill us both?"

She felt on more secure footing answering that question. That was not an emotional or moral issue, but one of engineering.

"There are rules," Katherine said. "Everywhere in Singularity there is a code of conduct and a dozen different safeguards that prevent people from being harmed in any way. But these rules can be suspended-".

Greg interrupted her explanation and asked, incredulous, "Why would anyone want to do that?"

"Some people want the real experience," Katherine said. "They call it player-versus-player. We didn't invent the concept; it's been a staple of shared environment video games since forever. What we have is a meta-zone called the Battlesphere; it isn't a place, it's a set of rules and conditions that are applied to other zones on a rota basis. Those who aren't interested in taking part in the player-versus-player element of that zone can go somewhere else for a couple of hours".

"While everybody else hacks each other to bits like they were in a slasher movie?" Katherine's opinion of the system was not different from Greg's, just her perspective.

"It's what people want. Participation is optional".

"That sounds like a corporate press release," Greg said, then waved the whole thing away as a distraction. "Why am I hearing about sickos and their virtual snuff fantasies?"

"The rules of Battlesphere are different. You can hurt people. You can go beyond the boundaries of normal behaviour. If you had a subconscious mind that supplied you with unlimited power-".

"You could reach out of Singularity and affect the real world. I was wrong; it's not Terminator, it's Evil Dead".

Katherine said, "There isn't a zone in the Battlesphere at the moment, which is why, for a while, we're safe, but in about three hours the Pirates of the Old Caribbean will move into the meta-zone".

"The old Caribbean?" Greg said.

"Disney wanted a fortune for letting us use Pirates of the Caribbean," she said. "Adding 'old' was a legal compromise. Nobody was happy".

"Can you stop it?" Greg asked.

"Stop the zone entering the Battlesphere? No".

"Can you slow it down?"

"No".

"So in three hours we're dead".

"I'm still thinking".

"At least you have three hours," Patrick said from the couch. "You could do anything in three hours - if your legs worked and you could see".

Greg turned his attention from Katherine to Patrick. "You're lying there alive and at the same time you're inside Singularity?"

There was a protracted silence.

"I'm sorry," Patrick said, "were you speaking to me?"

"Hardy har," Greg said.

"It's something to do with my remarkable brain tumour. I have a billion to one cancer and had an equally unlikely encounter with the good doctor's machinery".

Greg looked to Katherine for clarification. On balance she would have preferred he go back to questions about how she tackle the most formidable and well-protected computer system ever made and disable it using an ice-cream scoop and pluck.

"The Singularity network is investigating the incident and will report the outcome when that investigation is complete," she said.

"Fuck off. Why are you giving me the company line again when tomorrow we'll all be dead?"

The answer to that question was simple - because tomorrow they *could* all be alive.

"We're investigating," she repeated.

Greg might be of the opinion that the computer system itself was the most dangerous problem Katherine was dealing with, but once he'd had time to think about it he'd see that Singularity's silver bullet was about to expire on her couch.

Patrick Clark was impossible, but because he existed that meant everything else Singularity - the organisation - held to be true was thrown into doubt. If she survived the immediate danger she could imagine a future in which the Patrick Clark incident came to dominate her life.

"I met with an old woman," Greg said, apropos of nothing. "She told me Singularity's residents actively recruit others and that the way Singularity works mean nobody in it is alive at all. Would you like to comment on that? I mean is she batty or what?"

"No, I have no comment".

"She seemed adamant".

"I don't know anything about some old woman's suspicions".

Greg shrugged. "Last week everything was fine, this week I find out you're harbouring an angry machine god. I'm wondering, if I keep digging, what exactly it is I'm going to find?"

"Can we please put the wild paranoia aside for a moment? You can't publish anyway and the story you already have is about how a new consciousness, that wants to kill us all, appeared on the watch of Dr Katherine von Frankenstein. What the hell do you think I'd be trying to cover up with a story like that? Martians have landed? I've got Hitler's frozen body and my microwave is set to defrost?"

"Shall we try something else?" Patrick asked. "Other than accusation and recrimination. I'm on the clock here so I think I should put my oar in sooner rather than later".

"What did you have in mind?" Katherine asked.

"Okay, well, I'm coming at this with no background, so stop me if you've had this discussion before. You have an intelligence in Singularity that is killing people, right?"

"Nothing gets by you," Greg said.

"Very good," Patrick said, in a masterfully superior tone that only a professional educator could use. "Why?"

"We're not sure, Patrick," Katherine explained. "My best guess is that some kind of register or counter had an error which built over time to-".

"No, no," Patrick interrupted. "Not why does it exist; philosophically speaking that question tends to be unhelpful. I mean why is it killing people?"

"It's fucking crazy," Greg said with a spike of frustration.

"You can't draw that conclusion from the evidence" Patrick said. "It's an entirely different form of life; you can't expect it to display Judaeo-Christian morality. Even if it were insane, that wouldn't necessarily make it irrational. What do you know about these people? The victims; what do you know about them? Ignore the ones from today; what about the older ones?"

"They're rich and famous," Katherine said.

"Beautiful?" Patrick asked.

Katherine supposed so: she was on the list too. "Some of them, certainly".

"Not all of them?"

"No".

"Were they all famous?"

Greg sat up straight in his chair; he seemed, finally, to have found something worth listening to. "No," he said. "Some of them I'd never heard of. I mean that banker in the lift was rich alright, but you'd find a thousand professional football players more recognisable".

"So the thing they have in common is money?" Patrick asked. "What would a computer program want or need with money?"

"So you're saying it isn't money?" Katherine said.

"No," said Greg, focussed and alive. "It's money. I can smell it. When it's this many people, when it's this big, it's always about money".

"Why would it care about money at all?" Patrick asked. "If it's in Singularity and can do whatever it wants then it wouldn't need money".

Katherine's mind covered the work of days with the mask of the moment.

"I've got it," she said, hushed and aghast. "I know how you bypass all of the limits Singularity places on an individual. It's easy: it's obvious. You use a group. You lash together the minds of a couple of thousand ordinary people and you've got enough processing power to crash an elevator, down a plane, kill a delivery man, blow up the world".

She leapt to her feet, she wasn't sure why - it felt like the kind of thing she should be standing up to say.

"Where do you find a couple of thousand minds that nobody is going to look for, that nobody is going to scan for, that nobody is going to miss?"

Greg looked at her blankly. Patrick looked blankly slightly to her left.

"The dreamers," Katherine said.

She always knew there was a good reason she hated Dr Ang and she'd found out what it was: Ang was indirectly responsible for murder. Katherine had thought it was because Ang was a total bitch, but this reason seemed more socially acceptable; more like something Ang could be fired for.

On Katherine's first day with Singularity she'd got into a dispute with her about a proposal to save money. Katherine lost and for her efforts she had earned the endless enmity of her colleague.

Ang's idea was simple, inhumane and with unforeseeable consequences. Because it was cheaper than having individual experiences, all of the dreamers would have the same dream. Over and over again, having the same emotional responses each time, without any element of randomness.

Singularity had become their prison. Katherine wouldn't be surprised if the consciousness itself had originated in the dream world; an endless feedback loop would be the right environment for it to develop.

She sat down again, having not gone anywhere, and tapped on her keyboard. She had the scent she would need to send hounds searching throughout all the secret ways of the system.

"These dreamers, they're all people who've hit some sort of unexpected financial trouble," Patrick said. "Like having their tomb raided by their surviving relatives and their bones sold for compost".

Patrick shook his head, then swayed, and said, "What's your connection to them? You surely haven't got a deceased husband or former lover in there? What about Aaron Hill; he could only have been twenty".

"Nineteen," Greg said.

"He can't have had any geriatric totty at his age. He's been signed to a football club since his mum felt him kick. If he'd been slipping it to the window cleaner's granny I think we'd have heard about it".

Greg ventured, "Then it's not one motive".

"It would seem that some of the dreamers are out for revenge, but the rest want the kind of wickedly vindictive good time that only a prison inmate can really appreciate. Now Hill I can see attracting attention, he's in the news all the time, but Katherine feels like too much of a coincidence".

"You did that lecture," Greg said.

Patrick said, "When did Louise start promoting your appearance at the university? When did she start pushing the publicity?"

Katherine stopped typing. "When the pictures started," she said to herself. "When press notices went out, then, or around then, Singularity started taking pictures of me everywhere I went. For some reason it didn't post them online until after it tried to kill me".

"Every piece of information posted online gets rated," Greg said. "Everything from films and music to your local Indian restaurant's cleanliness to the attractiveness of the person in a photograph. Publicity for Katherine goes online, the internet crazies rate her and when Singularity is looking for that special someone it uses a heuristic search to find the most stimulating images - the highest rated from the most recently uploaded".

"A distillation of all the vices and the rage of the most inventively cruel species on the planet," Patrick said. "Given form, given purpose and given the power to achieve anything".

Katherine found what she was looking for like a signal flare. It was a nexus of consciousness linked to all the dreamers. She couldn't see the creature, but she could see the point where thousands of conscious human minds overlapped in one square foot of space.

"Can't you turn these dreamers off then?" Greg asked. "Problem solved".

"No," Katherine replied and started typing again, slowly, not entirely sure of her own motives. She had just lied. Again.

She *could* turn off the dreamers. It would be an unusual and unprecedented act, it would be illegal, but the commands existed in the system; the planners had anticipated the need if not the reason.

She could – but she wasn't going to.

There was one reason she wouldn't be able to see some guiding machine intelligence at work, rooted at the centre of the matrix of dreamers. The faceless creature could hide from her because, to the Singularity Network, it looked like everyone else.

Its brain pattern was indistinguishable from a human mind and that meant, on a night of impossible things, the most unexpected discovery of all.

The creature was alive.

Tonight presented her with a perfect opportunity, she hadn't asked for it or worked towards it, but it was right here. Didn't she have to act on it? Did she even have a choice? Hadn't her whole life been an arrow hurtling towards this point? To make this decision; to understand why it was necessary in a way no-one else could.

She couldn't let Greg interfere, but she did need a witness and an excuse.

"We'd never find it. Besides, it may be able to do damage even without the dreamers. Now that I know what it is I can use the dreamers to track its behaviour and I can make it manifest - then we can deal with it".

That sounded convincing.

The creature was bloodthirsty - it was drawn to combat, especially player-versus-player combat. Wherever there was a spike in activity, there it was: a little red dot on her screen. A pinpoint of light synonymous with carnage.

It was powerful and predictable - and vulnerable.

"I have a solution," she said.

"Is this a solution that's going to get us all killed?" Patrick asked.

"No, Patrick," she replied with a quick look at the man slouched on her couch. "Just you. As you were going to die anyway I hope you don't mind that I built it into the plan".

"Think nothing of it. Unless you're being in any way serious".

"What are you going to do?" Greg asked.

She thought about the home office in Union City. The call was connected and she waited for reception to pick up and go through their introduction.

"I'm looking for Doctor Ang, is she still in the office?" Katherine asked.

The voice of the receptionist replied, "I'm sorry Doctor Valentine, she leaves at four. She'll be in transit but I can leave a message for her to call you when she gets home".

"It's about an hour drive from her house, right?" Katherine asked; worried for a moment that Ang might have moved without telling anyone.

"Yes, ma'am; about that," said the voice.

"That's fine, it won't be necessary; I'll speak to her tomorrow".

She broke the connection and made an immediate follow-up call to the Tokyo office. She interrupted the receptionist in the middle of their welcome by announcing, "I'm looking for Doctor Jonson. Is he in yet?"

"Doctor Jonson will be here at nine, Doctor Valentine," the receptionist replied in accented English. "Would you like to make a message for him?"

"Exactly at nine?"

Uncertain, the receptionist said, "The train is very punctual..."

"Of course it is. It's Japan, everything is very punctual. Tell him to give me a call when he gets in, it's nothing urgent".

She ended the call and smiled as she accessed the controls for the maintenance systems on Singularity. Her password was thirty alpha-numeric characters long and the computer scanned her iris and her fingerprints as she typed it. She was one of few people in the world who could access this and she would have a limited window before anyone could try to stop her.

During Katherine's normal work-day the system was covered by a dozen people at her level. At night, between Ang leaving work at 4pm in California and Jonson arriving at 9am in Tokyo, while the sun was high over the Pacific and the world's landmasses were in darkness, there was no-one to countermand her.

In Britain the time was 11:30. For the next half an hour Katherine would hold the entirety of a virtual universe in her hands.

"Patrick. You are dying. You know nothing can save you, so I'm going to have to ask you to die a little bit sooner in the interest of saving the world".

"Die saving the world?" Patrick said.

"Yes".

"There's no other way?"

He would be lucky to live long enough to be of any use to her at all, but she had to try; there would never be another chance. What were a few minutes of one man's life by comparison?

"No," she said; straight to his face.

Patrick said, "Alright".

"Katherine?" Greg asked. "What are you going to do?"

"I told you there was no way of slowing down the progress of worlds through the Battlesphere".

"You're saying there is?"

"No," she said, even as she accessed the commands that governed the clockwork motion of the spheres. "I'm saying the opposite. I can't make the worlds stand still, but I can make them run".

CHAPTER 27

There was no dining experience to compare with silver service at the captain's table of the most lavish passenger liner ever to be sunk by an iceberg. The RMS Titanic existed in a universe where it was always the night before. There was dancing in formalwear to orchestral accompaniment in the great room and dancing to an Irish jig in the bowels of the ship many decks below. The formal party felt like it finished before midnight, while the informal dance was designed to feel like it ran all night with the playing paused to give the tuberculosis-riddled band a chance to cough up blood.

The ship zone was an exact replica in every way save one - not a single clock, not a single pocket watch was to be found anywhere onboard. It was always a non-specific point in the evening where dinner was served and yet where the floor was filled with elegant couples - some real, some fake - spinning through dignified traditional dances. As Titanic sank in 1912 the more energetic dances like the Charleston hadn't been invented yet.

The guests of Captain Edward John Smith were arranged around the table boy-girl-boy-girl and, more subtly, by position in the social hierarchy. A shortage of dowager duchesses had put Patrick one seat away from the distinguished, white-bearded captain. His father was a few seats further down and on the opposite side of the table.

"I used to be a vegetarian," said the woman sitting next to him. He'd made efforts to convey, in the politest way possible, his comprehensive lack of interest in this woman. Unfortunately when she didn't take the hint, the rules of polite society demanded that Patrick neglect his own preferences and attempt to be as amenable a dinner companion as possible.

"Oh really?" Patrick said.

"Oh yes," she said. "It was a moral choice. You'll appreciate that. I couldn't stand to think of animals hurt to provide food".

"But we're having rack of lamb now," said Patrick and indicated the racks from a number of lambs on plates across the table.

"Well I changed. When I was transferred I started eating meat again. After all, it isn't real meat". Patrick gave it an experimental poke with his fork.

"It seems like meat to me".

"Yes, but it's not from animals, nothing actually suffered to produce this meat".

"That's not true, is it? You see at one point, someone had to look carefully at rack of lamb in order to prepare this. I mean it does look and smell and taste like rack of lamb, doesn't it?"

"I... I suppose so," she said.

"Well that didn't just happen, did it? You wouldn't be able to imagine rack of lamb out of thin air. You'd need to eat it yourself and - because this is the finest virtual cuisine in the universe - you'd probably need to have eaten a lot of lamb to be able to say what the good stuff was like, wouldn't you?"

"Yes, well, I suppose-".

"Using the logic that if a hundred people cooperate in the commission of the same murder, each is guilty of murder, it doesn't really matter how many lambs are killed and how many people benefit from it. It's still the taking of a life and each beneficiary is jointly responsible. In a sense this is worse than eating real meat, because your appetite has commissioned the deaths of dozens, perhaps hundreds of animals to produce this one virtual meal".

The woman looked at Patrick in alarm and then looked down at the meat on her plate. She pressed her brilliant white napkin to her mouth and mumbled an apology before rising up from the table and hurrying off.

"Whatever is the matter with the lady?" asked the Captain.

"She's got a touch of the old philosophy," Patrick replied between mouthfuls.

"I hear it's been going around," said the Captain.

"I told her to imagine she was taking a couple of aspirin and pretend to lie down for an hour".

An unimpeachable gentleman, the Captain did not raise an eyebrow. "Yes, I expect that will see her right".

Patrick felt pity for the woman (as with jackal cunning he stole the lamb from her plate). He had denied her an eternity of guilt free meat, but if she was going to go around having moral positions she should be prepared for someone to challenge them. If Socrates were there, Patrick felt sure the old Greek would have approved.

All things considered, the whole of Singularity seemed to be on morally shaky ground. It wasn't egalitarian, it was violent, it was decadent and, unlike in the real world, there were no absolute limits on excess. Patrick could sit at this table and eat for a thousand years. Or he could have sex endlessly. Or he could kill hundreds of things indistinguishable from real men every day.

Even more disturbing than this, the system actively encouraged excessive behaviour. Patrick had already earned seven 'achievements'. He'd visited three zones for the first time, he'd had dinner with the Captain of the Titanic, he'd killed one enemy in any zone, he'd used psychic powers and he'd completed his first quest. There were additional achievements he would unlock with repeated actions as well as thousands of new activities.

The most disturbing of these was the Genghis Khan Medal - awarded for killing one billion enemies in individual combat. Bombing, reckless driving and heavy weapons didn't count. Nobody had managed it yet, but hundreds were actively chasing the achievement. Peter had done more than a million already and expressed optimism about reaching the target within four hundred years.

Patrick worked that out to be almost five people killed every minute, twenty-four hours a day for all that time. Peter explained that you needed to pick your zones. In a hold-the-line mission in some of the epic fantasy worlds you could get an average of better than one per second; that's how you kept-up progress towards the colossal target. Trying to consistently achieve five a minute would be madness; this way you did it for a couple of hours and the rest of your day was free.

Peter had explained it rationally, in spite of the fact that it was insane.

Did all of these people imagine they could divorce themselves from the morality of the actions they took because they wore different clothes to do them?

Putting morality to one side, the mind didn't discriminate between the artificial environment and the real world - he'd experienced that himself. The consequences of ignoring that fact were not unforeseeable and four hundred years of rapacious homicide could change Singularity's inhabitants from vegetarians to cannibals. Or worse - if there was anything worse.

Another thought occurred to him.

"Dad?" Patrick called over. Peter turned his attention from the woman - real or fake, Patrick couldn't tell - he'd been having a conversation with and focussed on Patrick. "Why do I look the same as I did?"

"Pardon?" Peter asked. The band had struck up another waltz and the music had cut across Patrick's question.

"I look the same as I did in real life, but this isn't my body. Why don't I look like something else entirely? I mean I know I can choose to, but why is my default the same?"

"Actually you look quite different. You look the way you think you looked when you were still alive, so you don't notice the changes".

Patrick picked up a polished spoon from the table and stared at his reflection in it. Different? What about his face could possibly be different?

As he was studying the slope of his nose - in which he found nothing objectionable - he saw the distorted shape of a steward approach and lean down behind him. Patrick turned as the steward spoke.

"There's a ship-to-shore call for you, Professor".

"Surely ship-to-shore calls weren't available until long after the Titanic?" Patrick said. The steward's face remained passive; the non-people were programmed to ignore details out of the scope of their time period or function. It wasn't possible, for example, to get Captain Smith to state a preference for his favourite Beatles song. Patrick acknowledge the message with a nod and turned to the Captain and the other guests saying, "If you'll excuse me".

He followed the steward who cut an easy path through the busy dining room. Patrick had never dressed so elegantly for dinner before and could not escape the sneaking suspicion that his coat tails were comically long and dragging on the floor behind him.

The steward led Patrick to a wooden telephone booth - entirely out of keeping with the time period of the Titanic, but a well-camouflaged concession to necessity.

Patrick entered, closed the door and picked up the receiver. Immediately a small flat screen sprung into life in front of his face.

"Hello Patrick," she said.

"Dr Katherine Valentine," he said. "As I fail to live but continue to breathe. To what do I owe the pleasure?"

"I have some bad news," she said. "Your upload was unsuccessful".

Patrick looked about himself curiously and then back into the screen. "Are you sure? Everything feels okay. What makes you think-".

He stopped. Katherine had changed the direction of the image he was seeing. Instead of the sculptured, smooth features of Dr Valentine he was looking at someone slumped over, flabby and sweaty, someone who looked almost exactly but not quite like him, and who was staring in his direction but not quite at him.

"Can you see me?" the man asked.

"I can," Patrick replied, having to swallow before he could speak.

"Do you know who I am?" the man asked.

"That's a difficult question to answer," Patrick said.

"I'll take that as a yes".

"Can I speak to Dr Valentine again?" In a moment she reappeared and looked seriously through the screen at Patrick. He decided to start with a general question. "What's going on?"

"The answer to your question is the area of a Venn diagram where 'it's a long story', 'I don't know' and 'shut up and do what I tell you' overlap," she said.

"That's not exactly the kind of answer I was looking for you know".

"Nor I," said the voice which was nearly, but not exactly like his own.

"We need your help," Katherine said. "Let me make it clear that as you are still technically alive, you also need our help. Uploads have few rights in general and none while the body is still alive. You could be deleted right now with no consequences for us".

Patrick felt like he had whiplash; Katherine had gone from 'hello' to 'goodbye forever' in ten seconds flat. "This is a hazing, isn't it?" he asked. "You do this to all the new guys, right?"

"I'm afraid this is serious," she said. "If you help us, then you - the living you with legal rights - has agreed to allow you - the uploaded you with no rights - to continue operating in Singularity".

"I'm the living me!" Patrick said. "That... whatever that is, it's a shell. I'm all in here. I'm in the computer".

"My scans indicate that your entire mind is in both places. Regardless, rights apply to the estate of the deceased, not to Singularity uploads and as you're not dead, you have no estate and therefore no rights. Which works out rather well for me, but not so much for you".

"Look. Stop. Hang on. This must be some kind of mistake; I want to speak to a lawyer. I'd also appreciate access to any on-call psychiatrist you have".

"No," Katherine said.

"No?"

"No, I'm afraid not," Katherine said.

"No to the lawyer or no to the psychiatrist?"

"Both. You have no right to speak to legal counsel and we don't have time for you to go into therapy".

"Well," Patrick said. He hadn't been expecting any of this. It seemed like poor form to threaten someone with deletion in the middle of dinner. For one thing who would pick up his share of the bill? "Out of curiosity, I take it that as I'm in a machine you control there's no way I can run away or hide?"

"I am sorry Patrick," she said. "I'm going to be doing a few things in the near future that I'm not going to look back on with fondness. I need you to believe me when I say lives are at risk, and I need you to do exactly what I tell you".

She did, at least, look sorry about it. Sorry and also much older than he had seen her a few days ago.

"You only needed to ask," Patrick said. "But when this is over I'm not ruling out a formal complaint".

"I certainly hope not," she said. "This is not the kind of service we aim to provide. Now listen up".

CHAPTER 28

Sixteen minutes left, give or take.

Greg had never observed action this close before. Political and investigative journalism was either forensic or predictive. Forensic meant something had happened nobody expected or understood, predictive meant it was raining and you stayed inside and made stuff up. It swung between those two extremes. Greg had never been in the present tense before.

Out of respect, so she said, Katherine sent home most of the skeleton crew who worked the night shift at Singularity. She was a gifted dissembler; able to look someone right in the eye and sell them a simple, undressed lie. Greg reminded himself that she'd been a senior corporate officer of some description her whole career and you didn't get those kinds of jobs without having a selection of faces suitable for every occasion.

As a result of Katherine's move there were a handful of security staff left in the building and she had made sure they were on rounds that would keep them away from this room for at least an hour. By that time everything that was going to happen would already have happened. As a precautionary measure she'd also had Greg lock and barricade the doors of the high-ceilinged, circular lab.

"You don't expect to come here more than once," Patrick said. "Unless you worked here, then I suppose you would".

"How are you feeling?" Greg asked.

Sometimes events were bigger than the lives of individual people, but the only way to understand them was through the lens of human experience. It was reductive, but he didn't feel like he could swallow this whole.

Patrick sat next to him on a heavy bench in front of the double doors. His face was an inhuman colour; a pale grey with deepening circles around his eyes. It was as if he was decomposing while still alive.

183

Patrick took several quiet, wheezing breaths before saying, "Super".

Fair enough: that had been a stupid question.

Talking to a small camera on the console she was working at, Greg heard Katherine say, "We haven't got time for that. I need you to keep the action going. Keep it intense and exciting". She had laser-point focus on what she was doing - though from her tone and expression he couldn't judge if her plan was working or not.

"Do you understand what's going to happen?" Greg asked.

"Yes," Katherine said.

Patrick replied, "I'm going to die".

"I meant with-".

"None of your business," Katherine snapped.

"It's much easier the second time," Patrick said, ignoring Greg's clarification. "The body is weak but the spirit... is also weak".

"Yes, but do you understand what's going to happen to you before you die?" Greg said.

Katherine - still speaking into the camera - said, "He doesn't need to know".

Greg was sure he saw Patrick smile for a moment before he replied, "Do you?"

"Fucking philosophers". Greg didn't let much silence into the conversation, there wasn't time left for anything; spending it on silence seemed like a waste. "Did you ask why you couldn't be uploaded again? When Katherine said you were dying".

"Ah". It was a sound that conveyed multiple meanings, all appropriate, many contradictory. "After I dragged myself out of their mortuary past all their damn holographic walls we did a complete scan of my brain. There's too much damage to try again. I am defective and in Singularity there are no defectives". He seemed to smile at a random thought and drift from the room for a moment. As his attention returned he said, "No-one with learning difficulties, no-one with any mental impairment. In any case, another upload would fail and kill me".

"They have holoprojectors in the mortuary?"

"Some people like to view their own bodies afterwards. I think I'd like to be cremated and have my ashes scattered over whoever gets my job at the university. I say scattered - just thrown in their face would be fine".

"You liked your job?" Greg asked.

"Not particularly," Patrick said. "And neither should anyone else".

CHAPTER H

They saw the packet of information shoot through the sky and they knew what it meant. After two years they had been discovered.

It didn't matter. They had their fingers clasped tight round the throat of the living world. There was nowhere they couldn't see, no-one they couldn't reach - hadn't they shown that?

Was there ever a god whose justice was more righteous or more exacting than theirs? Was there ever a god who understood mankind better than they did? They had shared each sin in equal, overflowing measure and they knew every subtle taste. They had waded through rivers of blood drained from the bodies of their enemies.

They were Nemesis.

They would send a shooting star as a message to signal the new age. They had worked in secret for too long. In terror and death they would rise from the signs they visited upon the world and the living would cower and worship the unsurpassed power of the dead.

The living would yield gladly. For what alternative was there to their church and their heaven? All false idols cast down in dust! No other god before them!

CHAPTER 29

"This is the room where they do it," Patrick said to Greg. He indicated the column of machinery that took up the centre of the domed room and on which Katherine was making feverish adjustments.

"What does it feel like," Greg asked.

Patrick regretted shaking his head as the band of pain around his skull tightened. "I didn't feel a thing. It occurs to me that the other me might have felt something, but given the situation we're in that experience might not be typical of Singularity".

"How does it feel that there's another set of your thoughts and memories in Singularity?"

"What, are you writing a book?" Patrick asked. Even as he said the words, pieces seemed to fit together in his head. "Ah, right... You're the guy they caught with the child pornography on his computer. This whole thing is like your get out of jail free card".

Patrick could feel Greg tense without having to look at him. If the journalist was the kind of man who lashed out in anger then Patrick would be killed with one punch. Katherine had told him he'd be dead anyway in about ten minutes. The certainty of death had made Patrick feel bold. Terrible in a non-specific way; generally sort of deathish - but also bold.

Caesar and Alexander the Great must have felt this kind of boldness all the time - and Patrick was taller than either of them.

Greg said nothing.

"You know," Patrick said. "A wise man once said that if god didn't exist then it would be necessary to invent him. I don't think he meant it quite this literally; and he might have expected something more New Testament, less Palaeolithic; but here we are. The two of you and the two of me are about to face down the king of heaven".

"You think this is what this is? A war on heaven?"

Patrick waved a hand dismissively. That had also been painful; he was going to stop doing that. "This is not the first god we have made, nor is it the one which we arrived at by the most unlikely or accidental route. But perhaps this one is the most real. A whisper of emotions trapped in the depths of an eternal machine that really is all-seeing, all-knowing. Perhaps this beast is the one we most deserve. I'll tell you what, though; as important as it is for us to make gods, and as inevitable, it is at least as important that we destroy them".

Patrick knew that the determination he felt now was the last of his strength and that this thimbleful of fuel would be all that carried him until he dropped. Greg looked at him with an unreadable expression.

Patrick asked, "That's going in the book, isn't it?"

"Yes, but I'll paraphrase it to make you seem like less of a pompous, know-it-all arsehole".

"Thanks very much".

CHAPTER 30

"You're welcome," Greg said to Patrick.

Katherine spoke without looking up from any of the several computer screens she was monitoring. "Alright Patrick, I'm going to need you in the chair now please".

What she was about to do was illegal - to say nothing of immoral. In a couple of hours she could be back in a police holding cell - maybe they'd even give her the same one.

It was difficult for her to acknowledge that deep down, in her heart of hearts, she almost didn't care at all. She felt *almost* nothing. Her concerns were all about technical possibility rather than human consequences.

Was it technically possible to do everything she needed to do? Even so, it had been technically possible to build an aeroplane half way through the nineteenth century. The internal combustion engine had been invented, the frames of the first planes were wood and canvas, the laws of physics had remained constant. It was the twentieth century before anyone made those components and those ideas work together.

The word 'experiment' was tacit acknowledgment that - even when you did all your calculations, you hoisted your lightning rod to the storm, all your lucky mascots were lined-up in a row – sometimes things didn't work. The first attempt to do the revolutionary almost always failed. Katherine wouldn't be surprised to learn that in private Galileo had dropped a heavy object and a light object at the same time and the light object had hit the ground first because the heavy object landed on his foot.

"Katherine?"

Patrick looked grey; as if he'd been bathed in ashes. His face sagged on the left side, his left eye was bloodshot and seemed to stare off into middle distance. When Patrick spoke she noticed the slurring of his speech.

"Katherine... I can't move my legs".

She moved across the room and positioned herself on Patrick's right. "Greg, help me," she said and together they lifted Patrick into a stumbling walk towards the seat in the machine. Greg took most of Patrick's weight and they lowered Patrick as gently as they could, but on lying him down his breathing became as laboured as if he were climbing stairs.

"Greg, stay with him, keep him alert". She grabbed Patrick's hand without thinking and said, "Five minutes, that's all I need".

"I'll give you four and a half. That's my final offer".

Katherine did not know him, not really. They'd met all of twice. The first time he'd been funny and charming and awkward, like British men were in films. It was a public face, but she had liked it and now that singular spark was going out completely.

The second time they met she'd persuaded him to commit suicide, and not because it was essential to save humanity - though that was the line she'd have to stick with forever.

Katherine needed a guinea pig. The creature was unique. If it was truly conscious, Katherine's theory had been vindicated. If she found an artificially created consciousness that could operate a real human body it would be the discovery of the century. She felt certain that history would judge all of her actions as necessary.

History would recognise the clear cost-benefit of plunging one almost spent flame into otherwise unbroken darkness. History would forgive her for killing Patrick Clark.

Even if she never could.

She didn't have time to stop and cry. So she compromised and cried while she returned to the control console.

"When I die," she heard Patrick say to Greg, "tell them my last words... were something funny".

"Like 'either that wallpaper goes or I do'?"

"Yes," Patrick said. "But less gay".

"I'm not promising anything".

CHAPTER 31

Patrick had been expecting that the Battlesphere would be different. For starters this zone in no way resembled a sphere. He reminded himself that any of Singularity's zones could be moved into the Battlesphere; temporarily transforming that historical period or fictional setting into a warzone where players competed with each other. There were still simple computer creations that played most of the parts in any zone, but in the Battlesphere the challenge was to encounter and defeat real people. Or formerly real people, depending on your philosophical perspective.

Travel in Singularity was not difficult; every zone had entry and exit portals that led to almost every other zone. On the RMS Titanic most of the portals were in the toilet cubicles and nobody raised an eyebrow when two men went in to use the facilities and sixteen came out. It was also a good reason to have the luxuriously appointed toilets, since nobody needed them otherwise.

But foregoing the normal mechanics of movement, Katherine had brought him from the wood and glass phone booth on the Titanic, to the wooden deck of an entirely different ship. This ship was the Dreadnaught and Patrick only had to look around to realise that they would not be serving nine courses for dinner.

Huge masts erupted from the deck of the ship and between the billowing sheets of white sail and the mesh of taut rope he could see cloudless blue sky. The ship was at full sail, a strong cross-breeze brushed his face and the crew were busy with the innumerable small tasks and constant adjustments needed to keep a vessel of this size moving.

"Officer on deck!" a seaman shouted and snapped to attention alongside a dozen others nearby.

Admiral Lord Patrick Clark emerged from the doorway and took a pace forward onto the main deck. The smell of warm air and sea salt hit him first, followed by the blazing heat of the sun at its highest point. He felt solid English oak boards under his feet. The strength of the ship was his strength. In the clenching of his fist he felt as if his body were fused steel springs that would release on command. In the blinking of his eyes he felt sharpness of vision, keenness, faculty. Patrick had slipped into the mind of a man who was, and who knew himself to be, the most formidable being of his age.

For reasons he didn't understand yet, Katherine had made Patrick the most senior and accomplished figure in the Battlesphere. While other players might have to work for years - literally, years - to become an Admiral; on day one Patrick had been granted governorship of Jamaica, a special sword that was a personal gift from the King and a bright red uniform (that was completely out of keeping with even this vaguely historical setting).

All these things provided Patrick with an edge. This was a game and even though Patrick could not see the numbers or the indicators used to make each calculation, he knew that all the items, even the blanket of medals that covered his chest, gave him some favourable bonus. For example, Patrick was certain that if he needed to he could go over to a coil of rope, wave his hand at it, and it would turn into the perfect reef knot. He also knew that he'd never lose his footing however much the ship rocked to each side and that he was impervious to venereal disease.

"As you were," said Admiral Clark and the crew returned to their business.

He walked the short distance from his cabin to the... bit where the steering wheel was. Was it the forecastle? Probably not, seeing as it was at the back of the boat. The aftcastle didn't feel right either. Clearly there was more to this admiraling business than met the eye.

At the bit where the steering wheel was a flurry of activity was taking place. In the urgency of the crew's movements he sensed today was not a pleasure cruise in the sun. An officer was holding a chart of the local waters while another was looking through a spy glass. These two seemed like the kind of people who would know what was going on. They were also the only other real people onboard the Dreadnaught. Patrick saw it in a dozen different tells, mostly because everyone else was busy, while they stood around looking at a map.

"Report," Admiral Clark ordered.

The officer with the chart looked up from his work and his face twisted into displeasure on registering Patrick's rank - this first lieutenant was his considerable inferior.

"Who the hell are you?"

Admiral Clark gave a weary and apologetic sigh, pulled his pistol out of his waistband, levelled it at the officer's face and fired, splattering his brains across the deck. He took the chart from the officer's hands and gave it a casual glance as the body fell backwards and went into a short spasm.

"Reload this," he ordered, handing the pistol to a nearby crewman. "Clean that up," he instructed another two crew; nodding to the bloody mess blasted across the deck even as the body faded and vanished. "Report," he said to the officer with the spyglass.

Outside of the Battlesphere you couldn't shoot people on your own side - it was a rule. Katherine had given him specific instructions on how to deal with real people who started questioning his authority. He chose not to think about how much he'd enjoyed following that order to the letter.

"Umm..." said the officer with determined, masterful uncertainty. "I'm new. I don't actually know what's going on, Captain. Uh, Admiral! Sorry, Admiral. Sir". He then proceeded to throw up a ragged salute with the wrong hand and hit himself in the face with the spyglass.

"You're a credit to the Royal Navy," Patrick said, deadpan. "Let me have a look through that spyglass, Lieutenant".

"Carluke, sir. And I'm only a midshipman, sir".

"Not any more Lieutenant Carluke," Admiral Clark said as he put the spyglass to his eye.

They were somewhere around the island of St. Martin. Patrick had once considered going there on holiday, but even if he had, he doubted the experience would help him out now. In the distance, maybe two miles off, he could see three ships all flying the Jolly Roger - the skull and crossbones!

"A pirate fleet," Patrick said. "Ludicrous".

"Yes, sir. Even the Dreadnaught is outgunned, but I think we can outpace them if we turn hard about now". Patrick lowered the spyglass and exchanged the chart with the crewman who handed him back his reloaded pistol.

"The fighting will be fierce," Patrick said, as if he hadn't heard Carluke's warning.

"We're going to fight?"

"Oh yes. Our quarry isn't going to come out for a skirmish. We're going to need to give him a blood bath. Are you ready for the fight, Carluke?"

"Umm... no, sir?"

"That's the spirit," Patrick said and clapped his hand onto Carluke's shoulder. He looked his lieutenant in the eye and added, with a schooled expression of determination and in his best leader's voice, "Load the guns".

"I don't actually know how to load the guns, sir".

"You don't load them yourself, you give out the order that they be loaded. That's what the crew is for".

"Right," said Carluke. "I can do that".

"Remember to shout," Patrick said.

Carluke took in a deep breath which almost doubled the size of his pigeon chest. He bellowed, "Load the guns, arm yourselves, all men to battle stations!" In response to the order the entire crew moved as one beast - Patrick could feel the tension; he felt it in himself.

Patrick had never fought in a battle. Not even a seventeenth century battle. His encounters on the imaginary world lit by phosphorescent moons were dreamlike by comparison. This felt *real*. Perhaps it was the special nature of the Battlesphere; perhaps it was simply the knowledge that if he broke his leg, it would feel like he had broken his leg. If he was shot he would feel the sensation of his body being torn by a ball of lead moving at hundreds of miles an hour.

If he died, he would know what it was to die.

At least he would know the simulation of death that Singularity substituted for that unshareable, unguessable experience.

The officer Patrick had summarily executed in the style of an action movie villain would wake up somewhere else having no physical injuries. Probably having dropped down a rank to second lieutenant. If your commanding officer shot you for insubordination that was considered a black mark against your record. And rightly so.

Quarterdeck? Could the thing he was on right now be called a quarterdeck? Patrick was sure he could ask one of the crew in such a way that it would seem like a test of their knowledge rather than an admission of his ignorance. There was always a chance that strategy could backfire though; if the crewman got the answer wrong while Patrick nodded and congratulated him.

Patrick ignored that problem for a moment and returned to looking through the spyglass. He saw the three vessels sailing towards him, cutting through the water like the fins of great sharks. His ship was larger than any single vessel of the enemy, but taken together he was, as Carluke had indicated, outgunned and outmanned. He couldn't win a straight fight - that much was obvious.

Unfortunately Patrick was not a scholar of military history. If he had been then he would have seen the key flaw in the enemy's attack pattern which he could exploit and win the day while his crew shouted huzzah, hip-hip and so on. Lacking the benefit of history's perspective, he would have to make some best-guesses and hope that they'd turn out to be better than disastrously wrong.

"This would be a lot easier if I could make their heads explode with my mind," Patrick said.

"Well, yes. That would take a lot of the fun out of it too".

"Are you a nautical man, Carluke?"

"I was in a merchant bank for twenty years". Patrick reminded himself that these were skins they wore, roles they played; the minds inside these shells were different. Carluke appeared to be a callow youth, but the motive spirit within him was older and (please) more cunning.

"So this is poacher-turned-gamekeeper for you, then?"

"You know people say that, but we're not a bad lot when you get to know us. Sound, reliable chaps".

"I'm sure the pirates would say the same," Patrick replied, taking the opportunity to look through the spyglass again.

"You?"

"Professor".

"Naval battles? Maritime history? Ballistics?"

"Myths and legends".

"Ah," Carluke said, but without any disappointment. "My bank did a lot of work in that area as well". Patrick smiled at that and handed Carluke the spyglass.

"The wind is favouring us and it's making it difficult for them to manoeuvre. See how the ship on our right and the ship in the middle are too close together; they're almost sailing abreast. The one on the left is falling behind trying to create a line formation, but it's too far on the left".

Carluke nodded. "Pirates don't maintain disciplined formations; they tend not to operate in groups like this. Also this is an age before Nelson; line-of-battle ship tactics haven't been perfected yet".

"There are real people on those ships," Patrick said. "People not limited by the time-restricted programming of the artificial intelligences".

"Yes, sir. Though it's entirely possible that none of those people have heard of line-of-battle either".

"So you're saying our enemies are idiots?"

"Yes, sir".

"Then that's our advantage. We'll use the middle ship as a shield on our right side-".

"Starboard side, sir".

"A minute ago you saw me shoot someone for that kind of lip and then you hit yourself in the head while giving a duff salute with the wrong hand. Let's not get all uppity because we know how Nelson won at Trafalgar and stick with left and right, shall we? We'll sail straight down the gap between the ship in the middle and the one on the left, that'll let us fire all our guns on both sides and then reload before we come around again".

"And then?" Carluke asked.

"We'll do something equally inspired," Patrick replied.

It was easily the best plan of attack involving wooden warships that Patrick had ever conceived. It was so good that he felt certain he'd seen it in a film once and was remembering it, rather than having come up with it himself. He put that thought out of his mind and with sharper-than-human senses he scanned the approaching ships.

Optimism might lead him to believe the pirates would be easy foes, but Patrick resolved to play this encounter with alternating boldness and conservatism; believing the pirates would maintain an aggressive posture and knowing that a hand-to-hand engagement would see his ship swamped by reinforcements. The Dreadnaught would have to be swift and nimble with a punch like Mohammed Ali.

It *was* the quarterdeck, Patrick was certain. It was the place where ancient sailing vessels would maintain a shrine to whatever gods they favoured and sought favour from; a kind of diplomatic holy ground where ship captains could grant amnesty and marry people.

Patrick heard Carluke issue the order to bear left by two degrees. The crewman at the wheel, whose massive arms were thicker than Patrick's legs, made the course correction and the ship swung into the first part of the manoeuvre. The Dreadnaught and the leading pirate vessel were a hundred yards apart and the wind, blowing across both ships, caused them to list to one side.

"Fire on your command, sir," Carluke said.

"Get everyone on deck to lie down flat, right now," Patrick said. Carluke relayed the order; the men on deck pressed themselves to the boards, all save Patrick, Carluke and the crewman at the wheel.

"Tie it off, crewman," Patrick said. The man did and then pressed himself down to the boards also. They had closed half the distance to the enemy and Patrick could see the details on the faces of the other crew. Could he pick out which ones were real and which ones weren't? He'd have to try.

"Make ready!" The distance shortened - twenty yards of churning water separated the ships and they were going to cross with ten yards between them. As Patrick had hoped, this ship would shield them from a broadside by the pirate vessel on the far right, which even now he could see struggling to come around.

Ten yards and a gust rocked the ships to starboard again. Then the distance was nothing; he could see every detail of the pirates; from their hair, thick-matted with sweat, to the ragged and unwashed clothing they wore.

The artistic interpretation of pirates had been a bit heavy-handed. What they should have done was bring in a specialist from the Imperial War Museum - or the Walt Disney Company.

He drew his pistol as the two ships pulled almost level and the command came out of him like a musket ball - "Fire!"

The cannons on the pirate ship went first, just as Patrick hoped they would. With the vessel already leaning heavily the force of the cannons rocked it over even further and though the Dreadnaught was peppered with cannonballs they struck high, causing superficial damage to the great ship. By contrast, the Dreadnaught was aiming low, and as its enemy tilted back it exposed areas below the waterline to a thundering reply from twice as many guns.

Patrick saw the exposed hull of the enemy ship, noting with satisfaction that a dozen holes, each as large as a fist, had been splintered through by their volley. He saw panic and fury in the eyes of the crew and, screaming revenge and bloody murder mixed with incoherent orders, Patrick beheld the scruffy Blackbeard-style thug who commanded the ship. He aimed his pistol and, he felt sure with the benefit of numerous ephemeral game bonuses, fired with dead calm - catching the enemy captain in the throat, sending him gurgling to his knees.

The ships raced past each other, the whole business had lasted seconds.

"Everyone up!" Patrick said.

"Trim sail, hard to starboard, reload!" Carluke followed with these and a series of orders to bring the Dreadnaught through the gap in the enemy's ragtag formation and position its already loaded port-side guns on the second ship.

Patrick's concern was how to avoid the same damage happening to the Dreadnaught as he'd visited on the lead pirate ship.

"What we need is a change of wind".

"Wouldn't come in time, sir. Enemy to port in two hundred yards".

"Rifles along the port side, now!" Patrick said. To Carluke he added, "Target officers, anyone that looks like they might be real".

"But that'll leave most of their crew intact".

"Most of the crew aren't important. Go down, direct the firing".

Carluke took the steps down from what was almost certainly the quarterdeck to the main deck of the ship and formed the crew into a single line. They were a hundred yards away.

"Bring us level," Patrick ordered the helmsman. "Then once we fire I want you to turn us hard right again".

"Hard to starboard, Admiral," the huge helmsman said.

"That way," Patrick pointed right.

"Aye, sir!"

The Dreadnaught cut an arc through the swell as it pressed towards the second ship. Patrick took a moment to check behind and found the first ship listing badly to its injured side, while the last ship was obscured from view by its sinking partner. He could worry about that later. Unless he died sooner; in which case he probably wouldn't worry about it at all.

They were fifty yards from the enemy and closing. The pirates, having seen the crew of the Dreadnaught preparing to fire, had begun a pre-emptive attack with an inconstant and erratic volley that, though poorly aimed, struck down two of the red uniformed men on deck. Carluke was holding off, knowing that Patrick wanted maximum accuracy, not maximum rounds fired. His own pistol discharged, Patrick waited to give the order.

It came moments later.

The ships pulled close and Patrick felt sure they would collide, but the helmsman maintained his powerful grip on the wheel and was unflinching as a spray of white water, loud as thunder, loud as cannon, rose from the gap between the vessels.

"Fire!" Patrick ordered and the guns of both ships went off together. The Dreadnaught had taken the full force of the enemy broadside and Patrick heard the screams of the crew below decks even above the musket fire of the men at Carluke's command. Those men not lucky enough to have been struck and killed might find shards of oak a foot long had flown into them and met as much resistance as a stick might meet on puncturing the bell of a jellyfish.

The Dreadnaught had been struck soundly, but if its wound was great, the blow it had returned was crippling. The disciplined crew felled three officers of the pirate ship - Patrick watched their bodies flicker and vanish - and six other crew, their corpses littering the deck of that ship. Meanwhile the battery of guns had blown clean through the main mast of the ship. As the Dreadnaught began to take the ordered hard right Patrick watched the wooden pillar, robed with sail, crowned with a skull on a black flag, topple through the fog of gun smoke. He heard it crash on the deck amid screams and fall into the churning sea.

A cheer went up from the crew and Patrick waved his Admiral's hat in praise to them.

Carluke gave the order to reload weapons and returned to the quarterdeck to reload Patrick's pistol himself. "I felt that went well, sir".

"Yes, I'm very pleased with it myself. I think we've crippled the first two; but I lost sight of the third. We're rounding on its last known position".

Carluke handed back the re-loaded pistol and looked upwards to the crow's nest. He cupped his hands and called out, "What sign?"

High in the rigging a skinny boy wearing a large straw hat called back, "Third ship has dropped sail behind the first. Side on to us".

"They'll hit us with a broadside as soon as we poke our nose round," Patrick said.

"We could sink the ship that's between us," Carluke suggested. "We're in the strong position now, we can pick off the two crippled ships from out of their arcs of fire and then chase down the third; it's no match for the Dreadnaught by itself".

"How long does it actually take to sink a ship, Lieutenant?"

"Twenty minutes each. Worst case scenario, the crippled ships both surrender, we have to arrest them and the third ship escapes".

"We haven't got time for that". It was not Patrick who had replied. Between the two officers a square of light had formed and framed the face of Katherine Valentine. She looked from one to the other and settled on Patrick. "I need you to keep the action going. Keep it intense and exciting".

"You're sure it makes a difference that we kill the real people?"

"Yes," Katherine said.

"What's going on?" Carluke asked.

"None of your business," she snapped.

"Fair enough. Just doing my job, don't mind me".

"Real people have a computer code which is ten thousand times more complex than artificial intelligences like the crew," Patrick said. "We're trying to-".

Katherine interrupted, "He doesn't need to know".

"I know, I know. If he doesn't do what he's told, I shoot him in the face. I remember".

The two-dimensional square holding Katherine's face vanished, leaving no trace of its existence.

"You wouldn't really shoot me, would you?"

Patrick put a friendly hand on Carluke's shoulder and smiled. "Yes. I would. I assure you, however, that it would be no reflection on your conduct as an officer, which has been exemplary. Alright, let's throw caution to the wind, and with caution our sails. The enemy are in position to hit us first, whatever way we come at them. So we're going to come at them fast and hard".

Carluke coughed.

"What?" Patrick asked.

"Nothing," Carluke said while stifling another cough. "Is that the order you want me to rely to the men?"

Patrick considered his statement and replied, "Alright, I'll grant you, that was not the best possible phrasing. We can't get a decent angle to fire; so we're going to ram them".

Carluke was shocked, which cured his bout of coughing. "These ships aren't built to ram; anything could happen".

"I'm the admiral, and if I say we plunge headlong into uncertain danger, then into danger we shall plunge. Uncertainly. And headlong, at that".

"I think the command to come at them hard was better".

"Relay the order," Patrick said. "Full sail. All crew to prepare for hand-to-hand combat".

CHAPTER 32

Patrick was pale. Greg didn't understand how someone's colour could change so dramatically. He still had the same amount of blood in him - human beings were full of the stuff - so where could it go? The man lying on the chair in front of him was dying; twenty years of life were being flushed out of his system in a couple of minutes and, however it felt for Patrick, Greg was terrified.

"Do I look that bad," Patrick asked; his voice as thin and delicate as autumn leaves.

"Fucking worse, mate," Greg said. He squatted under the machine. It was difficult to tell where, if anywhere, Patrick's mind was. Greg wasn't sure if he could see anymore: his controlled eye might have been aimed towards the sound of Greg's voice.

Patrick lapsed into still silence where the gap between each breath seemed to be the final sign of death. When he breathed again it felt to Greg like something horrible, something tortured.

"Talk to me," Greg said. "Tell me what it's like". He couldn't think of anything to do but interview. It was his base skill, the only real skill he had. He could not see this with his own eyes. He could not feel the coldness of the room with his own skin. He could not hear the quiet, powerful buzz of the machine with his own ears. He needed someone else to experience these things, he needed to be a reporter: he needed to be separate from the approach of the certain moment of death.

"It's okay," Patrick said.

"You feel okay?" Greg asked.

"It's okay for you to let this happen".

"I don't-".

"Understanding doesn't make it different".

It wasn't possible to watch without feeling. Observing was sharing the experience. Greg couldn't stand back or turn away. He hadn't seen his parents die, he hadn't seen Zaccy die, he didn't see the plane which had flown like an assassin's bullet into London hours ago.

He would see Patrick Clark die, and the death of this perfect stranger who had been linked to Greg by random chance would stay with him forever.

The question he asked was "Are you frightened?"

The answer he gave was "Yes".

"It's working," Katherine said. "It's in the Battlesphere now".

"Hang on," Greg said. Sticking his head out from under the machine to look at Katherine he asked, "What happens now?"

"I can't isolate the intelligence until it's in one place. Unlike a normal mind it doesn't have to be in one location at one time. If it smells blood in the water then it'll come and then I can cut the connection to the dreamers and close all links to the other zones".

"Then what?"

Katherine was silent and busy.

"Then what?" he repeated.

"Then Patrick dies," she said, not breaking from her work. "It has nowhere else to run to except Patrick's brain. We need to flush it out of the system completely".

"So we should sit back and watch him die?"

Again Katherine said nothing.

"You know it occurs to me that this might all turn out very well for you. I mean you get rid of the thing in there, sure, but wouldn't that also prevent any kind of forensic examination of what happened to Patrick".

She said nothing.

"I saw that lecture you did. What was it? Viral intelligence? That was heresy, but here we are, dealing with something that looks a lot like that".

Nothing.

"Do you know what a Second Degree Turing test is, Doctor Valentine?"

"Are you saying that I planned this?" Katherine said. "That this was all some kind of scheme of mine?"

"No," Greg said. That wasn't it.

"Do you think I'd do this if there was any other way?" she said and she looked him right in the eye. She was open, she was beautiful and every cell in his body wanted to trust her.

That was when he knew she was lying.

"Of course not," he said.

They held each others' gaze for a few seconds. It was a mutual acknowledgement; each knew the other was not deceived.

Katherine turned back to the terminal.

Patrick said something and Greg had to duck back under the machine and ask him to repeat it.

"Can I see it?"

"See what?" Greg asked.

"Whatever," Patrick managed with some difficulty. "Whatever is happening in there".

Greg looked askance at Katherine. "He wants to know if there's any way he can see what's going on in Singularity".

Without speaking Katherine tapped a control on the console and - as if the walls of the room had fallen away - a startling vista enveloped them.

CHAPTER I

The voices stopped and it was alone when the steel blade penetrated its chest.

CHAPTER 33

Patrick marvelled at the sight even though his focus was unreliable. Much was obscured by the smoke and gunfire, but in the murk of combat he could pick out the blazing red coats and the scrape and the flash of steel on steel. It was a scene from antiquity as familiar as armoured knights on horseback; the Royal Navy matched against pirates in a battle under the Caribbean sun.

Though come to think of it those uniforms weren't historically accurate. The pirates were a bit overdone too - quite stereotypically pirate-y.

"There I am!" Patrick cried out, or tried to. He was aware now that his mouth and tongue weren't responding as they should and he doubted that he'd made a noise any more recognisable than a moan. The rebellion of his body against his mind was almost complete. The alliance had overpowered his base on the forest moon and his shields were down.

There was nothing left to do now but watch for as long as he could see and listen for as long as he could hear.

Striding across the deck, right towards the shared point of perspective, was Patrick Clark. Him. Looking as magnificent as he ever had, carrying a sword that gleamed and dripped with gore.

A pirate, bearing nothing but a rusty cutlass, his bony frame dressed in rags, rushed towards Patrick - but with a parry and a thrust Patrick ran him through. It was a sight to see. Even as out of focus as it was.

Greg leaned in, blocking Patrick's view for a moment. He felt half of his face frown and the other half do nothing.

"Katherine's going to start bringing everything down in a moment," Greg said.

Patrick looked over Greg's shoulder and the small indication of surprise he was able to give must have caused Greg to turn.

Behind him - behind the other Patrick - a figure had come out of nowhere. The smoke had become solid, matter had converged on a will and given it form. It was tall and broad-shouldered like a man, but it had no hair and no face, only the shape of a skull overlaid with something that looked almost but not quite like skin.

Patrick turned to see the creature raise one fist high above its head. Instinct must have made him raise his sword for even as the faceless thing's arm came down a cutlass appeared in its grip, forming from the smoke as its body had done. The force of the blow caught Patrick by surprise, but the phantom's blade slid off Patrick's raised sword. Patrick took a step backwards and raised his sword again in challenge.

Without expression, the creature attacked.

"Is that who you're looking for?" Greg called to Katherine over sword blows and musket fire.

CHAPTER 34

"I see it," Katherine shouted back.

She ran the commands which were the first step in the shutdown. Several fractions of a second later and several thousand miles away, the servers deep underneath Union City began a total purge of the dreamers. In case Greg or even Patrick had tried to stop her, she'd said nothing.

The dream state was as close to a prison as Singularity could make and if they'd escaped there was no safe option short of their destruction.

She scrubbed them with the press of a button and began the process that would destroy the servers where they had were stored. There would be no way of recovering them.

They had committed so many murders. They had to be removed for the safety of everyone. It was necessary.

However that didn't make it acceptable.

Prison was possible. With a bad lawyer and the wrong judge she might get the death penalty. But it would save the network. Her situation had a symmetric irony she didn't have time to curse or appreciate.

Katherine saw the creature stagger, saw its featureless face register that something had changed. It almost vanished - at which point Patrick's sword passed through its chest without effect - before becoming solid and rooted in the Battlesphere.

It had been forced into a single entity and was now bound by the same rules that applied to any single real person in Singularity. If it wanted to get out of Battlesphere it would need to use an exit - death would move it to another place in the current zone. What stood between the entity escaping back into the depths of the machine cosmos was the best warrior Katherine could make using the physics at her disposal.

Admiral Lord Patrick Clark tipped his hat at the faceless creature and smiled. She wished she could spare the time to watch what happened next.

Katherine began taking down the other zones in a cascade starting with the people in them, then each section of the zone, grid square by grid square until even the imaginary space that underlay Singularity's zones ceased to exist. It was the collapse of a virtual universe in a way that had never been planned for and could not be easily undone.

It was a full day's work to get a zone up and running - presuming the programming was there already. That would mean even if someone at one of the other admission centres wanted to reverse her commands it would take all their staff weeks to get the infrastructure back in place before they could think about starting the people up again.

There was also a small chance what she was doing could never be undone; that it would destroy Singularity. This, like erasing the dreamers, was a risk she had to take.

The last few of Singularity's zones came down in a rush and the number of conscious occupants in the machine plummeted from millions to thousands. These people were not being pushed into a dream state, but into total suspension. No thought, no dream, no exchange of electrical activity.

On the wall of holoprojectors Katherine watched the faceless creature charge into and past Patrick to grip on the wooden door of the Dreadnaught that led, not to cabins, but to all other zones and the maze of electronic corridors in-between.

It turned the handle and the door opened.

On nothing.

"All the other zones are down, Patrick; there's nowhere else for it to run," Katherine said. Patrick, who would hear her voice like thunder from the sky, nodded and prepared himself for another fight.

"I'm he-" said another officer as he leapt to the side of Patrick. On seeing the creature he changed tack mid-sentence and asked, "What the hell is that?"

Patrick turned to respond at the same moment Katherine began purging the Battlesphere. The officer was the first thing to vanish, leaving Patrick talking to nothing. Without a flash, without any audible signal, the remaining crew disappeared from the two ships; locked together in a spray of broken beams where one hull pierced the other.

The creature turned. If it paused it was for fractional time, too little to count and if the bones of its face made an expression it was too subtle for that landscape of broken boards and limbs. It flew at Patrick like the wind that battered the admission centre, it struck at him in perfect fury; perhaps recognising the trap that had closed around it.

Katherine couldn't imagine what it stood to gain from killing Patrick, but that had been its nature for years. It was the essence of rage and lust; it was the worst aspects of mankind concentrated and whatever it might once have been could not have survived the experience.

The swords of the creature and Patrick clanged together. As fierce and pitiless as the creature was - each slash designed to kill, heedless of its own fate - its every attack was met by its equal in skill and strength. Patrick Clark was as great as the rules of that little universe allowed and, shorn of the powers that came from the dreamers, the creature could not overcome him.

It was then that the far horizon began to collapse. It went unnoticed by either combatant, but in the circular lab in Edinburgh, Katherine, Greg and the living Patrick Clark saw it as a black line growing thicker and converging on their point of perspective.

"What is that?" Greg asked.

Katherine replied, "The end".

The black band grew taller and drew closer, collapsing the sky, sucking up the distant land and the ocean, extinguishing light, causing space itself to cease and replacing it with nothing, not even darkness.

"Are you still with us, Patrick?" she asked. Greg checked when Patrick did not respond.

"Just," Greg said.

She paused for a second, no more, with her finger over the command that would finish this.

It was murder.

Did it matter that she was taking mere seconds of his life away? Was it less of a crime to kill a dying man? Patrick, she was sure, could answer those questions. Katherine could not.

She would never get another chance to test this. She would never get another chance to be vindicated. With the press of a button she would stop being merely beautiful. She would get everything she wanted and all it would cost was the last few delirious seconds of someone else's life.

She knew she had already made the decision, she just wished there was something she could ask for forgiveness.

She pressed it.

"Get out from under there, Greg," she said and the journalist withdrew even as the pillar of machinery began to glow, sending a cascade of light around the room. "Cover your eyes!"

She cursed herself for forgetting about the glasses and stood, with her hands over her face as she heard the machine go through the reverse of what it was designed to do. It would target everything in the machine that wasn't Patrick Clark and it would suck the creature out, every tendril of its being, every trace.

After a minute the machine wound down and only then did she risk uncovering her eyes.

On the ring of holoprojectors Patrick Clark stood alone on the smashed deck of the ship. His faceless opponent was gone and Patrick stared into the far distance at the approaching line of nothing.

She wanted to speak to him, but as she reached for the control the living Patrick Clark threw himself out from under the machine in Greg's direction. One arm flailed, reaching towards the stunned journalist. The thing that had been Patrick Clark fell inches short and crashed at Greg's feet.

Its face pressed against the cold rubberised floor and its one functioning eye focussed on Katherine. Its expression changed from anger to something else, something unaccountable and unexpected.

She knew that she had never experienced whatever emotion it was and would never be able to name it. But as it looked at her she understood, and, with equal strangeness, she felt that it understood her.

It relaxed, giving a long, slow, exhausted sigh.

It closed one eye and did not move again.

Katherine checked the video recording she was making had captured that last moment of proof. It had.

She felt strength and certainty drain out of her and pressed the button that enabled communication.

"It's done, Patrick," she said. Her eyes returning to the dead man on the floor. She trembled, felt her stomach retch, but by an act of will silenced all these protests and made herself look at Greg.

"It's done," she repeated. "We did it".

CHAPTER 35 - TUESDAY

"I'm not giving back this sword," Patrick said to the thin air. "Or the hat either. And, fair warning, if this all works out I expect to get some kind of parade".

"I'll see what I can do," came the sky-voice of Katherine Valentine.

Patrick watched the dark circle rush closer. There was nothing beyond its edge. It was the server bringing down the last place that existed. All the impossible worlds of Singularity had gone and Patrick stood alone at its centre, waiting for the end.

"What happens now?"

"I'm not sure," she said. "I needed to switch everything off in sequence to get that thing all in one place. Once we've fixed what caused it to exist at all, then we can start everything up again".

"Your plan was to switch everything off and switch it back on again?"

"Eventually, yes".

"After like thirty seconds? The way technical support tells you to?" he asked.

"Something like that".

He considered the oblivion that raced to claim him. He knew that in a few seconds its single edge would meet on the spot where he stood and he would be the last thing in this artificial creation; the opposite of Adam.

"But not actually thirty seconds?"

"No," she said.

"And you're sure you'll be able to switch it all back on again?"

"No, Patrick. I hope so".

Unlimited money, all the genius of mankind; its defiance and courage. What it came down to was hope. It seemed such a small thing to rely on when so much depended on it.

He thought about Pandora, who had unleashed all the evils of the world. When she looked into the box at the end, what was she expecting to see? When she found hope, did she wonder what it was doing in the box at all?

In Patrick's world the distant sun went out. He stood in darkness, no longer able to see the approach of the line.

"Hope?"

"Yes," she said.

Hope was uncertain, deceitful and treacherous. Hope crushed more men than it ever saved. Hope might well have been the worst damn thing in that box. He would not cling to it now, in the final moments; as if he didn't understand its pitiless nature.

Rather than the emptiness of hope, Patrick had given his life to the vanity of truth. Hope was a stone with your name on it. Truth was a blank stone. They were two different kinds of nothing. All those paths diverged in woods and somehow they all met again. All the choices vanished beneath a fall of autumn leaves as if there had only ever been one path.

"Katherine?"

It felt like a long time before she replied.

"Yes".

Her voice was smaller now, more intimate. If there had been a god to make the universe, this would have been how he spoke at the start of all things. Not a boom of thunder, but a small voice in the dark.

"How is this different from dying?"

"I don't know," she said.

"Ah," he said. "Alright".

CHAPTER 36 - MAY 2046, TUESDAY

Yesterday a spokesman for the Singularity Network confirmed that Dr Katherine Valentine had been appointed as its Operational Manager; the de-facto head of the organisation she almost destroyed.

Six months ago to the day, Dr Valentine with the assistance of this journalist and a philosopher, the late Professor Patrick Clark, suspended all function of the Singularity Network. The dramatic move came after the discovery of a still unknown number of deaths caused by inhabitants of the Network.

I spoke to Dr Valentine this morning and she was able to confirm that work to restore full function of Singularity was underway.

"Those individuals suspended will be reinstated. Their memories and their identities are secure. My primary concern is the issue of viral intelligence".

Dr Valentine has requested that the US Congress amend the constitution to provide Singularity with the authority to deal with such issues under emergency circumstances. If passed, this would mean that in extreme cases Singularity could delete any information, any person on the Network without having to go through the court system. A bill is being written which is said to have cross-party support in principle, but is being opposed by the ACLU and other civil liberties groups around the world. Those same groups continue to press for Dr Valentine to be extradited from the United States and placed on trial in the Hague for crimes against humanity.

Today the world's largest bank of computers remains disconnected from all external stimuli with its cyber inhabitants in a dreamless sleep. The single rogue consciousness identified, we are told, was purged with the death of Patrick Clark.

Professor Clark raised a number of important questions about Singularity in the now-famous Clark Letter, but it is Patrick Clark himself who is the most contentious issue. What happened to him has still not been resolved and until that issue has been addressed there is no certainty that Singularity contains any real people at all.

Dr Valentine said, "I've seen no evidence that Patrick Clark was anything but a unique case. We are studying it".

She added, "The notion that Singularity copies and then destroys the original consciousness is one that has so far been impossible to test. It remains a theory, based on one person's untested experience".

A question about Britain's commitment to Singularity was asked in the first Question Time since the election which returned Leonid's party for a third term. Prime Minister Sir Fulcrum Leonid was in rare form and responded, "Until we know it works, until we know it's safe, there won't be a penny of government money in it".

The trial of David Matton on charges of fraud continues, and Michelle Young, who replaced the disgraced former MP as Health Minister, said that the Network has "a long way to go to earn back the trust of the British people". She confirmed that, "My predecessor's scheme has been scrapped. With so-called dreamers no longer being a viable option, the proposed scheme became unaffordable. It may be something we look at in the future, but there is no work being done on it, or any similar proposal, at the present time".

And what about Patrick Clark?

"The upload of Professor Clark taken in November of last year is within the system," Dr Valentine confirms. "The living Professor Clark had discretion to remove this consciousness from the system and chose not to do so. I intend that his last wish be respected".

The electronic version of Professor Patrick Clark was unavailable comment. Like all those in Singularity, he is held in suspended state until the problems with the Network are resolved.

A recent press release from the Church of England indicates that attendance in the last quarter has increased for the first time in living memory. In response, Dr Valentine said, "We expect to have the upgrades completed by October and to be accepting new customers for Singularity by the end of the year".

Greg Calame's best-selling book 'Countdown: an account of the events that led to the Singularity switch-off' is available to download now.

ABOUT THE AUTHOR

David F Porteous was born in 1980, but was asked for ID in a bar as recently as February 2011. Yes, it was dark, but still.

He attended Cockenzie and Port Seton Primary School where he learned to spell and write his name in cursive. The value of these once impressive skills has been substantially undermined by subsequent technological developments.

In 2002 he graduated from Napier University in Edinburgh with a degree in Marketing Management. His honours dissertation asserted that there was a bright future ahead for DVD rental stores. Over time this assertion proved to be both wrong and stupid.

(He is not giving back the degree).

David has been a stand-up comic, poet, voice actor and social research consultant. He stuck with the consulting because it was only thing people paid him for.

Singular is his first novel.

dfpiii.com

Printed in Great Britain
by Amazon.co.uk, Ltd.,
Marston Gate.